Posthumous Works

Ann Bleecker

LITERATURE HOUSE / GREGG PRESS
Upper Saddle River, N. J.

Republished in 1970 by
LITERATURE HOUSE
an imprint of The Gregg Press
121 Pleasant Avenue
Upper Saddle River, N. J. 07458

Reprinted from original edition in
Rare Book Collection
Rutgers University

Standard Book Number—8398-0167-X
Library of Congress Card—70-104419

Printed in United States of America

M^{rs} ANN ELIZA BLEECKER.

THE

POSTHUMOUS WORKS

O F

ANN ELIZA BLEECKER,

I N

PROSE AND VERSE.

To which is added,

A COLLECTION OF ESSAYS,

PROSE AND POETICAL,

B Y

MARGARETTA V. FAUGERES.

N E W - Y O R K :
Printed by T. and J. Swords, No. 27, William-Street.
—1793.—

To the Public.

IN the publication of *Poſthumous Works*, it has been uſual for the Editors or Publiſhers to accompany them with a Prefatory Addreſs,—generally explaining the particular reaſons for offering them to the world, or relating their peculiar merits, and conſequently their claim to the patronage of the lovers of ſcience. In compliance with this general cuſtom we think it neceſſary merely to note, that having been frequently ſolicited to publiſh, in a ſeparate volume, a part of thoſe writings of Mrs. BLEECKER which had appeared in the *New-York Magazine*, we conceived a collection of all ſuch of her poems and eſſays as might with propriety come before the public, would be more likely to meet the approbation both of *her* friends, and of the friends of American literature. Having ſuggeſted this idea to thoſe who appeared moſt ſtrenuous for the meaſure, we were pleaſed to find it met their hearty concurrence; and through the obliging diſpoſition of her huſband and daughter, we are now happy in being able to preſent this volume to our fellow citizens.

We

TO THE PUBLIC.

We are indebted to a friend for the idea of adding a number of profe and poetical effays, which likewife firft appeared in the *New-York Magazine*, moft of them under the fignature of ELLA, and which are the production of Mrs. MARGARETTA V. FAUGERES, the daughter of Mrs. BLEECKER. Our obligations to this lady are much increafed by the addition of feveral Original Effays in verfe, which the reader will find interfperfed in that part of the collection which comprehends her writings

It is not our intention to recommend this volume by an elaborate difplay of its particular merits or peculiar excellencies: the beft recommendation we can give it, is an attentive perufal: and when this is done, that the reader of tafte and elegance will join in afferting, that though it is not faultlefs, yet that its merits preponderate, and entitle it to the patronage of every true American, is the candid opinion of

The PUBLISHERS.

New-York, September, 1793.

SUBSCRIBERS

SUBSCRIBERS NAMES.

Thomas Allen, 6 cop
Athenian Society,
Andrew Anderfon,
William Bache,
Gardiner Baker,
Eleazer Ball,
John Banks,
Andrew D. Barclay,
Edward Bartlett,
Anthony Bartow,
Johanna Bayard, 2 cop.
Chriftian Beakley,
Cornelius Bergen,
Anthony L. Blanchard,
John R. Bleecker, jun.
Alexander Bleecker,
Nathaniel Bloodgood,
Robert Boggs,
John Bolen,
George Bowne, jun.
Walter Bowne,
Samuel Boyd.
Lætitia Bradifh,
Andrew Bradifh,
Sufan V. Bradford,
Gafherie Brafher,
George Brewerton,
James Brewerton,

Henry Brewerton,
Catharine Bridgen,
William Brifkcoa,
Michael Brooks,
William Broome,
John Burger, jun.
Lancafter Burling, jun.
William Bunce,
Samuel Burrowe,
Thomas C. Butler,
Eliza Caldwell,
Calliopean Society,
Robert Campbell,
Nicholas G. Carmer,
Maria Charles,
Mrs. Childs,
John Clark,
Benjamin Clark,
De Witt Clinton,
Peter Cole,
Richard F. Cooper,
Mifs Cooper,
Peter S. Cortelyou,
Catharine Cox,
John Cruger,
James Davidfon,
Richard B. Davis,
Matthew L. Davis,

A 3
William

SUBSCRIBERS NAMES.

William A. Davis,
Peter Deall,
Mrs. Delancey,
Thomas Demilt,
John De Wint,
Henry Dodd,
Nathaniel Forfter,
Abraham Fowler,
Mrs. Fraunces,
Hugh Gaine,
William Gilliland,
Charles D. Gold,
Sol. Goodwin,
Oliver Goodwin,
Thomas Greenleaf,
Benjamin Haight,
Thomas Hamerfley,
Nicholas Hammond,
John Harriffon,
Ann Julia Hatton,
H. Haydock, jun. 2 cop.
William Hervey,
Sarah Higginfon,
Robert Hinchman,
Peter Hines,
Jacob Hochftroffer,
Robert Hodge,
Mary Hodgdon,
Horanian Liter. Society,
William Hurft,
E. Jones,
Epaphrus Jones,
John B. Johnfon,
Ifaac L. Kip,
Ifaac Kip, jun.
James Kirkland,

Jane Kirkpatrick,
Jeremiah Lanfingh,
Jonathan Lawrence, jun.
John Leonard,
Edmund Ludlow,
Peter Mabie,
Elizabeth Mann,
Thomas Marfhall,
John M. Mafon,
Benjamin G. Minturn,
Jacob Moon,
Benjamin I. Moore,
Jacob Morton,
Robert Mott,
Townfend M'Coun,
Archibald M'Cullum,
Dennis M'Gahagan,
Eliza O. Millen,
John W. Mulligan,
John Neilfon,
John L. Norton,
Daniel Paris,
Euphemia Paterfon,
Nathaniel Pearfall,
Henry Poft, jun. 3 copies.
Abraham Prall,
William Rainey,
John Read,
John Reid,
James Riker,
Jofeph Roberts,
Sufannah Rodgers,
John Ryers,
Jofhua Sands,
George Service,
H. P. Schuyler,

Philip

SUBSCRIBERS NAMES.

Philip Schuyler,
Peter C. Schuyler,
G. V. Schoonhoven,
Maria Scott,
James Seaman,
Richard Seaman,
J. Slidell, jun.
Thomas R. Smith,
George Snowdon, jun.
Jofeph M. Stanbury,
Daniel Steele,
Thomas Stoutenburgh,
Samuel Suydam,
Mary Swords,
Abraham C. Ten Broeck,
Anthony Ten Eyck,
Jacob Ten Eyck,
Cornelius Tiebout,
James Tillery,
John V. Thomas,
Chriftian Tupper,

John Utt,
Ifaac Vanderbeck, jun.
Samuel B. Vanderbilt,
Cornelius C. Van Alen,
Daniel L. Van Antwerp,
Anna Maria Van Wyck,
Gebafh Viffcher,
Harman Vofburgh,
James Walker,
Sarah Wallace,
George J. Warner,
George Wattles,
C.R.&G.Webfter, 6 cop.
Ifaac H. Whitney,
Benjamin Williamfon,
Nathaniel Woodward,
William Wyche,
Jofeph Youle,
Jofeph Young,
Samuel Young.

☞ But few returns have been made of the fub-
fcription-papers fent out of this city; many likewife that were delivered to individuals, we have
heard nothing of: Should, therefore, any who have
fubfcribed for this volume find their names omitted, they will be pleafed to afcribe it to the caufe
above mentioned.

CONTENTS.

CONTENTS.

CONTENTS.

By

CONTENTS.

By Mrs. FAUGERES.

CONTENTS.

MEMOIRS

MEMOIRS

OF

Mrs. ANN ELIZA BLEECKER.

Mrs. ANN ELIZA BLEECKER was the youngest child of Mr. BRANDT SCHUYLER, of this city, (the place of her nativity;) she was born in October, anno Domini 1752; and though in her early years she never displayed any partiality for school, yet she was passionately fond of books, insomuch that she read with propriety any book that came to hand long before the time that children in common pass their Spelling-Books. But though her poetical productions (which made their appearance very early) displayed a taste far superior to her years; yet, so great was her diffidence of

B   her

her own abilities, that none but her moſt
intimate acquaintance were ever indulged
with a view of any of her performances,
and *then* they were no ſooner peruſed than
ſhe deſtroyed them.

Hence it comes, that none of her com-
poſitions previous to the year 1769, are
extant: in that year ſhe married JOHN J.
BLEECKER, Eſq; of *New-Rochelle*; and
being willing *now* to cheriſh her genius,
after a ſhort reſidence in the capital, they
retired to *Poughkeepſie*, where they ſtayed
a year or two; and then taking a liking
to the northern parts of this ſtate, they
removed to *Tomhanick*, a beautiful ſolitary
little village eighteen miles above *Albany*.
Here Mr. BLEECKER built him an houſe
on a little eminence, which commanded a
pleaſing proſpect. On the *eaſt* ſide of it
was an elegantly ſimple *garden*, where fruits
and flowers, exotics as well as natives,
flouriſhed with beauty; and a little beyond
it the roaring river of *Tomhanick* daſhed
                                    with

with rapidity its foaming waters among the broken rocks; toward the *weft*, lay wide cultivated fields; in the *rear*, a young orchard, bounded by a thick foreft; and in *front*, (after crofling the main road) a meadow, through which wandered a dimpling ftream, ftretched itfelf to join a ridge of tall nodding pines, which rofe in awful grandeur on the fhelving brow of a grafly mountain. Through the openings of this wood you might defcry little cottages fcattered up and down the country, whofe environs the hard hand of Induftry had transformed into rich fields and blooming gardens, and literally caufed the wildernefs to bloflom as the rofe—It is to this fcene fhe alludes where fhe fo beautifully fays,

Caft your eyes beyond this meadow,
   Painted by a hand Divine,
And obferve the ample fhadow
   Of that folemn ridge of pine.

This was fuch a retreat as fhe had always defired—the dark foreft, the rufhing river,

and the green valley had more charms for
her than the gay metropolis fhe had left,
and in which fhe was fo well calculated to
fhine: and fhe was fo much attached to
rural pleafures, that no birds (thofe of
prey excepted) were ever fuffered to be
fhot near her habitation if fhe could prevent it—indeed, they built their nefts un-
molefted in the very porch of the houfe.

And the cultivation of flowers had likewife a large fhare of her attention, fo much,
that where *Flora* had been remifs in deck-
.ing the fod, fhe took upon herfelf that
office, by gathering feeds from her own
garden and ftrewing them promifcuoufly
in the woods and fields, and along the clovery borders of her favourite brook.

'Till the memorable 1777, they lived in
the moft perfect tranquillity—fair profpects were opening on every fide—Her
mother, a widow, (an ornament to the
fex) lived with her—her half-fifter, Mifs
TEN EYCK, was her cheerful fprightly
companion

companion—and her attentive hufband and prattling children clofed the circle, and left her fcarce another wifh on this fide of the grave—*Then*, indeed, the clamorous thunders of *War* frighted them from their peaceful dwelling, and the blafting hand of *Defolation* difperfed them as a flock in the defert.

Mr. BLEECKER, hearing of the approaches of the infatuated BURGOYNE, had left Mrs. BLEECKER with the children and fervants, while he went to *Albany* to feek a place for them, (her mother and fifter having juft quitted her.) But he had fcarce been gone a day when, as fhe fat at breakfaft, fhe received intelligence that the enemy were within two miles of the village, burning and murdering all before them. Terrified beyond defcription fhe rofe from the table, and taking her ABELLA on her arm, and her other daughter (about four years old) by the hand, fhe fet off on foot, with a young mulatto girl, leav-

B 3   ing

ing the houfe and furniture to the mercy
of the approaching favages. The roads
were crouded with carriages loaded with
women and children, but none could afford
her affiftance—diftrefs was depictured on
every countenance, and tears of heartfelt
anguifh moiftened every cheek. They
paffed on—no one fpoke to another—and
no found but the difmal creaking of bur-
dened wheels and the trampling of horfes
interrupted the mournful filence. After a
tedious walk of four or five miles, fhe obtained a feat for the children upon one of
the waggons, and fhe walked on to *Stony-
Arabia*, where fhe expected to find many
friends; but fhe was deceived—no door
was open to *her*, whofe houfe by many of
them had been made ufe of as a home—
fhe wandered from houfe to houfe, and at
length obtained a place in the garret of a
rich old acquaintance, where a couple of
blankets, ftretched upon fome boards, were
offered her as a bed; fhe, however, fat up

all

all night and wept, and the next morning Mr. BLEECKER coming from *Albany*, met with them and returned to that city, from whence they fet off with feveral other families by water. At twelve miles below *Albany* little ABELLA was taken fo ill that they were obliged to go on fhore, where fhe died. The *impreffions* this event made on Mrs. BLEECKER's mind were never effaced. The remembrance of every circumftance that led to it—the return of the feafon—the voice of an infant—or even the calm approach of a fummer's evening, never failed to awaken all her forrows; and fhe being naturally of a penfive turn of mind, *too* freely indulged them.

From this they proceeded to *Red-Hook*, where fhe met with her mother, who was declining very faft, and died a little after her daughter's arrival. The capture of BURGOYNE foon after taking place, they again fet off to vifit their little folitude; but, in their journey thither, fhe had the
forrowful

forrowful office of clofing the eyes of her laft remaining fifter.*

The defcription fhe has given of thefe events, in a letter to a friend, may not be unacceptable.

Tomhanick, December 15, 1777.

" CURST be the heart that is callous
" to the feelings of humanity, and which,
" concentered in itfelf, regards not the wail-
" ings of affliction! Excufe my enthufi-
" afm—it is the effect of repeated injuries
" received in my flight; but thank heaven
" I have fupported every fhock with tole-
" rable fortitude, except the death of my
" ABELLA—fhe indeed had wound herfelf
" round every fibre of my heart—I loved,
" I idolized her—however, my little love
" languifhed and died, and I believe I
                                    " could

* Her own fifter, Mrs. SWITS—her half-fifter, Mrs. DARBE, (then Mifs TEN EYCK,) is ftill living.

" could then have beheld with lefs anguifh
" the diffolution of Nature than the laft
" gafp of my infant. The fenfations I felt
" at the death of my dear parent were of a
" different nature—it was a *tranquil forrow*,
" a *melancholy* which I have heard obferv-
" ed *foothes* the foul inftead of corroding
" it. While I held the expiring faint in
" my arms, and faw her juft verging into
" eternity—while I dropt tear after tear in
" folemn filence over her livid countenance,
" oh how fincerely did I wifh to accom-
" pany her from thofe fcenes of vanity,
" from which her admirable precepts had
" fo much detached my affections! *Oh*
" *my mother! cried I*, you *lately wept for*
" *my* ABELLA, *we now pay the fame mourn-*
" *ful tribute to* you! Oh Death! thou
" greateft evil annexed to human nature,
" how doft thou diffolve the fweet connec-
" tions among men, and burft away the
" filken bands of Friendfhip! I thought
" I had *now* defcended the loweft vale of
                                    " mortal

" mortal forrow, but the deception vanifh-
" ed at the bed-fide of my expiring fifter.
" To enhance the diftrefs, fix tender in-
" fants were clamouring round their infen-
" fible mother, the one half unconfcious
" of the occafion of the general grief, and
" only lamenting becaufe the reft did.

" After her interment I returned hither,
" truly convinced how vifionary the eclat
" of *this* world is, and defiring to pafs the
" remainder of my life in a tranquil enjoy-
" ment of the bounties of heaven, neither
" elated to the extravagance of *mirth*, nor
" funk to the meannefs of *dejeEtion*.

" A. E. B."

From this period till the year 1781,
they lived in tolerable tranquillity, when, in
the beginning of Auguft, as Mr. BLEECKER
was affifting in the harveft, he, with two
of his men, were made prifoners by a party
from

from *Canada*, and taken off immediately. As it was late in the afternoon, Mrs. BLEECKER expected him with a degree of impatience, and began to be apprehenfive that fomething uncommon had occurred: a fervant was therefore difpatched, who foon returned with the forrowful account, that he could not fee any of them, and that the waggon and horfes were in the road tied to a tree.

She was at no lofs to conjecture what was become of him, for a number of fmall parties from *Canada* were known to be fculking in the woods, for the fole purpofe of carrying off the moft active citizens. The neighbours therefore were immediately alarmed, and the woods, as far as was practicable, were fearched; but they could not difcover a fingle trace of the party. Mrs. BLEECKER, giving him up for loft, fet off for *Albany* directly, though it was then near night, and abandoned herfelf to the moft hopelefs grief; but, by a
                                           wonderful

wonderful train of events, Mr. BLEECKER was re-taken by a party from *Bennington,* after having paſſed the laſt habitation on this ſide of the *Green-Mountains,* and when his conductors for the *firſt time* had conſidered themſelves as perfectly ſecure. He returned to her in ſix days, and the joy ſhe felt at finding him operating more powerfully than the grief ſhe experienced at his loſs, a fit of ſickneſs enſued, which nearly proved fatal. They again returned to *Tombanick.*

Though Mrs. BLEECKER was witneſs to many ſcenes of diſtreſs during the late war, in many of which ſhe was the principal ſufferer; yet, the idea of a *far diſtant* peace, which ſhould again reſtore her to her friends, gilt the ſolitary ſhades which encompaſſed her, and bore her up under frequent and poignant griefs.

In the year 1783, (the ſpring after the peace,) ſhe re-viſited *New-York,* in hopes of ſeeing her old acquaintance and friends; but

but her hopes were far from being realized—some were dead; others had left the continent; and the few who remained were in different states: She saw her half-fister, Miſs TEN EYCK, but once, and then but for a few minutes, as one party was embarking for *New-York* juſt as the other arrived at *Albany*. Her principal correſpondents and much-loved relatives, the Miſs V** W***'s, were in *Jerſey*; and as the Britiſh were ſtill here, ſhe could not (without the greateſt difficulty) viſit them. But the ruinous condition of her native city gave ſuch a ſhock to her ſpirits as the united efforts of her reaſon and fortitude were not able to ward off. The places which ſhe once knew as the ſcenes of feſtivity, were now ſunk into duſt—the place that once knew them knowing them no more; or if by hard ſearching ſhe at laſt deſcried them, they only met her eye as monuments of her paſt pleaſures—dreary piles, mouldering faſt beneath the relentleſs hand of

C   *Time*

Time and *War*. Her fenfibility was too
keen for her peace—She had ftruggled on
through the war, and had fuffered *Hope* to
beguile the hours devoted to diftrefs: but
now the fcene was changed—the illufion
vanifhed, and fhe concluded *now* fhe fhould
fee no more good upon earth. She returned again to her cottage, where fhe found
her health very rapidly decline; and on the
23d of the following November, about
noon-day, (after two days confinement to
her bed) her calm fpirit took its flight
from its fhattered habitation, without a
ftruggle or a groan. She retained her fen-
fes till within a few minutes of her death;
and the laft words fhe uttered to her weeping hufband and family, were affurances
of the pleafing profpect *Immortality* offered
her.

It is needlefs to fay her lofs was feverely
felt—it may be naturally fuppofed. The
benevolence of her difpofition had extended itfelf to all claffes of people; and in
the

the village where she dwelt, there were several families who might be called her dependants. To the aged and infirm she was a physician and a friend—to the orphan she was a mother—and a soother of the widow's woes; all loved—all honoured her: and when they followed her to the grave, they weeping said, (though differently expressed, still meaning the same,) " *We have lost* HER *whose equal we shall never see again!*"

It is to be regretted that the writings which we now have are but a small part of what she composed: she was frequently very lively, and would then give way to the flights of her fertile fancy, and write songs, satires, and burlesque: but, as drawing a cord too tight will make it break, thus she would no sooner cease to be *merry*, than the heaviest *dejection* would succeed, and then all the pieces which were not as melancholy as herself, she destroyed. As she seldom kept copies of her poetical epis-

tles,

tles, the moft of *them* are loft; one in particular, written fome little time before fhe
fled from *Tomhanick*, in 1777, and directed
to General BURGOYNE, was left in her bureau; the bureau was broken open and its
contents plundered by his men; but whether the letter ever reached him or not, is
unknown. In the winters of 1779 and
1780, fhe amufed herfelf and friends by
writing what fhe called the *Albany Gazette*,
which was fent by every opportunity to
Fifhkill, where feveral of her relations lived.
This lively and ingenious performance was
much admired, and being handed about
from one company to another, is entirely
loft. Several political and fatirical pieces
fhared a fimilar fate.

Some of thofe, however, which are left,
are here prefented to the public. The political fentiments difplayed in feveral of them
will, it is probable, recommend them to the
notice and favour of the Patriot, and the
reft may pleafe the lovers of artlefs ftyle.

Many

Many of them are faulty, but their merits are more numerous than their *defects*, and *these* will be eafily pardoned and forgotten by all who knew her; for *Detraction* will not rife up againft *her*, after death, whofe virtues, when alive, endeared her to fo many admiring *friends*, and whofe *enemies* (and *Envy* created her fome) could not fpeak evil of her.

As moft of thefe pieces were intended for the amufement of herfelf and particular friends, and not for the public eye, they appear as they flowed extempore from her pen. Frequently fhe wrote while with company, at the defire of fome one prefent, without premeditation, and at the fame time bearing a part in the converfation.

Mrs. BLEECKER poffeffed a confiderable fhare of beauty; her countenance was animated, and expreffive of her benevolent, feeling mind; her perfon, rather tall, was graceful and elegant; her eafy, unaffected deportment and engaging manners pro-

C 3   cured

cured her the efteem of moft perfons at firft fight, which generally increafed on a more intimate acquaintance.

M. V. F.

New-York, May, 1793.

THE

THE
HISTORY

OF

MARIA KITTLE.

In a Letter to Mifs Ten Eyck.

Tomhànick, December, 1779.

DEAR SUSAN,

HOWEVER fond of novels and romances you may be, the unfortunate adventures of one of my neighbours, who died yefterday, will make you defpife that fiction, in which, knowing the fubject to be fabulous, we can never be fo truly interefted. While this lady was expiring, Mrs. C----- V-------, her near kinfwoman, related to me her unhappy hiftory, in which I fhall now take the liberty of interefting your benevolent and feeling heart.

MARIA KITTLE was the only iffue of her parents, who cultivated a large farm on the
banks

banks of the *Hudfon*, eighteen miles above *Albany*. They were perfons of good natural abilities, improved by fome learning ; yet, confcious of a deficiency in their education, they ſtudied nothing ſo much as to render their little daughter truly accompliſhed.

MARIA was born in the year 1721. Her promiſing infancy preſaged a maturity of excellencies ; every amiable quality dawned through her liſping prattle ; every perſonal grace attended her attitudes and played over her features. As ſhe advanced through the playful ſtage of childhood, ſhe became more eminent than a Penelope for her induſtry ; yet, ſoon as the ſun declined, ſhe always retired with her books until the time of repoſe, by which means ſhe ſoon informed her opening mind with the principles of every uſeful ſcience. She was beloved by all her female companions, who, though they eaſily diſcovered her ſuperior elegance of manners, inſtead of envying, were excited to imitate her. As ſhe always made one in their little parties of pleaſure on feſtival days, it is no wonder that ſhe ſoon became the reigning goddeſs among the ſwains. She was importuned to admit the addreſſes of numbers,

whom

whom fhe politely difcarded, and withdrew
herfelf awhile from public obfervation. However, the fame of her charms attracted feveral
gentlemen of family from *Albany*, who intruded
on her retirement, foliciting her hand. But
this happinefs was referved for a near relation
of her's, one Mr. KITTLE, whofe merits had
made an impreffion on her heart. He, although
not-handfome, was poffeffed of a moft engaging
addrefs; while his learning and moral virtues
more particularly recommended him to her
efteem. Their parents foon difcovered their
reciprocal paffion, and highly approving of it,
haftened their marriage, which was celebrated
under the moft happy aufpices.

MARIA was fifteen when married. They
removed to his farm, on which he had built a
fmall neat houfe, furrounded by tall cedars,
which gave it a contemplative air. It was fituated on an eminence, with a green inclofure
in the front, graced by a well cultivated garden on one fide, and on the other by a clear
ftream, which, rufhing over a bed of white
pebble, gave them a high polifh, that caft a
foft gleam through the water.

Here

Here they refided in the tranquil enjoyment of that happinefs which fo much merit and innocence deferved: the indigent, the forrowful, the unfortunate were always fure of confolation when they entered thofe peaceful doors. They were almoft adored by their neighbours, and even the wild favages themfelves, who often reforted thither for refrefhments when hunting, expreffed the greateft regard for them, and admiration of their virtues.

In little more than a year they were bleffed with a daughter, the lovelier refemblance of her lovely mother: as fhe grew up, her graces increafing, promifed a bloom and underftanding equal to her's; the Indians, in particular, were extremely fond of the fmiling ANNA ; whenever they found a young fawn, or caught a brood of wood-ducks, or furprifed the young beaver in their daily excurfions through the forefts, they prefented them with pleafure to her; they brought her the earlieft ftrawberries, the fcarlet plumb, and other delicate wild fruits in painted bafkets.

How did the fond parents hearts delight to fee their beloved one fo univerfally careffed ! When they fauntered over the vernal fields with

with the little prattler wantoning before them
collecting flowers and purfuing the velvet elu-
five butterfly, MARIA's cheek fuffufing with
rapture, " Oh my dear," fhe would fay, " we
" are happier than human beings can expect
" to be; how trivial are the evils annexed to
" our fituation! may God avert that our hea-
" ven be limited to this life !"

Eleven years now elapfed before Mrs. KIT-
TLE difcovered any figns of pregnancy : her
fpoufe filently wifhed for a fon, and his defires
were at length gratified; fhe was delivered of
a charming boy, who was named, after him,
WILLIAM.

A French and Indian war had commenced
fometime before; but about eight months
after her delivery, the favages began to commit
the moft horrid depredations on the Englifh
frontiers. Mr. KITTLE, alarmed at the danger
of his brothers, who dwelt near *Fort-Edward*,
(the eldeft being juft married to a very agreeable young woman) invited them to refide with
him during the war.

They were fcarce arrived when the enemy
made further incurfions in the country, burning the villages and fcalping the inhabitants,
neither

neither refpecting age or fex. This terribly
alarmed Mrs. KITTLE; fhe began to prepare
for flight, and the next evening after receiving
this intelligence, as fhe and Mr. KITTLE were
bufily employed in packing up china and other
things, they were accofted by feveral Indians,
whofe wigwams were contiguous to the village
of *Schochticook*, and who always feemed well
affected to the Englifh. An elderly favage
undertook to be prolocutor, and defired the
family to compofe themfelves, affuring them
they fhould be cautioned againft any approaching danger. To inforce his argument, he prefented MARIA with a belt interwoven with
filk and beads, faying, " There, receive my
" token of friendfhip: we go to dig up the
" hatchet, to fink i' in the heads of your ene-
" mies; we fhall guard this wood with a wall
" of fire---you fhall be fafe." A warm glow
of hope deepened in MARIA's cheek at this---
Then ordering wine to be brought to the
friendly favages, with a fmile of diffidence,
" I am afraid," faid fhe, " neceffity may oblige
" you to abandon us, or neglect of your pro-
" mife may deprive us of your protection."---
" Neglect of my promife!" retorted he with
                                        fome

some acrimony: " No, MARIA, I am a true
" man; I shoot the arrow up to the Great
" Captain every new moon: depend upon it,
" I will trample down the briars round your
" dwelling, that you do not hurt your feet."
MARIA now retired, bowing a grateful acknowledgment, and leaving the savages to indulge their festivity, who passed the night in
the most vociferous mirth.

Mrs. KITTLE, with a sort of exultation, related the subject of their conference to her husband, who had absented himself on their first
appearance, having formed some suspicion of
the sincerity of their friendship, and not being
willing to be duped by their dissimulation.
" And now," added MARIA smiling, " our
" fears may again subside: Oh my dear! my
" happiness is trebled into rapture, by seeing
" you and my sweet babes out of danger." He
only sighed, and reaching his arm round her
polished neck, pressed her to his bosom. After
a short pause, " My love," said he, " be not
" too confident of their fidelity; you surely
" know what a small dependence is to be placed
" on their promises: however, to appear sus-
" picious might be suddenly fatal to us; we

D " will

" will therefore fufpend our journey to *Albany*
" for a few days." Though MARIA's foul
faddened at the conviction of this truth; though
her fears again urged her to propofe immediate
flight, yet fhe acquiefced; and having fupped
with the family, this tender pair funk afleep
on the bofom of reft.

Early the next morning Mr. KITTLE arofe,
firft impreffing a kifs on MARIA's foft cheek,
as fhe flumbered with her infant in her arms.
He then awaked his brother, reminding him
that he had propofed a hunting match the preceding evening. " It is true," replied PETER,
" but fince hoftilities have commenced fo near
" us as the Indians inform, I think it rather
" imprudent to quit the family."---" Come,
" come," replied the other, " do not let us
" intimidate the neighbours by cloiftering our-
" felves up with women and children."---" I
" reject the thought," rejoined PETER, " of
" being afraid." Then having dreffed himfelf, while his brother charged their pieces,
they left the houfe, and traverfed the pathlefs
grafs for many hours without perceiving any
thing but fmall birds, who filled the fragrant
air with melody. " PETER," faid Mr. KIT-

TLE,

TLE, cafting his eyes around the lovely landfcape, " what a profufion of fweets does Na-
" ture exhale to pleafe her intelligent crea-
" tures! I feel my heart expand with love and
" gratitude to heaven every moment, nor can'
" I ever be grateful enough. I have health
" and competence, a lovely fond wife whofe
" fmile would calm the rudeft ftorm of paffion,
" and two infants bloffoming into perfection;
" all my focial ties are yet unbroken---PETER,
" I anticipate my heaven---But why, my bro-
" ther, do you turn pale? what dreadful idea
" ftiffens your features with amazement? what
" in God's name ails you, PETER? are you
" unwell? fit down under this tree awhile."
---To thefe interrogatories PETER replied,
" Excufe my weaknefs, I am not unwell, but
" an unufual horror chilled my blood; I felt
" as if the damps of death preft already round
" my foul; but the vapour is gone off again,
" I feel quite better." Mr. KITTLE cheered
his brother, attributing his emotion to fear;
who, by this time, having re-affumed his compofure, entered into difcourfe with cheerfulnefs, refufing to return home without having
killed any thing.

D 2   Then

Then rising, they proceeded through lofty groves of pine, and open fields that seemed to bend under the heavy hand of Ceres. At laſt, diſappointment and fatigue prevailed on them to return home. they had gone farther than they apprehended; but paſſing along the bank of the river within a few miles of Mr. KIT-TLE's, they eſpied a fat doe walking ſecurely on the beach, which PETER ſoftly approaching, levelled his piece with ſo good an aim that the animal dropped inſtantly at the exploſion. This ſeeming ſucceſs was, however, the origin of their calamities; for immediately after, two ſavages appeared, directed in their courſe by the firing. Setting up a loud yell, they ran up to the brothers and diſcharged their fire-arms. Mr. KITTLE ſtarted back, but PETER received a brace of balls in his boſom. He recoiled a few ſteps back, and then ſunk down incompaſſed by thoſe deadly horrors of which in the morning he had a preſentiment. Mr. KITTLE ſtood awhile aghaſt, like a perſon juſt waked from a frightful dream; but on ſeeing the Indian advancing to tear the ſcalp from his dying brother, he ſuddenly recollected himſelf, and ſhot a bullet through his head: then grappling
with

with the other, who was loading again, he wrefted his firelock from him, and felled him to the ground with the but-end of it. This was no time for reflection or unavailing laments; the danger was eminent: fo leaving the favages for dead, with a mournful filence Mr. KITTLE haftened to throw the deer from off his horfe, and laid his bleeding brother acrofs him.

When our fouls are gloomy, they feem to caft a fhade over the objects that furround us, and make nature correfpondent to our feelings: fo Mr. KITTLE thought the night fell with a deeper gloom than ufual. The foft notes of evening birds feemed to be the refpoufes of fa-vage yells. The echo of his tread, which he never before regarded, now rung difmally hol-low in his ears. Even the ruftling of the winds through the leaves feemed attended with a fo-lemnity that chilled him with cold tremors. As he proceeded with his mournful charge, his feelings were alarmed for his dear MARIA; he dreaded the agitation and diftrefs this ad-venture would throw her in: but it was un-avoidable!

The found of his horfes feet no fooner in-vaded the ears of MARIA, than feizing a light

D 3   fhe

she sprung with a joyful impatience to the door, and was met by her partner pale and bloody, who endeavoured to prevent too sudden a discovery of this calamity. But at the first glance she comprehended the whole affair, and retiring a few steps, with the most exquisite agony in her countenance, " Oh Mr. KITTLE !" she cried, clasping her hands together, " it is " all over---we are betrayed---your brother is " killed !"---" Too true, oh, too fatally true !" replied he, falling on his knees beside her as she funk down, " my angel! the very savages " that solemnly engaged to protect us have de- " prived him of life; but I am yet alive, my " MARIA, be comforted---I will instantly pro- " cure carriages, and before morning you and " your innocents shall be beyond the reach of " their malevolence."

By this time the family had crouded about them, and with grievous wailings were inquiring the particulars of this sad adventure. Mr. KITTLE having related every circumstance with brevity, ordered the corpse to be laid in a remote chamber, desiring at the same time a horse to be saddled for him. Then, more oppressed by his wife's griefs than his own, he

led

led the difconfolate fair to her chamber, where,
being feated, fhe fighing demanded where he
intended to go at that time of night. "Only,"
faid he, " to the village of *Schochticook* to hire
" a couple of waggons; I fhall return in an
" hour I hope, with a proper guard to fecure
" our retreat from this hoftile place." MARIA
was filent; at length fhe burft into a flood of
tears, which his endearments only augmented.
Then expoftulating with him, " Is it not
" enough," cried fhe, " that you have efcaped
" one danger, but muft you be fo very eager,
" to encounter others? befides, you are fpent
" with forrow and fatigue---let one of your
" brothers perform this filent expedition."---
" It is impoffible," replied the tender hufband;
" how can I dare to propofe a danger to them
" from which I would fhrink myfelf? their
" lives are equally precious with mine : but
" God may difappoint our fears, my love!"
He would have continued, but his fpoufe, rifing
from her feat, interrupted him---" At leaft,
" my dear, before you leave us give your lovely
" babes a farewell embrace, that if fate fhould
" ---fhould feparate us, *that* yet fhall fweeten
" our hours of abfence." Here fhe found
herfelf

herfelf clafped in her confort's arms, who exclaimed, "My MARIA! I love you paffion-
"ately, and if the leaft fhadow of danger did
"appear to attend this night's travel, for your
"fake, for my bleffed children's fake I would
"decline it: but I have left the Indians lifelefs,
"who no doubt attacked us from fome private
"pique; nor will they be difcovered until
"morning."---"Well then," MARIA anfwered, "I no longer oppofe you ; forgive my
"fears." Meanwhile, as fhe ftept to the cradle for her fuckling, the fair ANNA, who was
liftening at the door anxious to hear her parents
fentiments on this occafion, quitted her ftation
and flew to them fwift as light; dropping on
her knees before her father, and looked up in
his face with the moft attractive graces and the
perfuafive eloquence of fimplicity. Her neck
and features were elegantly turned, her complexion fairer than the tuberofe, and contrafted
by the moft fhining ringlets of dark hair. Her
eyes, whofe brilliancy was foftened through
the medium of tears, for a while dwelt tenderly
on his countenance. At length, with a voice
fcarce audible, fhe fighed out, "Oh papa! do
"not leave us; if any accident fhould happen
"to

" to you, mamma will die of grief, and what
" will become of poor ANNA and BILLY?
" who will care for me? who will teach me
" when my papa, my mamma's papa is gone?"
" ---" My sweet child," replied he, embracing her and holding her to his bosom, " there
" is no danger; I shall return in an hour, and
" before to-morrow you shall be safe on the
" plains of *Albany*, and my heart shall exult
" over the happiness of my family."

Mrs. KITTLE now approached with her
playful infant in her arms; but its winning actions extorted nothing but groans from her pain-
ed bosom, which was more stormy than On-
tario-Lake, when agitated by fierce winds.
Mr. KITTLE perciving this uncommon emotion, gently took the child from her, and repeatedly kissed it, while new smiles dimpled
its lovely aspect. " Oh!" said he to himself,
" this gloom that darkens MARIA's soul is su-
" pernatural!---it seems dreadfully portenti-
" ous!---Shall I yet stay?" But here a servant
informing him that his horse was ready, he
blushed at his want of fortitude; and having
conquered his irresolution, after the most affecting and solemn parting, he quitted his house,
never to review it more!

MARIA

MARIA then walked fadly back again, and having affembled the family in a little hall, they clofed and barred the doors. Mrs. CO-MELIA KITTLE, MARIA's fifter-in-law, was far advanced in her pregnancy, which increaf-ed her hufband's uneafinefs for her; and they were debating in what manner to accommo-date her at *Albany*, when the trampling of feet about the houfe, and a yell of complicated voices, announced the Indians arrival. Struck with horror and confternation, the little family crouded together in the center of the hall, while the fervants at this alarm, being in a kitchen diftant from the houfe, faved them-felves by a precipitate flight. The little BIL-LY, frightened at fuch dreadful founds, clung faft to his mother's throbbing breaft, while ANNA, in a filent agony of amazement, clafp-ed her trembling knees. The echo of their yells yet rung in long vibrations through the foreft, when, with a thundering peal of ftrokes at the door, they demanded entrance. Diftrac-tion and defpair fat upon every face. MARIA and her companions gazed wildly at each other, till, upon repeated menaces and efforts to break open the door, GOMELIA's hufband, giving all

for loft, leifurely advanced to the door. Co-
MELIA feeing this, uttered a great fhriek, and
cried out, " O God! what are your doing, my
" rafh, rafh, unfortunate hufband! you will
" be facrificed!" Then falling on her knees,
fhe caught hold of his hand and fobbed out,
" O pity me! have mercy on yourfelf, on me,
" on my child!"---" Alas! my love," faid he,
half turning with a look of diftraction, " what
" can we do? let us be refigned to the will of
" God." So faying he unbarred the door, and
that inftant received a fatal bullet in his bofom,
and fell backward writhing in agonies of death;
the reft recoiled at this horrible fpectacle, and
huddled in a corner, fending forth the moft
piercing cries: in the interim the favages rufhing in with great fhouts, proceeded to mangle
the corpfe, and having made an incifion round
his head with a crooked knife, they tugged
off his bloody fcalp with barbarous triumph.
While this was perpetrating, an Indian hi-
deoufly painted, ftrode ferocioufly up to COME-
LIA, (who funk away at the fight, and fainted
on a chair) and cleft her white forehead deeply with his tomahack. Her fine azure eyes
juft opened, and then fuddenly clofing for ever,
fhe

she tumbled lifeless at his feet. His sanguinary soul was not yet satisfied with blood; he deformed her lovely body with deep gashes; and, tearing her unborn babe away, dashed it to pieces against the stone wall; with many additional circumstances of infernal cruelty.

During this horrid carnage, the dead were stripped, and dragged from the house, when one of the hellish band advanced to MARIA, who circling her babes with her white arms, was sending hopeless petitions to heaven, and bemoaning their cruelly lost situation: as he approached, expecting the fatal stroke, she endeavoured to guard her children, and with supplicating looks, implored for mercy. The savage attempted not to strike; but the astonished ANNA sheltered herself behind her mamma, while her blooming suckling quitting her breast, gazed with a pleasing wonder on the painted stranger.---MARIA soon recognized her old friend that presented her with the belt, through the loads of shells and feathers that disguised him. This was no time, however, to irritate him, by reminding him of his promise; yet, guessing her thoughts, he anticipated her remonstrance. "MARIA," said he, "be not afraid, I have promised to protect you;

"you

" you shall live and dance with us around the
" fire at *Canada:* but you have one small in-
" cumbrance, which, if not removed, will
" much impede your progress thither." So
saying he seized her laughing babe by the wrists,
and forcibly endeavoured to draw him from her
arms. At this, terrified beyond conception, she
exclaimed, " O God! leave me, leave me my
" child! he shall not go, though a legion of de-
" vils should try to separate us!" Holding him
still fast, while the Indian applied his strength
to tear him away, gnashing his teeth at her op-
position; " Help! God of heaven!" screamed
she, " help! have pity, have mercy on this
" infant! O God! O Christ! can you bear
" to see this? O mercy! mercy! mercy! let
" a little spark of compassion save this inoffend-
" ing, this lovely angel!" By this time the
breathless babe dropt its head on its bosom; the
wrists were nigh pinched off, and seeing him just
expiring, with a dreadful shriek she resigned
him to the merciless hands of the savage, who
instantly dashed his little forehead against the
stones, and casting his bleeding body at some
distance from the house, left him to make his
exit in feeble and unheard groans.---Then in-

E   deed,

deed, in the unutterable anguifh of her foul,
fhe fell proftrate, and rending away her hair,
fhe roared out her forrows with a voice louder
than natural, and rendered awfully hollow by
too great an exertion.   " O barbarians!"
fhe exclaimed, " furpaffing devils in wicked-
" nefs! fo may a tenfold night of mifery en-
" wrap your black fouls, as you have deprived
" the babe of my bofom, the comfort of my
" cares, my bleffed cherub, of light and life---
" O hell! are not thy flames impatient to
" cleave the center and engulph thefe wretches
" in thy ever burning waves? are there no thun-
" ders in Heaven---no avenging Angel---no
" God to take notice of fuch Heaven defying
" cruelties?" Then rufhing to her dead infant
with redoubled cries, and clapping her hands,
fhe laid herfelf over his mangled body; again
foftened in tears and moans, fhe wiped the
blood from his ghaftly countenance, and preft
him to her heaving bofom, alternately careffing
him and her trembling ANNA, who, clinging
to her with bitter wailings, and kiffing her
hands and face, entreated her to implore the favages for mercy.   " Do, my angel mamma,"
fhe urged, " do beg them yet to pity---beg
" them yet to fave you for my poor, poor papa's
                                    " fake!

" fake!---Alas! if we are all killed, his heart
" will break!---Oh! they can't be rocks and
" ftones!---Don't cry mamma, they will
" fpare us!"---Thus the little orator endeavoured to confole her afflicted mother; but
their melancholy endearments were foon interrupted by the relentlefs favages, who having plundered the houfe of every valuable thing
that was portable, returned to MARIA, and
rudely catching her arm, commanded her to
follow them; but repulfing them with the boldnefs of defpair, " Leave me, leave me," fhe
faid, " I cannot go---I never will quit my
" murdered child! Too cruel in your mercies,
" you have given me life only to prolong my
" miferies!"---Meanwhile the lovely ANNA,
terrified at the hoftile appearance of the enemy,
left her mamma ftruggling to difengage herfelf from the Indians, and fled precipitately to
the houfe. She had already concealed herfelf
in a clofet, when Mrs. KITTLE purfuing her,
was intercepted by flames, the favages having
fired the houfe. The wretched child foon difcovered her deplorable fituation, and almoft fuffocated by the fmoke, with piercing cries called
for help to her dear, dear mother.---Alas!

E 2   what

what could the unhappy parent do? whole
fheets of flames rolled between them, while
in a phrenzy of grief fhe fcreamed out, " O
" my laft treafure! my beloyed ANNA! try
" to efcape the devouring fire---come to me
" my fweet child---the Indians will not kill
" us---O my peiifhing babe! have pity on
" your mother---do not leave me quite defti-
" tute!" Then turning to the calm villains
who attended her, fhe cried, " Why do you
" not attempt to refcue my fweet innocent?
" can your unfeeling hearts not bear to leave
" me one---a folitary fingle one?" Again
calling to her ANNA, fhe received no anfwer,
which being a prefumption of her death, the
Indians obliged MARIA and her brother HEN-
RY to quit the houfe, which they effected with
fome difficulty, the glowing beams falling a-
round them and thick volumes of fmoke ob-
fcuring their paffage. The flames now ftruck
a long fplendor through the humid atmofphere,
and blufhed to open the tragical fcene on the
face of heaven. They had fcarce advanced two
hundred yards with their reluctant captives,
when the flaming ftructure tumbled to the earth
with a dreadful crafh. Our travellers by in-
                                            ftinct

ftin&t turned their eyes to the mournful blaze;
and MARIA, burfting afresh into grievous lamentations, cried, " There, there my brother,
" my children are wrapt in arching fheets of
" flames, that used to be circled in my arms!
" they are entombed in ruins that breathed
" their flumbers on my bofom! yet, oh! their
" fpotlefs fouls even now rife from this chaos
" of blood and fire, and are pleading our injur-
" ed caufe before our God, my brother!" He
replied only in fighs and groans, he fcarcely
heard her; horror had froze up the avenues of
his foul; and all amazed and trembling, he followed his leaders like a perfon in a troublefome
dream.

The diftant flames now caft a fainter light,
and the northern breeze bent the columns of
fmoke over the fouth horizon. Sad and benighted they wandered through almoft impe-
netrable fwamps, forded the broad ftream of
Tomhanick and the rapid river of *Hofack*; they
paffed through deferted fettlements, where the
yelling of folitary dogs increafed the folemnity
of midnight, nor halted till the ftars, emitting
a-feebler luftre, prefaged the approach of day.
MARIA, overcome by forrow and fatigue, im-

E 3   mediately

mediately funk helplefs at the foot of a tree, while the favages (who were fix in number) kindled a fire, and prepared their meal, (in a ealabafh) which confifted only of fome parched maize pulverized and enriched with the fat of bears flefh. Coterving MARIA had fallen afleep, they offered not to difturb her, but invited HENRY KITTLE to partake of their repaft. He durft not refufe them; and having fwallowed a few mouthfuls of their unpalatable food, and accepted of a pipe of tobacco, he defired leave to repofe himfelf, which being readily granted, they foon followed his example, and funk afleep, leaving two centinels to guard againft furprife, which precaution they always make ufe of.

I am forry, dear SUSAN, to quit MARIA in this interefting part of her hiftory; but order requires that we fhould now return to her fpoufe, whom we left on his way through the wood.

The village of *Schochticook* is fituated on a circular plain, furrounded by high hills, rifing in form of an amphitheatre. Mr. KITTLE had juft gained the verge, when, chancing to caft his eyes around, he perceived the whole fouthern

ern hemifphere fuddenly illuminated with a bright blaze; however, being accuftomed to the foreft's being often fired to clear it from the under-wood, he was not much furprifed, but proceeded to defcend the hill. On his arriving with the account of his brother's murder, the place was put in the higheft commotion; the men fitting up their arms, and the women clamouring about them, highly importunate to be removed to *Albany*; but the night being very dark, this manœuvre was deferred till morning; nor could Mr. KITTLE prevail on a fingle perfon to return with him during the darknefs: he felt himfelf ftrangely agitated at this difappointment, and refufing to repofe himfelf, with great impatience he watched the firft orient beam of Phofphor, which appearing, he fat off for home with two waggons and a guard of three Indians. As he approached his late happy dwelling, his bofom dilated with the pleafing hope of foon extricating his beloved family from danger; he chid the flownefs of the carriages, and felt impatient to diffipate the apprehenfions of MARIA, to kifs the pendant tear from her eye, and prefs his fportive innocents to his bofom. While thefe bright ideas

played

played round his soul, he lifted up his eyes,
and through an opening in the woods beheld
his farm: but what language can exprefs his
furprife and confternation at feeing his habitation fo fuddenly defolated! a loud exclamation
of amaze burft from the whole company at fo
unexpected a view---the blood revolted from
Mr. KITTLE's cheek---his heart throbbed under the big emotion, and all aghaft, fpurring
on his horfe, he entered the inclofure with
full fpeed.---Stop here unhappy man! here let
the fibres of thy heart crack with excruciat-
ing mifery---let the cruel view of mangled
wretches, fo nearly allied to thee, extort drops
of blood from thy cleaving bofom!---It did---
it did. Uttering a deep groan he fell infenfible
from his horfe, while his attendants, haftening
towards him, were fhocked beyond conception at the difmal fpectacle; and, ftarting back
with averted eyes from the dead, were thunder ftruck, not having power to move or
fpeak. After awhile two Indians (who being
ufed to fanguinary fcenes, recovered themfelves firft) took a blanket, and walking backward to the mangled COMELIA, threw it
over her naked body; the others then timidly
                                        advanced,

advanced, and Mr. KITTLE opening his eyes, groaned again bitterly; then raifing himfelf on his knees, with a look of unutterable anguifh, he called upon his dear MARIA. Alas! no voice but the folemn repetition of his own cries was articulated to him: then rifing with an air of diftraction, he ftalked round the bloody fcene, and examined the dead bodies; firft uncovering the pale vifage of COMELIA, he furveyed in filence her diftorted features; but perceiving it was not MARIA, he gently laid the cloth over again, and turning furioufly, caught up his ghaftly infant, whofe little body was black with contufions, and his fkull horribly fractured. Almoft fainting under his mournful load, and ftaggering at the dreadful difcovery, he depofited it again on the bloody earth, and clapping his hands together repeatedly with violence, " O hell! " hell!" he cried, " you cannot inflict tor- " ments fo exquifite as thofe I now fuffer! " how am I crufhed to the center! how " deeply am I degraded below the worms of " the fod! O my children! my children! " where are you now? O my wife! my " MARIA! the beloved of my bofom, are you,

" too

" too fallen a facrifice? Why do I furvive
" thefe miferies, my God? how can mortality
" fupport them? Burft---burft my fhrinking
" heart, and punifh a wretch for not having
" died in the defence of fuch lovely and in-
" nocent beings! Oh! why was I abfent in
" this fatal hour? why did not their groans
" vibrate on my foul that I might have flown
" to their aid?" Thus wildly lamenting and
wandering among the fmoaking ruins, he
picked up fome of the calcined bones of his
once beautiful ANNA. At this fight defpair
fhook his foul afrefh, new agonies convulfed
his features, and dropping the fad evidence of
his miferies, he extended his arms to Heaven,
and roared out, " Revenge! great God! re-
" venge if thou art juft and kind as reprefent-
" ed! Oh! that I had the power of an arch-
" angel to thunder eternal horrors on the
" guilty wretches who have blafted the bud
" of my happinefs, who have darkened the
" brighteft eyes that ever opened on the light!"

The men here interfering, to confole him
obferved, the bones were probably thofe of his
brother PETER; but on finding his fkeleton
entire, Mr. KITTLE infifted that it muft have
been

been MARIA and ANNA, who, having hid themfelves, had doubtlefs perifhed in the flames. Again, in the furious extravagance of paffion, he tore the hair from his head, and cafting himfelf proftrate on the afhes, he gathered the crumbling bones to his bofom, while the big drops of anguifh iffued at every pore, till life, unable longer to fuftain the mental conflict, fufpended her powers, and once more deprived him of fenfation. His companions having laid him on a waggon, now conferred together in what manner to proceed, and apprehending an attack from the favages, they unanimoufly concluded to lay the dead bodies on the remaining carriage, and make the beft of their way to *Schochticook*, which they accordingly performed with great filence and expedition.

You may judge, my dear, what a panic the appearance of this mournful cavalcade ftruck over the inhabitants of this defencelefs village. Mr. KITTLE was gently laid on a bed, and being let blood, his refpiration became lefs obftructed, though he continued fenfelefs till his unfortunate family were interred. Six weeks elapfed before he recovered any degree

of

of ftrength; but even then he appeared pale
and emaciated, like a fecond LAZARUS; his
difpofition was entirely changed, his looks were
fierce, his attitudes wild and extravagant, and
his converfation, which formerly was fenfible,
commanding attention by a mufical voice, now
was incoherent, and his cadence deep and hollow, rather infpiring terror than any pleafing
fenfation. Thirfting for revenge, and perceiving that folitude only tended to corrode his moments with the blackeft melancholy, he foon
after entered the Britifh fervice in the capacity
of gentleman volunteer, and fignalized himfelf by his prudence and intrepidity, attract-
ing the particular notice of his officers, who
being affected with his misfortunes, proffered
their fervices to him with fo much friendfhip
and candour, as obliged him to accept of them,
and yet lightened the obligation.

But doubtlefs, my dear, your generous fenfibility is alarmed at my filence about Mrs.
KITTLE; I think we left her repofing under
a tree: fhe was the firft that awaked as the
fun began to exhale the cryftal globules of
morning, when half rifing, and reclining on
her elbow, fhe furveyed the lovely landfcape
around

around her with a deep figh; they were on an eminence that commanded an unlimited profpect of the country every way. The birds were cheerful; the deer bounded fearlefs over the hills; the meadows blufhed with the enamel of FLORA: but grief had faddened every object in her fight; the whole creation feemed a dark blank to the fair mourner. Again recollection unlocked the fluices of her eyes, and her foft complaints difturbed her favage companions, who, rifing and kindling up the dying embers, began to prepare their victuals, which they invited her to partake of. This fhe declined with vifible deteftation; and turning to her brother, with the dignity of confcious merit in diftrefs, "No," faid fhe, "I never will " receive a morfel from thofe bloody hands yet " dropping with recent murder!---let me pe- " rifh---let the iron hand of famine firft pinch " out my vitals and fend me after my chil- " dren!" Notwithftanding this, HENRY added his folicitations that fhe fhould accept of fome refrefhment, reminding her of the confequence of her fatal refolution, which could be deemed no otherwife than fuicide. Finding this had no effect, he tried to touch her feelings on a fofter key---" Remember, MA-

F   " RIA,"

" RIA," said he, " you have a tender husband
" yet living; would you wish to deprive him
" of every earthly consolation? Would you
" add affliction to affliction, and after he
" has performed the sorrowful obsequies of
" his children, to crush all his remaining hope
" by the news of your voluntary death? No,
" live my sister! be assured he will soon get
" us exchanged, when soft sympathies shall
" wash away your sorrows; and after a few
" years, who knows but the smiles of a new
" lovely progeny may again dawn a paradise
" of happiness on you." MARIA was affected, and half raising her eyes from the earth,
she replied, " O my brother! how confoling
" do your words sink on my heart! though
" my reason tells me your arguments are im-
" probable and fallacious, yet it soothes the
" tempest of my soul---I will try to live---
" perhaps I may again behold my dear, dear,
" dear husband!" Here a flood of tears interrupted her.

As this conversation was held in English,
the savages were inquisitive to know the subject of it, at the same time enjoining them both
never to utter a syllable in their presence except

cept in their own uncouth dialect, which, as
they perfectly underſtood, they could not excuſe themſelves from. HENRY then informed
them that his ſiſter, objecting to their method
of preparing food, had deſired him to prevail
with them to indulge her in dreſſing her meals
herſelf. This they readily granted, and farther
to ingratiate themſelves in the priſoners' favour, they diſpatched a young Indian to hunt
for partridges or quails in the groves adjoining
them : He inſtantly returned with a brood of
wood-pigeons, ſcarcely fledged, which he preſented to HENRY, who cleaned and broiled
them on ſticks, with an officious ſolicitude to
pleaſe his ſiſter, which ſhe obſerved with a
look of gratitude, and taking a pigeon from the
ſtick, began to eat more from complaiſance
than inclination. HENRY was delighted at her
ready acquieſcence, and their repaſt being ended, they proceeded on their tireſome journey
with leſs repining than the preceding night.
MARIA was exempted from carrying a burden, yet ſhe found the fatigue almoſt intolera-
ble. They continually paſſed through a ſcene
of conflagration, the ſavages firing every cottage in their way, whoſe mournful blaze catch-

ing

ing the dry fields of grain, would fcorch off hundreds of acres in a few moments, and form a burning path for their deftroyers. As the fun advanced to his zenith, its rays beat fierce- ly on our travellers, augmented by the crack- ling flames around them; when meeting with a cool ftream of water, MARIA was com- manded to fit down (being over-heated) while the reft approached the rivulet: the Indian that guarded MARIA was ftooping down to drink, when a loud ruftling among the leaves and trampling of bufhes attracted his attention; he liftened awhile feemingly much alarmed, then ftarting up fuddenly, he flew to MARIA, and caught hold of her hair, aiming his hatchet at her head: the confequence was obvious, and her fate feemed inevitable; yet, with a ftoical compofure, fhe folded her arms acrofs, and waited the fatal ftroke with perfect refigna- tion; but while the weapon was yet fufpended over her, chancing to look around, he perceived the noife to proceed from a large deer, whofe antlers were entangled in the branches of a thicket. Though an uncivilized inhabitant of the foreft, he blufhed at his precipitancy, and returning the inftrument of death to his

girdle,

girdle, after some hesitation made this apology:
" MARIA, this sudden discovery is well for
" you; I thought we had been pursued, and
" we never suffer our prisoners to be re-taken;
" however, I was imprudent to attempt your
" life before there was a probability of your
" being rescued:" then desiring her to rise
and drink, he quickly shot the deer, his associ-
ates helping him to skin it. Instead of quench-
ing her thirst she sat down pensive on the flowery margin, casting he eyes carelessly on the
stream: she knew not whether to esteem her
late deliverance from death a happy providence or protraction of misery. Observing
the spotted trout, and other fish, to dart spor-
tively across the water, she could not help
exclaiming, " Happy! happy animals! you
" have not the fatal gift of reason to embit-
" ter your pleasures; you cannot anticipate
" your difficulties by apprehension, or pro-
" long them by recollection; incapable of of-
" fending your Creator, the blessings of your
" existence are secured to you: Alas! I envy
" the meanest among ye!" A gush of tears
concluded her soliloquy; and being called to
attend the company, she arose, and they began
F 3 their

their journey for the afternoon. HENRY defiring to have a piece of venifon (having left
it behind, feldom incommoding themfelves
with more than the hide and tallow) they returned and obliged him with a haunch, which
was very fat: at the next interval of travel he
dreffed it for himfelf and MARIA. In the
evening they croffed the river fomewhat below *Fort-Edward*, in a canoe left hid under
fome bufhes for that purpofe. They obferved
the moft profound filence until they entered
the woods again; but it was very late before
they halted, which they did in a deep hollow,
furrounded by pines whofe tops feemed to be
loft in the clouds. It was neceffary here to
light a fire, for the wolves howled moft dreadfully, and the whole foreft rung with the cries
of wild beafts of various forts. The confines
of hell could not have given MARIA more
difmal ideas than her prefent fituation: the
horrid gloom of the place, the fcowling looks
of her murderous companions, the fhrill
fhrieks of owls, the loud cries of the wolf,
and mournful fcreams of panthers, which were
redoubled by diftant echoes as the terrible
founds feemed dying away, fhook her frame
with

with cold tremors---fhe funk under the oppreffion of terror, and almoft fainted in
HENRY's arms; however, on perceiving the
beafts durft not approach the light, but began
to retire, fhe became a little more affured,
and helped HENRY to erect a booth of pine
branches, making a bed of the fame materials
in it while he prepared their fupper: having
eaten, and kindled a large fire in the front of
her arbour, fhe laid down and foon fell in a
deep fleep. She felt herfelf refrefhed by this
unexpected repofe, and the next morning,
with fome alacrity, continued her journey,
hoping at laft to arrive at fome Chriftian fet-
tlement. Arriving at *Lake-Champlain*, they
raifed a wigwam on the bank, expecting the
coming of Indians from the oppofite fhore to
carry them over.

Here our unfortunate captives were ftript of
their habits, already rent to pieces by briers,
and attired each with remnants of old blankets.
In this new drefs Mrs. KITTLE ventured to
expoftulate with the favages, but it was talking to the ftormy ocean; her complaints ferv-
ed only to divert them; fo retiring among the
bufhes, fhe adjufted her coarfe drefs fomewhat
decently,

decently, and then feating herfelf filently under a fpreading tree, indulged herfelf in the
luxury of forrow. HENRY, fenfible that they
expected more fortitude from him, and that if
he funk under his adverfe fortune he fhould
be worfe treated, affected to be cheerful; he
affifted them in catching falmon, with which
the lake abounds; an incredible quantity of
wild fowl frequenting the lake alfo, he laid
fnares for thofe of the leffer fort, (not being
allowed fire-arms) and fucceeded fo well, that
his dexterity was highly commended, and
night coming on, they regaled themfelves on
the fruits of their induftry. The night was
exceedingly dark, but calm; a thick mift ho-
vered over the woods, and the fmall ridgy
waves foftly rolled to the fhore, when fuddenly a large meteor, or fiery exhalation, paffed
by them with furprifing velocity, cafting on
every fide fhowers of brilliant fparkles. At
fight of this phænomenon the Indians put their
heads between their knees, crying out in a lamentable voice, " Do not! do not! do not!"
continuing in the fame attitude until the vapour difappeared. HENRY, with fome furprife, demanded the reafon of this exclamation,

tion; to which they replied, " What he had
" feen was a fiery dragon on his paffage to
" his den, who was of fo malevolent a tem-
" per, that he never failed, on his arrival there,
" to inflict fome peculiar calamity on man-
" kind." In about five minutes after the
earth was violently agitated, the waves of the
lake tumbled about in a ftrange manner, feem-
ing to emit flashes of fire, all the while attended with moft tremendous roarings, intermixed
with loud noifes, not unlike the explofion of
heavy cannon. Soon as the Indians perceived
it was an earthquake, they cried out, " Now
" he comes home!" and cafting themfelves
in their former pofture, filled the air with difmal howlings. This was a terrible fcene to
MARIA, who had never been witnefs to fo
dreadful a convulfion of Nature before; fhe
ftarted up and fled from her favage companions
towards an eminence at fome diftance, where,
dropping on her knees, fhe emphatically implored the protection of Heaven: however,
fhe was followed by an Indian and HENRY;
the latter, highly affected with her diftreffes,
taking hold of her trembling hand, " But why,
" my fifter!" faid he, " have you fled from
" us

" us? is the gloom of a foreſt more cheering
" than the ſympathiſing looks of a friend?"
" No, my brother!" replied MARIA; " but
" the thought was ſuggeſted to me, that the
" ſupreme God perhaps. was preparing to
" avenge himſelf of theſe murderers by ſome
" awful and uncommon judgment, and I fled
" from them as LOT did from *Sodom*, leſt I
" might be involved in the puniſhment of their
" guilt." They converſed in Engliſh, which
diſpleaſing the Indian, he ordered them to return to the wigwam, threatening to bind MA-
RIA faſt if ſhe offered to elope again. The
ſhock being over, ſilence again ſpread through
the realms of darkneſs, when a high wind
aroſe from the north and chilled our half-naked
travellers with exceſſive cold. The ſavages
(whoſe callous ſkins were proof againſt the in-
clement weather) not caring to continue their
fires, leſt they ſhould be diſcovered and ſurpriſed by ſome Engliſh party, they paſſed here
a very uncomfortable night; but the wind ſub-
ſiding, and the ſky growing clear, the ſun roſe
peculiarly warm and pleaſant, ſtreaming ten
thouſand rays of gold acroſs the lake. MARIA
had ſcarcely performed her oraiſons, when the
                                        ſavages,

favages, forming a circle round her and HENRY, began to dance in a moſt extravagant manner, and with antic geſtures that at another time would have afforded mirth to our travellers. Having continued their exerciſe ſome time, they incontinently drew out boxes of paint, and began to ornament their captives with a variety of colours; one having croſſed their faces with a ſtroke of vermilion, another would interſect it with a line of black, and ſo on until the whole company had given a ſpecimen of their ſkill or fancy.

Soon after two canoes arrived, in which they paſſed over the lake, which was uncommonly ſerene and pleaſant. They proceeded not far on their way before they were obliged to halt for two days, on account of MARIA's inability to travel, her feet being greatly ſwoln and lacerated by the flinty path. At length, by eaſy ſtages, they came in view of an Indian ſettlement, when MARIA's long unbent features relaxed into a half ſmile, and turning to HENRY, " Here, my brother!" ſaid ſhe, " I " ſhall find ſome of my own ſex, to whom ſim- " ple Nature, no doubt, has taught humanity ; " this is the firſt precept ſhe inculcates in the " female

" female mind, and this they generally retain
" through life, in spite of every evil propen-
" sity." As she uttered this elogium in favour
of the fair, the tawny villagers, perceiving
their approach, rushed promiscuously from
their huts with an execrable din, and fell upon
the weary captives with clubs and a shower
of stones, accompanying their strokes with
the most virulent language; among the rest an
old deformed squaw, with the rage of a Tisi-
phone, flew to MARIA, aiming a pine-knot
at her head, and would certainly have given
the wretched mourner her quietus had she not
been opposed by the savage that guarded Mrs.
KITTLE: he at first mildly expostulated with
his passionate countrywoman; but finding the
old hag frantic, and insatiable of blood, he
twisted the pine-knot from her hand and
whirled it away to some distance, then seizing
her arm roughly and tripping up her heels,
he laid her prostrate, leaving her to howl and
yell at leisure, which she performed without a
prompter.---MARIA was all in a tremor, and
hastily followed her deliverer, not caring to
risk another encounter with the exasperated
virago. By this time the rage and tumult of
the

the favages fubfiding, the new-comers were admitted into a large wigwam, in the center of which blazed a fire. After they were feated, feveral young Indians entered with bafkets of green maize in the ear, which, having roafted before the fire, they diftributed among the company.

Mrs. KITTLE and her brother complaining of the bruifes they met with at their reception, an old Indian feemed to attend with great concern; then leaving the place, in a little time returned with a bundle of aromatic herbs under his arm, the juice of which he expreffed by rubbing them between two ftones with flat furfaces; this he gave them to drink, applying the leaves externally. They inftantly found relief from the medical quality of this extraordinary plant, and compofing themfelves to fleep, expected a good night's repofe; but they were miftaken, for their entertainers growing intoxicated with fpirituous liquors, which operating differently, it produced a moft complicated noife of yelling, talking, finging, and quarrelling: this was a charm more powerful than the wand of Hermes to drive away fleep: but grown familiar with forrow and difappointment, MARIA regarded this as a trifle,

G   and

and when HENRY expreffed his concern for her, fmiling, fhe replied, " We muft arm our-" felves with patience, my brother! we can " combat with fate in no other manner."

It were endlefs to recapitulate minutely every diftrefs that attended the prifoners in their tedious journey ; let it fuffice, that having paffed through uncommon mifery, and imminent danger, they arrived at *Montreal*.--- Here the favages were joined by feveral fcalping parties of their tribe, and having previoufly frefh painted themfelves, appeared in hideous pomp, and performed a kind of triumphal entry. The throng of people that came out to meet them, threw MARIA in the moft painful fenfations of embarraffment; but as the clamours and infults of the populace increafed, a freezing torpor fucceeded, and bedewed her limbs with a cold fweat---ftrange chimeras danced before her fight---the actings of her foul were fufpended---fhe feemed to move mechanically, nor recollected herfelf till fhe found fhe was feated in the Governor's hall, furrounded by an impertinent, inquifitive circle of people, who were inquiring into the caufe of her diforder, without attempting any thing towards her relief. Difcovering her
fituation.

fituation, fhe blufhingly withdrew to a dark corner from the public gaze, and could not help fighing to herfelf, " Alas! but a very few " days ago I was hailed as the happieft of wo- " men---my fond hufband anticipated all my " defires---my children fmiled round me with " filial delight---my very fervants paid me the " homage due to an angel---O my God! what " a fudden, what a deplorable tranfition! I " am fallen below contempt!" As fhe thus moralized on her fituation, an Englifh woman (whom humanity more than curiofity had drawn to the place) approached MARIA, and obferving her tears and deep dejection, took hold of her hand, and endeavoured to fmile; but the foft impulfes of nature were too ftrong for the efforts of diffimulation---her features inftantly faddened again, and fhe burft into tears, exclaiming, (with a hefitating voice,) " Poor, forlorn creature! where are thy " friends! perhaps the dying moments of thy " fond parent, or hufband, have been cruelly " embittered with the fight of thy captivity! " perhaps now thy helplefs orphan is mourn- " ing for the breaft which gave him nourifh- " ment! or thy plaintive little ones are won-

G 2 " dering

" dering at the long abſence of their miſerable
" mother!"---" Oh! no more! no more!"
interrupted MARIA; " your pity is ſeverer
" than ſavage cruelty----I could ſtand the
" ſhock of fortune with ſome degree of firm-
" neſs, but your ſoft ſympathy opens afreſh
" the wounds of my ſoul! my loſſes are be-
" yond your conjecture---I have no parent,
" no ſportive children, and, I believe, no
" huſband, to mourn and wiſh for me!"
Theſe words were ſucceeded by an affecting
ſilence on both ſides: meanwhile the Indians
teſtified their impatience to be admitted to the
Governor by frequent ſhouts; at length his
Excellency appeared, and having held a long
conference with the ſavages, they retired with
his Secretary, and our priſoners ſaw them no
more.

After their exit the Governor turning round
to MARIA and HENRY, demanded who they
were? Mrs. KITTLE's perplexity prevented
her reply; but HENRY, in a moſt reſpectful
manner, gave him a ſuccinct account of their
misfortunes. The Governor perceiving him
ſenſible and communicative, interrogated him
farther, but he modeſtly declined giving any
political

political intelligence. Obferving that MARIA fuffered greatly in this interview, he foon concluded it, after having prefented feveral pieces of calicoes and ftuffs to them, defiring they would accept what they had occafion for. Mrs. KITTLE immediately fingled out a piece of black calimanco with tears of gratitude to her benefactor; who, fmiling, obferved fhe might chufe a gayer colour, as he hoped her diftreffes were now over. MARIA fhook her head in token of diffent, but could make no reply. He then difmiffed them, with a fmall guard, who was directed to provide them with decent lodgings.

HENRY was accommodated at a baker's, while his fifter, to her no fmall fatisfaction, found herfelf placed at the Englifh woman's who, on her arrival, had expreffed fo much good nature. She had fcarcely entered, when Mrs. D-----, prefenting her with a cordial, led her to a couch, infifting on her repofing there a little, " for," fays fhe, " your wafte " of fpirits requires it."

This tendernefs, which MARIA had long been a ftranger to, relaxed every fibre of her heart: fhe again melted into tears; but it was a

gufh

gush of grateful acknowledgment, that called
a modeft blush of pleafure and perplexity on
Mrs. D------'s cheek. Being left alone, fhe
foon fell in a profound fleep; and her friend
having prepared a comfortable repaft, in lefs
than an hour awaked her, with an invitation
to dinner---" And how do you find yourfelf,
" my fifter?" faid fhe inftinctively, feizing
MARIA's hand and compreffing it between
her's; " may we hope that you will affift us
" in conquering your dejection?"---MARIA
fmiled benignly through a cryftal atmofphere
of tears, and.kiffing the hand of her friend,
arofe. Having dined, and being now equip-
ped in decent apparel, MARIA became the admiration and efteem of the whole family. The
tempeft of her foul fubfided in a folemn calm ;
and though fhe did not regain her vivacity, fhe
became agreeably converfable.

In a few days, however, fhe felt the fymp-
toms of an approaching fever. She was alarmed
at this, and intimating to Mrs. D----- her fears
of becoming troublefome, " Do not be con-
" cerned," returned that kind creature; " my
" God did not plant humanity in my breaft to
" remain there an inactive principle." MA-
                                        RIA

RIA felt her oppreffion relieved by this generous fentiment; and indeed found her friendfhip did not confift in profeffion, as fhe inceffantly tended her during her illnefs with in-
expreffible delicacy and folicitude. When fhe
was again on the recovery, Mrs. D----- one
day ordered a fmall trunk covered with Mo-
rocco leather to be brought before her, and
opening it, produced feveral fets of fine linen,
with fome elegant ftuffs and other neceffaries.
---" See," faid fhe, " what the benevolence
" of *Montreal* has done for you. The ladies
" that beg your acceptance of thefe things,
" intend likewife to enhance the favour, by
" waiting on you this afternoon."---" Ah!"
interrupted MARIA, " I want them not; this
" one plain habit is enough to anfwer the pur-
" pofe of drefs for me. Shut the cheft, my
" dear Mrs. D-----, and keep them as a fmall
" compenfation for the immenfe trouble I have
" been to you."---" If this is your real fen-
" timent," replied her friend, (fhutting the
cheft, and prefenting her the key,) " return
" your gifts to the donors ; and fince you will
" reward me for my little offices of friendfhip,
" only love me, and believe me difinterefted,
" and

" and I fhall be overpaid."---" I fee I have
" wronged your generofity," anfwered MA-
RIA. " Pardon me, my fifter, I will offend
" no more. I did not think you mercenary---
" but---but---I meant only to difengage my
" heart of a little of its burden."---As this
tender conteft was painful to both parties, Mrs.
D----- rifing abruptly, pretended fome bufinefs, promifing to return again directly.

In the afternoon MARIA received her vifi-
tants in a neat little parlour. She was dreffed
in a plain fuit of mourning, and wore a fmall
muflin cap, from which her hair fell in artlefs
curls on her fine neck : her face was pale, though
not emaciated, and her eyes ftreamed a foft
languor over her countenance, more bewitch-
ing than the fprightlieft glances of vivacity.
As they entered fhe arofe, and advancing,
modeftly received their civilities, while Mrs.
D---- handed them to chairs: but hearing a
well-known voice, fhe haftily lifted up her
eyes, and fcreamed out in an accent of furprife, " Good Heaven! may I credit my fen-
" fes? My dear Mrs BRATT, my kind neigh-
" bour, is it really you that I fee?" Here
fhe found herfelf clafped in her friend's arms,
who,

who, after a long fubfiding figh, broke into tears. The tumult of paffion at length abating ---" Could I have gueffed, my MARIA," faid fhe, " that you was here, my vifit fhould not " have been deferred a moment after your arri- " val; but I have mourned with a fifter in " affliction, (permit me to prefent her to you,) " and while our hearts were wrung with each " other's diftrefs, alas! we inquired after no " foreign calamity." Being all feated, " I " dare not," refumed MARIA, " afk after " your family; I am afraid you only have " efcaped to tell me of them."---" Not fo, my " fifter," cried Mrs. BRATT; " but if you " can bear the recollection of your misfor- " tunes, do oblige me with the recital." The ladies joined their intreaty, and Mrs. KITTLE complied in a graceful manner.

After fome time fpent in tears, and pleaf- ing melancholy, tea was brought in; and to- wards fun-fet Mrs. D----- invited the com- pany to walk in the garden, which being very fmall, confifted only of a parterre, at the far- ther end of which ftood an arbour covered with a grape-vine. Here being feated, after fome chat on indifferent fubjects, MARIA de- fired

fired Mrs. BRATT, (if agreeable to the company) to acquaint her with the circumstances of her capture. They all bowed approbation; and after some hesitation Mrs. BRATT began:---

" My heart, ladies, shall ever retain a sense
" of the happiness I enjoyed in the society
" of Mrs. KITTLE and several other amia-
" ble persons in the vicinage of *Schochticook*,
" where I resided. She in particular cheered
" my lonely hours of widowhood, and omit-
" ted nothing that she thought might conduce
" to my serenity. I had two sons; she recom-
" mended the education of them to my leisure
" hours. I accepted of her advice, and found
" a suspension of my sorrows in the execution
" of my duty. They soon improved beyond
" my capacity of teaching. RICHARD, my
" eldest, was passionately fond of books, which
" he studied with intense application. This
" naturally attached him to a sedentary life,
" and he became the constant instructive com-
" panion of my evening hours. My youngest
" son, CHARLES, was more volatile, yet not
" less agreeable; his person was charming,
" his wit sprightly, and his address elegant.
                                    " They

" They often importuned me, at the com-
" mencement of this war, to withdraw to
" *Albany*; but, as I apprehended no danger,
" (the Britith troops being ftationed above us,
" quite from *Saratoga* to the Lake) I ridicul-
" ed their fears.

" One evening as my fons were come in
" from reaping, and I was bufied in preparing
" them a difh of tea, we were furprifed by a
" difcharge of mufketry near us We all
" three ran to the door, and beheld a party of
" Indians not twenty paces from us. Struck
" with aftonifhment, we had no power to
" move; and the favages again firing that in-
" ftant, my CHARLES dropped down dead
" befide me. Good God! what were my
" emotions! But language would fail, fhould
" I attempt to defcribe them. My furviving
" fon then turning to me, with a countenance
" expreffive of the deepeft horror, urged me
" to fly. " Let us be gone this inftant," faid
" he; " a moment determines our fate. O
" my mother! you are already loft." But
" defpair had fwallowed up my fears; I fell
" fhrieking on the body of my child, and
" rending away my hair, endeavoured to re-
" call

" call him to life with unavailing laments.
" RICHARD, in the meanwhile, had quitted
" me, and the moment after I beheld him
" mounted on horfeback, and ftretching away
" to the city. The Indians fired a volley at
" him, but miffed, and, I flatter myfelf that
" he arrived fafe. And now, not all my
" prayers and tears could prevent the wretches
" from fcalping my precious child. But when
" they rent me away from him, and dragged
" me from the houfe, my grief and rage
" burft forth like a hurricane. I execrated
" their whole race, and called for eternal ven-
" geance to cruih them to atoms. After a
" while I grew afhamed of my impetuofity:
" the tears began again to flow filently on my
" cheek; and, as I walked through the foreft
" between two Indians, my foul grew fudden-
" ly fick and groaned in me; a darknefs, more
" fubftantial than Egyptian night, fell upon
" it, and my exiftence became an infupport-
" able burthen to me. I looked up to Hea-
" ven with a hopelefs kind of awe, but I
" murmured no more at the difpenfations of
" my God; and in this frame of fullen refigna-
" tion I paffed the reft of my journey, which
                                        " being

"being nearly fimilar to Mrs. KITTLE's, I
" fhall avoid the repetition of. And now per-
" mit me (faid fhe, turning to the French la-
" dies) to acknowledge your extreme goodnefs
" to me. I was a ftranger, fick and naked, and
" you took me in. You indeed have proved
" the good Samaritan to me, pouring oil and
" wine in my wounds."---" Hufh, hufh! (cri-
" ed Madame DE ROCHE,) you eftimate our
" fervices at too high a rate. I fee you are no
" connoiffeur in minds; there is a great deal
" of honeft hofpitality in the world, though
" you have met with fo little."

" I now rejeƈt, (interrupted Mrs. BRATT,)
" all prejudices of education. From my in-
" fancy have I been taught that the French
" were a cruel perfidious enemy, but I have
" found them quite the reverfe."

Madame DE R. willing to change the fubjeƈt,
accofted the other ftranger,---" Dear Mrs.
" WILLIS, fhall we not be interefted likewife
" in your misfortunes?"---" Ah! do, (added
Mademoifelle V.) " my heart is now fweetly
" tunéd to melancholy. I love to indulge thefe
" divine fenfibilities, which your affeƈting hif-
" tories are fo capable of infpiring."---MA-

H   RIA

RIA then took hold of Mrs. WILLIS's hand,
and preffed her to oblige them.---Mrs. WIL-
LIS bowed. She dropt a few tears; but af-
fuming a compofed look, fhe began:---

" I am the daughter of a poor clergyman,
" who being confined to his chamber by fick-
" nefs, for feveral years, amufed himfelf by
" educating me. At his death, finding my-
" felf friendlefs, and without money, I ac-
" cepted the hand of a young man who had
" taken a leafed farm in Pennfylvania. He
" was very agreeable, and extravagantly fond
" of me. We lived happily for many years
" in a kind of frugal affluence. When the
" favages began to commit outrages on the
" frontier fettlements, our neighbours, intimi-
" dated at their rapid approaches, erected a
" fmall fort, furrounded by a high palifade.
" Into this the more timorous drove their cat-
" tle at night; and one evening, as we were
" at fupper, my hufband (being ordered on
" guard) infifted that I fhould accompany him
" with the children (for I had two lovely
" girls, one turned of thirteen years, and an-
" other of fix months.) My SOPHIA affented
" to the propofal with joy. " Mamma,
(faid

" (faid fhe,) what a merry woman the Cap-
" tain's wife is; fhe will divert us the whole
" evening, and fhe is very fond of your com-
" pany: come, I will take our little CHAR-
" LOTTE on my arm, and papa will carry the
" lantern." I acceded with a nod; and al-
" ready the dear charmer had handed me my
" hat and gloves, when fomebody thundered
" at the door. We were filent as death, and
" inftantly after plainly could diftinguifh the
" voices of favages conferring together. Chil-
" led as I was with fear, I flew to the cradle,
" and catching my infant, ran up into a loft.
" SOPHIA followed me all trembling, and
" panting for breath caft herfelf in my bofom.
" Hearing the Indians enter, I looked through
" a crevice in the floor, and faw them, with
" menacing looks, feat themfelves round the
" table, and now and then addrefs them-
" felves to Mr. WILLIS, who, all pale and
" aftonifhed, neither underftood nor had
" power to anfwer them. I obferved they
" took a great pleafure in terrifying him, by
" flourifhing their knives, and gafhing the
" table with their hatchets. Alas! this fight
" fhot icicles to my foul; and, to increafe my

H 2   " diftrefs,

" diftrefs, my Sophia's little heart beat
" againft my breaft, with redoubled ftrokes,
" at every word they uttered.

" Having finifhed their repaft in a glutti-
" nous manner, they laid a fire-brand in each
" corner of the chamber, and then departed,
" driving poor Mr. Willis before them.
" The fmoke foon incommoded us; but we
" dreaded our barbarous enemy more than the
" fire. At length, however, the flames be-
" ginning to invade our retreat, trembling and
" apprehenfive, we ventured down ftairs; the
" whole houfe now glowed like a furnace;
" the flames rolled towards the ftairs, which
" we haftily defcended; but juft as I fat my
" foot on the threfhold of the door, a piece of
" timber, nearly confumed through, gave way,
" and fell on my left arm, which fupported my
" infant, miferably fracturing the bone. I in-
" ftantly caught up my fallen lamb, and haf-
" tened to overtake my Sophia. There was a
" large hollow tree contiguous to our houfe,
" with an aperture juft large enough to admit
" fo fmall a woman as I am. Here we had
" often laughingly propofed to hide our chil-
" dren, in cafe of a vifit from the olive colour-
                                        " ed

" ed natives. In this we now took shelter;
" and being seated some time, my soul seemed
" to awake as it were from a vision of horror:
" I lifted up my eyes, and beheld the cottage
" that lately circumscribed all my worldly
" wealth and delight, melting away before the
" devouring fire. I dropt a tear as our apostate
" first parents did when thrust out from *Eden.*

" The world lay all before them, where to
" chuse their place of rest, and Providence
" their guide. Ah, EVE! thought I, hadst
" thou been like me, solitary, maimed, and
" unprotected, thy situation had been deplo-
" rable indeed. Then pressing my babe to my
" heart, " How quiet art thou, my angel, (said
" I;) sure---sure, Heaven has stilled thy lit-
" tle plaints in mercy to us."---" Ah! (sobbed
" SOPHIA,) now I am comforted again that
" I hear my dear mamma's voice. I was
" afraid grief would have forever deprived me
" of that happiness." And here she kissed
" my babe and me with vehemence. When
" her transports were moderated, " How cold
" my sister is, (said she,) do wrap her up
" warmer, mamma; poor thing, she is not
" used to such uncomfortable lodging."

H 3   " The

" The pain of my arm now called for all
" my fortitude and attention; but I forbore to
" mention this afflicting circumstance to my
" daughter.

" The cheerful swallow now began to usher
" in the dawn with melody; we timidly pre-
" pared to quit our hiding place; and turning
" round to the light, I cast an anxious eye of
" love on my innocent, wondering that she
" slept so long. But oh! horror and misery!
" I beheld her a pale, stiff corpse in my arms;
" (suffer me to weep, ladies, at the cruel re-
" collection.) It seems the piece of wood that
" disabled me, had also crushed my CHAR-
" LOTTE's tender skull, and no wonder my
" hapless babe was quiet. I could no longer
" sustain my sorrowful burden, but falling
" prostrate, almost insensible at the dreadful
" discovery, uttered nothing but groans. So-
" PHIA's little heart was too susceptible for
" so moving a scene. Distracted between her
" concern for me, and her grief for the loss
" of her dear sister, she cast herself beside me,
" and with the softest voice of sorrow, bewail-
" ed the fate of her beloved CHARLOTTE---
" her sweet companion---her innocent, laugh-
" ing

" ing play-fellow. At length we rofe, and
" Sophia, clafping all that remained of my
" cherub in her arms, " Ah! (faid fhe,) I did
" engage to carry you, my fifter, but little
" did I expect in this diftreffing manner."
" When we came in fight of the fort, though
" I endeavoured to fpirit up my grieved child,
" yet I found my fprings of action begin to
" move heavily, my heart fluttered, and I
" fuddenly fainted away. Sophia, conclud-
" ing I was dead, uttered fo piercing a cry,
" that the centinel looking up, immediately
" called to thofe in the fort to affift us. When
" I recovered, I found myfelf in a bed encir-
" cled by my kind neighbours, who divided
" their expreffions of love and condolement
" between me and my child. I remained in
" the fort after this; but, ladies, you may think,
" that bereft as I was of fo kind a hufband and
" endearing child, I foon found myfelf foli-
" tary and deftitute. I wept inceffantly; and
" hearing nothing from my dear Willis, I
" at length refolved to traverfe the wilds of
" Canada in purfuit of him. When I com-
" municated this to my friends, they all ftrong-
" ly oppofed it; but finding me inflexible,
" they

" they furnished me with some money and ne-
" cessaries, and obtained a permission from
" the Governor to let me go under protection
" of a flag that was on the way. Hearing
" likewise that a cartel was drawn for an ex-
" change of prisoners, I sat out, flushed with
" hope, and with indefatigable industry and
" painful solicitude, arrived at *Montreal*, worn
" to a skeleton (as you see ladies) with fatigue.

" I omitted not to inquire of every officer,
" the names of prisoners who had been brought
" in. At length I understood that Mr. WIL-
" LIS had perished in jail, on his first arrival,
" of a dysentery.---Here my expectations ter-
" minated in despair. I had no money to re-
" turn with, and indeed but for my SOPHIA
" no inclination---the whole world seemed
" dark and cheerless to me as the fabled re-
" gion of Cimmeria, and I was nigh perishing
" for very want, when Mrs. BRATT, hearing
" of my distress, sought my acquaintance: she
" kindly participated my sorrows, and too---
" too generously shared her purse and bed with
" me. This, ladies, is the story of a broken-
" hearted woman; nor should I have intruded
" it in any other but the house of mourning."

Here

Here she concluded, while the ladies severally embracing her, expreſſed their acknowledgments for the painful taſk ſhe had complied with to oblige their curioſity.----
" Would to Heaven!" ſaid Madame DE R̊.
" that the brutal nations were extinct, for
" never---never can the united humanity of
" *France* and *Britain* compenſate for the horrid
" cruelties of their ſavage allies."

They were ſoon after ſummoned to an elegant coilation; and having ſpent beſt part of the night together, the gueſts retired to their reſpective homes.

During two years, in which the French ladies continued their bounty and friendſhip to Mrs. KITTLE, ſhe never could gain the leaſt intelligence of her huſband. Her letters, after wandering through ſeveral provinces, would often return to her hands unopened. Deſpairing at length of ever ſeeing him, " Ah!" ſhe would ſay to Mrs. D----, " my
" poor huſband has undoubtedly periſhed, per-
" haps in his fruitleſs ſearch after me, and I
" am left to be a long---long burden on your
" goodneſs, a very unprofitable dependant."

In

In her friend's abfence fhe would defcend
into the kitchen, and fubmit to the moft me-
nial offices; nor could the fervants prevent her;
however, they apprifed Mrs. D---- of it, who
feized an opportunity of detecting her at her
labour. Being baffled in her humble attempt
by the gentle reproaches of her indulgent pa-
tronefs, fhe fat down on the ftep of the door,
and began to weep. " I believe, good Mrs.
" D-----," faid fhe, " were you a hard tafk-
" mafter, that exacted from thefe ufelefs hands
" the moft flavifh bufinefs, I could acquit my-
" felf with cheerfulnefs: my heart is like ice,
" that brightens and grows firmer by tempefts,
" but cannot ftand the warm rays of a kind
" fun." Mrs. D----- was beginning to anfwer, when hearing a tumult in the ftreet, they
both hafted to the door, and MARIA, cafting
her eyes careleffly over the crowd, in an inftant
recognized the features of her long-lamented
hufband, who fprang towards her with an un-
defcribable and involuntary rapture: but the
tide of joy and furprife was too ftrong for the
delicacy of her frame: fhe gave a faint exclamation, and ftretching out her arms to receive
him, dropped fenfelefs at his feet. The fuc-
ceffion

ceffion of his ideas was too rapid to admit
defcribing. He caught her up, and bearing
her in the hall, laid his precious burden on a
fettee, kneeling befide her in a fpeechlefs a-
gony of delight and concern. Meanwhile the
fpectators found themfelves wonderfully affect-
ed---the tender contagion ran from bofom to
bofom---they wept aloud; and the houfe of
joy feemed to be the houfe of lamentation.
At length MARIA opened her eyes and burft
into a violent fit of tears---Mr. KITTLE, with
anfwering emotions, filently accompanying
her; then clafping his arms endearingly round
her, " It is enough, my love," faid he, " we
" have had our night of affliction, and furely
" this bleffed meeting is a prefage of a long
" day of future happinefs; let me kifs off thofe
" tears, and fhew by your fmiles that I am
" indeed welcome." MARIA then bending
fondly forward to his bofom, replied, fighing,
" Alas! how can your beggared wife give you
" a proper reception? fhe cannot reftore your
" prattling babes to your arms---fhe comes a-
" lone! Alas! her prefence will only ferve
" to remind you of the treafures---the filial
" delights you have loft!"---" God forbid,"
                                    anfwered

anfwered he, " that I fhould repine at the lefs
" of my fmaller comforts, when fo capital a
" bleffing as my beloved MARIA is fo won-
" derfully reftored to me." Here he was in
civility obliged to rife and receive the compliments of Mrs. BRATT, Mrs. WILLIS, and
Madame DE R----, who, hearing of his arrival, entered juft then, half breathlefs with
impatience and joy. The company increafed; an elegant dinner was prepared: in fhort,
the day was devoted to pleafure; and never
was fatisfaction more general---feftivity glowed on every face, and complacency dimpled
every cheek.

After tea MARIA withdrew in the garden,
to give her beloved an account of what had befallen her during their feparation. The eloquence of forrow is irrefiftible. Mr. KITTLE
wept, he groaned, while all impaffioned (with
long interruptions of grief in her voice) fhe
ftammered through her doleful hiftory; and
yet fhe felt a great fatisfaction in pouring her
complaints into a bofom whofe feelings were
in unifon with her's---they wept---they fmiled
---they mourned, and rejoiced alternately,
with an abrupt tranfition from one paffion to
another.

Mr.

Mr. KITTLE, in return, informed her, that having thrown himfelf into the army, in hopes of ending a being that grew infupportable under the reflection of paft happinefs, he tempted death in every action wherein he was engaged, and being difappointed, gave himfelf up to the blackeft melancholy. " This " gloomy fcene," he obferved, " would foon " have been clofed by fome act of defpera- " tion; but one evening, fitting penfive in his " tent, and attentively running over the cir- " cumftances of his misfortunes, a thought " darted on his mind that poffibly his brother " HENRY might be alive." This was the firft time the idea of any one of his family's furviving the general murder had prefented itfelf to him, and he caught at the flattering fug- geftion as a drowning wretch would at a plank. " Surely, furely," faid he, " my brother " lives---it is fome divine emanation lights up " the thought in my foul---it carries convic- " tion with it: I will go after him---it fhall " be the comfort and employment of my life " to find out this dear brother---this laft and " only treafure." Perfuaded of the reality of his fancy, he communicated his defign to a

I   few

few of his military friends; but they only
laughed at his extravagance, and strongly dif-
fuaded him from fo wild an undertaking. Being difcouraged, he defifted; but fhortly after,
bearing that a company of prifoners (who
were enfranchifed) were returning to *Quebec*,
he got permiffion to accompany them. After
a very fatiguing journey he arrived at *Montreal*, and was immediately introduced to the
General Officer, who patiently heard his ftory,
and treated him with great clemency. Having obtained leave to remain a few days in
town, he refpectfully withdrew, and turning
down a ftreet he inquired of a man who was
walking before him, where lodgings were to
be, let? The ftranger turned about, civilly
taking off his hat, when Mr. KITTLE, ftarting back, grew as pale as afhes---" Oh, my
" God!" cried he, panting, " oh! HENRY,
" is it you! is it indeed you! No, it cannot
" be." Here he was ready to fall; but HEN-
RY, with little lefs agitation, fupported him;
and a tavern being at hand, he led him in.
The mafter of the hotel brought in wine, and
they drank off many glaffes to congratulate fo
happy a meeting. When their tranfports were
abated,

abated, HENRY ventured to tell him that his
MARIA was living and well. This was a
weight of joy too ftrong for his enfeebled pow-
ers---he ftared wildly about. At length, recovering himfelf, "Take care, HENRY," faid
he, "this is too tender a point to trifle upon."
---"My brother," replied HENRY, "be calm,
"let not your joy have a worfe effect than
"your grief---they both came fudden, and it
"behoves a man and a chriftian to fhew as
"much fortitude under the one as the other."
---"Alas! I am prepared for fome woeful de-
"ception," cried Mr. KITTLE; but, HEN-
"RY, this fufpence is cruel."---"By the eter-
"nal God!" rejoined his brother, "your
"MARIA, your wife, is in this town, and if
"you are compofed enough, you fhall imme-
"diately fee her." Mr. KITTLE could not
fpeak---he gave his hand to HENRY, and
while (like the Apoftles friends) he believed
not for joy, he was conducted to her arms,
and found his blifs wonderfully real.

I 2   THE

THE
STORY
OF
HENRY AND ANNE.

FOUNDED ON FACT.

HENRY and ANNE were born in *Germany*, in the Marquifate of *Baden:* their parents dwelt contiguous to each other, and the moft fentimental friendfhip fubfifted between the two families. ANNE was graceful even in infancy; HENRY tall and majeftic, ftrong and active, though not regularly beautiful: their poverty early introduced them on the fields: their little hands were lacerated by the bearded grain, and their tender feet wounded by the afperities of a flinty foil. ANNE's lovely complexion foon loft its delicate whitenefs, but was amply recompenfed by the bloom

I 3

of luxuriant health. Whilſt they toiled together in gathering the ſtones from the green
ſurface of a meadow, or weeding the vines,
the courtly paſſenger would ſtop and gaze with
pity to ſee ſo much elegance and beauty of
form joined to the ſervility of unremitted labour. HENRY redoubled his exertions con-
ſtantly to leſſen little ANNE's fatigue; and
when their taſk was done, they rejoined their
companions, aſſiſted them to complete their
work, and with gleeful hearts ſported themſelves to ſleep.

Nor were the old farmers diſpleaſed to ſee
the growing affection between their children:
" We ſhall ſoon be cloſer united," ſaid they;
" HENRY and ANNE (our only offspring)
" ſhall cement our friendſhip, and perpetuate
" our names to remoteſt centuries." Alas!
in the midſt of this inchanting viſion, an officer, attended by a file of muſqueteers, demanded HENRY. He was now ſeventeen, full
grown, and muſt enter his Lord's ſervice. It
was in vain to expoſtulate. Without a farewell ſigh from ANNE, or ſcarce an embrace
from his diſtracted parents, he muſt depart.
Being eſcorted to a diſtant town, he was there

initiated

initiated into all the military manœuvers, and three weeks after joined his regiment, which left that part of *Germany* foon after. HENRY's difappointed love funk him into melancholy--- he grew defperate, and negligent of life. In a very warm action, being engaged with the enemy in fight of the General, he ventured himfelf rafhly, and fought without caution. It was called intrepidity, and he was advanced to the rank of ferjeant. Having acquitted himfelf with honour, and the time of his fervice being elapfed, his Captain gave him his difcharge, with previous offers of promotion if he would continue in his company. " I " blufh to decline my officer's generous pro- " pofal," faid HENRY ; " but it is better to be " virtuous than fortunate--- I have left three " broken hearts at home, I muft haften to heal " them---the foft voice of my ANNE calls me " from the thunder of *Bellona*."---" Go," faid his commander in a foftened tone, " I " know what love is---my HENRY can be " happy, I only great;" then dropping a tear, " Go HENRY---farewell---I know you de- " ferve to be happier than I am."

The

The interview between the lovers was ten‑ der and romantic.‑‑‑ANNE, to confole her HENRY's parents, remitted not her affiduities to pleafe them. She cultivated their garden; fhe culled the richeft fruit and brighteft flowers to amufe them: her active fingers extended an imperceptible thread of flax to provide them linen of finer texture than the product of Egyptian looms: fhe refifted the importunity of HENRY's rivals heroically, while her old father, weeping for joy, commended her con‑ ftancy. " My child," faid he, " thou art no " difgrace to thy lineage; HENRY loves thee, " he is worthy of thee, and worthy of every " facrifice thou canft make him; cheer up my " little one, he will foon return."‑‑‑" No, " my father, fome inexorable fhot will cleave " his brave heart." So faying, fhe rofe agi‑ tated from weeding a bed of lupins, when a foot foldier approached. Scarce had the old man civilly accofted the ftranger over the hedge, when ANNE fcreamed out, " Oh heaven! " father, it is our HENRY, our own HEN‑ " RY."‑‑‑In an inftant the family was con‑ vened; from tears they made abrupt tranfitions to mirth, which foon caught the ears of the
                                                    good

good neighbours, who came in crouds to feli-
citate the foldier's arrival. His parents invited
them to return the next day and fhare the general feftivity, which they freely accepted,
and affifted to flaughter the poultry and fatteft
lambs. The entertainment was truly paftoral.
The tables were fpread in the vineyard, beneath verdant arches that were impurpled by
weighty clufters of grapes; a gufhing fountain
clofe by difpenfed a delicious coolnefs, and bafkets of flowers filled the air with balmy fweet-
nefs. To heighten the fcene, the filvery airs
of mufic, from the violin, harp, and melli-
fluous flute, foftly circled through the fky.
In fhort, a prieft was called and our lovers
married.

For two years peace and plenty were their
houfhold gods; but then HENRY feeing a family increafing, began to reflect on the means
of fupporting them. He had no land, and
had never been taught any mechanical branch
of bufinefs; however, after taking advice,
he purchafed a fmall flock of merchandife,
and prepared to follow the army. The good
parents exhaufted themfelves to increafe his
commodities. " Be frugal and cautious, fon,"'
                                        faid

said they; " remember ANNE and her babe."
—" Ah!" cried HENRY, embracing them,
" if I dishonour my parents, take ANNE from
" my bosom, give my paradise to a stranger,
" and let me die the death of a villain !"

HENRY visited his beloved friends frequently, but the army being stationed at a consider-
able distance from them, after an interval of
three years, he sighed in absence near eleven
months; he had accumulated eight hundred
pounds in cash by extraordinary application,
which compensated in some measure this painful separation, when he received a summons to
return home.   It seems his father-in-law had
been dispossessed of his farm, through inability to discharge his rent.   The good old man
retired with his child to HENRY's parents,
where they were cordially received; but grief
made insensible inroads in his constitution; in
less than three weeks (having languished a
few days) he died in ANNE's arms.

HENRY burst into tears at the news. " Cru-
" el parent," said he, " you knew my happy
" situation---why did you let the canker of
" disappointment abridge your days? my trea-
" sure was your own---I am infinitely your
                                    " debtor

" debtor---I never yet earned my RACHEL."
---Having paid a tribute of fincere drops of
gratitude and love, he fighed and went to bed;
he flumbered, and faw his ANNE fmile with
joy at the gold and filver he poured at her feet:
his little ones climbed his knees, and feemed
to be delighted with the glitter of his treafures:
his enamoured fancy called up every pleafing
idea to fport round his innocent family, when
he was fuddenly awaked by four ruffians, who
entered his tent well armed; and, advancing
to his bed, bade him be filent, at the peril of
immediate deftruction. Regardlefs of their
menaces, he ftarted up and demanded their
bufinefs; upon which they feized and bound
him hand and foot, then fell to rummaging the
tent. They foon difcovered his money---
what a glorious booty! In vain did he plead,
foothe, and threaten. " Leave me a few
" pieces: leave me but a little, a very little,
" to carry me to my poor wife and children."
His rhetoric made no impreffion---they left
him not a fous.

Being at fome diftance from the camp, his
repeated calls for help were not heard; at
length, in the filence of midnight, a centinel
diftinguifhed

distinguished a mournful cry for affistance, and sent a couple of veterans to reconnoitre. HENRY, now relieved from corporeal confinement, began to feel his heart contracted and shrunk by ideas of approaching beggary. He looked round him; the whole creation seemed comfortlefs and defolate. " How shall " I behold my domeftic bleffings? how shall " I look ANNE in the face? would to God I " had tilled fome fterile fpot of ground, we " would have been content in indigence; na-" ture would have been fatisfied with herbs " and lentils. Curfed ambition to be rich has " ruined me, and I am a traitor to my fami-" ly." With thefe bitter reflections the day broke, and having collected the little furniture of his tent, he difpofed of it to advantage to the humane foldiery, who univerfally loved him and pitied his misfortunes. Having fecured his cafh in a fmall bag, he fet off with a reluctant ftep for home. In vain did the birds carol on the elms that shaded the road. In vain did the ploughman whiftle gleefully, and the lambs wanton o'er the green hillocks. No enlivening fcene could diffipate his melancholy.

He

He protracted his journey through fear of being too foon the meffenger of ill tidings. On the fecond day at noon, having bought a loaf of bread, he fat down by a rivulet to eat; his tears flowed apace, and he began to deliberate whether he fhould return to ANNE or not. He counted his little ftore, and fell liftlefs on the grafs through defpondency. While thus he lay fadly ruminating, a handfome couple (thinking themfelves unobferved) paffed through the bufhes. "Alas!" faid the man, "for fix years my EMMA you have fuftained "the moft bitter poverty with your unfortu- "nate hufband. My heart breaks under the "oppreffion of your mifery; I cannot bear it "---return I befeech you, to the Baron; afk "his fatherly forgivenefs; he will reinftate "you to favour---and lovely EMMA I fhall "die content."---"I fmile," replied the fair one, "at your ignorance; gold and gems and "banquets have no charms for me; my "heart was formed for focial happinefs; I "love you, and deprived of your company "I fhould languifh and die, whereas I feel "no uneafinefs at the abfence of riches; we "have enough to fubfift comfortably on,

K   "though

" though it be coarfe; fo pray, my dear, drop
" this unwelcome delicacy." Here they
went out of hearing, and HENRY, ftruck
with the lady's fentimens, began to refume
courage. " I am afhamed," faid he, " at
" my want of fortitude; here is voluntary po-
" verty accepted in preference of an anxious
" mind: furely ANNE will have as much
" philofophy in that article as the unfortunate
" EMMA: what a deftruction have I efcap-
" ed! had I wandered away from my defolate
" family, we had all been miferable indeed."
So thinking, he took his pack on his fhoulders
and proceeded on his journey.

The fourth evening, paffing leifurely by
his deceafed parent's door, he involuntarily
turned back and walked in. Here his feelings
received a new fhock. Strange faces accofted
him---rudenefs and dirt had ufurped the place
where ANNE once reigned the goddefs of civility and neatnefs. The green inclofure,
furrounded by jeffamine, was trampled on by
fwine, and lean cattle browzed on the vines
that mantled over ANNE's window. He turned with grief and difguft from this mortifying
fcene, and had gone but a little farther, when

ANNE.

Anne defcrying him at a diftance, flew like
a bird acrofs the meadow, and fell into his
arms. After the firft emotions of tranfport
were fubfided, Henry affectionately em-
braced his lovely babes and tender parents,
who met him on the road. " I mifs but one
" from this beloved company," faid Henry.
---Anne burft into tears. " My Henry,
" you will mifs the chief of our good neigh-
" bourhood---our indulgent old Lord is dead;
" his tyrannical heir oppreffes his tenants with
" heavy rents and fevere exactions, and they
" have unanimoufly agreed to fhelter them-
" felves from this great burden, by flying to
" the wilds of *America*."

After they were feated in the houfe, " What
" your fpoufe advances," faid the old man,
" is true; and your aged parents would have
" alfo been forced to venture their trembling
" limbs and grey hairs over the dangerous
" ocean, had not our bleffed Henry's induf-
" try fecured us a competency." This trial
was too fevere. Henry changed countenance, and caft his eyes around with an
alarming wildnefs. " What is the matter
" with my child?" cried his mother. Alas!
K 2   this

this encounter was too fudden. " Old and
" experienced as I am, I feel almoft over-
" come with joy myfelf."---" Ah!" exclaimed her fon (recollecting himfelf) " fain
" would I conceal from fuch endearing friends
" the motive of my diftrefs; but I fhould ex-
" pire in the effort: forgive and pity a wretch
" who brings home nothing but mifery---
" who can fee his family fall to ruin, and yet
" live."---All aftonifhed they gazed at each
other in filence, while HENRY fobbed, unable to articulate a word. At length ANNE,
all fhining through tears, drew nigh and
kneeled before him---" Keep us not in fuf-
" pence, my hufband; pour your griefs into
" our bofoms, and wrong us not by referve;
" you can never bring mifery to us whilft you
" remain virtuous and loving as now."---
HENRY clafped the fad orator with paffionate
fondnefs in his arms; and after a little hefita-
tion acquainted them with the particulars of
his misfortune.

It was in vain to try to conceal their furprife
and difappointment, though HENRY's affliction forbad them to fall into repining, or any
expreffion of difcontent. By degrees their
chagrin

chagrin fubfided. The poor acquiefce with
greater refignation to calamity than the rich,
who feldomer meet with difappointment. At
laft, by an infenfible gradation, our penfive
affociates became bleft and eafy. A fmall repaft was provided, and fhutting out corrofive
Care, they indulged the hour of feftivity with
as much glee as if the robbers had reftored the
money ten fold.

The ftory of HENRY's robbery was foon
known, and his parents concluded that their
Lord would fhew fome lenity to them; but
finding him invariably cruel and oppreffive,
they began to attend to the flattering informa-
tions about the New World.---"At leaft,"
faid ANNE, " we fhall go into a land of fim-
" plicity.---the artlefs favages fubfift not by
" rapine and deceit: pride and hypocrify and
" avarice are ftrangers where luxury and
" titles are unknown."---The old man dif-
fented from this opinion. " Wherever the
" print of human footfteps have appeared,
" there certainly, my child, all human vices
" follow, though often under different appel-
" latives; however, we muft hazard this ad-
" venture. As the Lepers faid at Samaria,

K 3   " if

" if we ftay here we fhall certainly perifh,
" and if we go away, at the worft, we can
" but die."

The enfuing week, as they were merrily
chatting on the green before the door, a fudden cloud overfpread the heavens with black-
nefs, which foon fell in a torrent of rain, in-
termingled with thunder and lightning. The
family retired in the houfe; but HENRY hafted to drive the cattle and fheep to a place of
fecurity. All wet and dropping with rain he
was returning to the houfe, when an elegant
phæton, attended by a number of domeftics,
ftopped at the gate. A gentleman handed out
a lady, who feemed much affrighted with the
ftorm, and conducted her, with a delicate tendernefs, to the door. HENRY opened it wide,
and bowing to the ground, defired them to
walk in, prefenting them each with a chair.
The noble air, and rich dreffes of the new
guefts, awed our humble rufties, who fcarcely
durft lift up their eyes at them, until the gentleman, faluting the lady, inquired how his
fair EMMA did after her fright. HENRY then
inftantly recollecting the lady's countenance,
with a modeft apology for his boldnefs, re-
counted

counted his adventure at the brook---" I pre-
" fume," added he, " this lady is the very fame
" lovely EMMA whofe noble difinterefted-
" nefs made me blufh at my want of fortitude,
" and in effect faved my family from ruin."
Here EMMA, ftarting up, feized his hand---
" I little thought, my kind friend, that our
" converfation had an auditor at that time;
" but fince you have been a witnefs of my
" diftrefs, rejoice with me in my prefent hap-
" py fituation." Here, refuming her feat,
while her fpoufe hung enamoured over her
chair, fhe favoured the attentive circle with
an abridgment of her hiftory.---

" I am the only child of the prefent Baron
" of *Schauffhoufen*, who was particularly cau-
" tious that my education fhould render me
" up an accomplifhed lady to the world. On
" my firft introduction into the *grande monde*,
" I found myfelf encompaffed by admirers,
" whofe addreffes I permitted from vanity;
" but advancing to my twentieth year, my
" father grew folicitous that I fhould felect a
" hufband from the number. It was in vain
" to remonftrate to him that my heart was dif-
" engaged. He infifted on my accepting a
" partner

" partner for life.---" Chufe, my child, (faid
" he,) throughout all the empire; you can
" ennoble a peafant by your alliance with
" him, or caft a new luftre over the efcut-
" cheon of a prince."

" Seven months after this I became ac-
" quainted with my prefent hufband; and not
" doubting but that the Baron would accede
" to our union, I permitted the moft violent
" love to fteal into my bofom. I acquainted
" him in a dutiful and affectionate manner of
" my attachment, to which he made no reply;
" but turning from me with a ftern look (to
" my furprife) fhut his clofet door full in my
" face. In ten minutes I received this note---

" If you are determined, Mifs, to debafe
" the nobility of your birth, by a marriage
" with your prefent object, I renounce you
" forever. Take your jewels and clothes,
" and be miferable.

".Lodovicus Strelitz."

" I wept inceffantly on the perufal of this
" cruel billet. I wrote one to my lover, de-
" firing him to forget me; but before I could
" difpatch it, my coufin CHARLOTTE enter-
                                    " ed

" ed the room in great confusion. " Begone,
" EMMA," said she, " your father is exaf-
" perated to a degree of madnefs. He bids
" me to give you this purfe of piftoles, and
" commands you to quit the caftle inftantly."
---" Alas!" said I, finking on the floor, " I
" facrifice my love to my duty. My dear
" coufin, tell my old parent I am no longer
" a rebel to his will." Here I wept bitter-
" ly; but the cruel CHARLOTTE called out,
" Here, JOSEPH, if the chaife is ready, hand
" your young lady in. I am commiffioned,
" dear EMMA, to wait on you to another
" lodging. The angry Baron is from home,
" and I forfeit his favour if I do not oblige
" you to fubmit."---I then rofe from my
" knees, and fullenly giving my hand to her,
" said faintly, " I fee, CHARLOTTE, you
" have fupplanted me ; your undermining arts
" have ruined me." She made no reply, and
" I fuffered myfelf to be conducted to the
" chaife. In two hours we came to a neat
" farm-houfe. CHARLOTTE formally took
" leave of me, and I was fhewn to a fmall, clean
" apartment, where, in a fit of agonizing def-
" pair, I threw myfelf upon a little bed.
" The

" The woman of the houſe, coming in, in-
" formed me that CHARLOTTE had advanced
" the pay for my year's board at her houſe ;
" and concluding I was ſome refractory child,
" gave me a long lecture on obedience to pa-
" rents. I ſcarcely heard her.

" After a few days I wrote to my father.
" I begged the interceſſion of my relations, but
" in vain ; CHARLOTTE had ſtopped up every
" avenue to mercy. Finding myſelf rejected
" totally, I at length yielded to the emotions
" of a ſoft paſſion, and accepted the hand of
" my preſent huſband. We lived happily
" during ſix years, when, being ſeized with
" a pleuriſy, my phyſician made a report of
" my danger and poverty to my father. We
" had a ſmall hut on the common. The
" Baron's coach drove up to the door. He
" ſtooped as he entered, and walked cautiouſ-
" ly over the looſe uneven floor of my poor
" bed-room. I roſe up ſurpriſed to ſee him ;
" and as I ſat leaning againſt a pillow, the old
" man, in a guſh of grief and remorſe, fell
" on my bed ſobbing and unable to ſpeak.
" My two little ones ſeeing me weep, came
" up with viſible concern. The eldeſt kiſſed
                                    " my

" my hand and faid, " Don't cry any more,
" mamma, Mrs. MORELY has fent us bread
" and milk enough for two days." Here the
" Baron redoubled his fighs and feemed nearly
" fuffocated, when I feebly bent towards him.
" O my father! am I then forgiven?" But
" what he replied I know not---I fainted on
" the pillow. To be fhort, he took us all
" home. CHARLOTTE's indifcretions drew
" the odium of the family on her, and a bro-
" ken lieutenant carried her off to _England_.
" My father became exceffively fond of my
" fpoufe and children, and we are now upon
" a vifit to an old aunt, who lays a dying, and
" to whom I am fole heirefs. My friends,"
" continued fhe, " I fee by your looks my
" hiftory is not impertinent, and I acknow-
" ledge myfelf yet indebted to HENRY for his
" obliging partiality to me."

ANNE, with pleafed looks, immediately
fpread a table with a clean diaper cloth, and
placed on it feveral earthen plates, filled with
the moft delicious fruits, fome bifcuits, a plate
with honey-combs, and a flafk of wine; while
HENRY, bowing low, thanked the lady for
the honour fhe had done him. " I blefs the
" Almighty," faid HENRY, " for fo fignally
" rewarding

" rewarding virtue. I even rejoice that the
" Baron's cruelty gave your excellent qualities
" an opportunity to shine out so philosophical-
" ly in the test of poverty. Believe me, Ma-
" dam, the lustre of many a soul lies hidden
" beneath the splendor of affluence, like the
" Grand Duke's gems in the green vault."
The gentleman smiled---" And many a senti-
" mental mind, my HENRY," said he, " is
" circumscribed by poverty, and is of little
" utility to mankind beyond the limits of his
" own family. I heartily wish you, my friend,
" a fortune equal to your merit; in the mean-
" while accept this trifle," handing him a
purse with twenty pistoles. HENRY, amid the
highest confusion of blushing gratitude, received the gift gracefully, and pressed his be-
nefactors to accept of his little regale. When
they had eat, the sun began to shine out with
new lustre after the rain, and EMMA proposed
to proceed on their journey. She took a tender leave of HENRY, and kissing ANNE, stept
into the carriage, which instantly drove out
of sight.

Soon after this agreeable interview, they
prepared for their long voyage. The pensive
neighbours

neighbours affembled, and having delivered
their cattle to the Marquis's fteward, they all
embarked in a fmall veffel on the *Rhine* After
a tedious fail down the river, they were taken
aboard a fhip bound for *New-York*, in *America*.
A fair wind fprung up; they foon loft fight of
the Imperial fhores, and found themfelves furrounded by a horizon of waters.   The poor
cottagers viewed the uncommon fcene with
pleafure, mixed with dread; but in a few days
were accuftomed to the profpect, and great
agitation of the veffel.   HENRY, to leffen the
expence, had conditioned to work out his paffage; but he could procure only very indifferent accommodations for his family, the fhip
being fo crouded.   After a few weeks fail
ANNE's eldeft fon fickened and died, and the
mournful parents, with agonizing hearts, committed the babe of their hopes the darling of
their bofoms, to the waves.   " There finks
" my child," cried ANNE, weeping, " in the
" depth of the wild ocean: inftead of flumber-
" ing in my arms, he is gone to be the food
" of fea monfters."   HENRY fupported and
comforted her.   " We have another, my
" beloved; let us not fin away the only re-
            L   " maining

" maining little one by fruitlefs repinings;
" our fon is afcended to his Creator; it is not
" him that welters in the deep: O! grieve
" not that he is taken from the evil to come;
" from evils which we fhall yet forrow over!
" Wifely and mercifully has Providence pro-
" portioned our fufferings to our ftrength, and
" given the lenient hand of Time power to
" mollify thofe griefs he cannot cure." In a
little fpace ANNE's forrows funk into a languid ferenity. She began to fmile as ufual,
and HENRY was happy.

They had a tedious paffage; but at length,
one moonfhine night, the failors cried out,
" land!" In a moment they all crouded upon
deck: it was very calm, and near day: a gentle fouth breeze arofe foon after, and by fun-
rife they clearly diftinguifhed the little iflands
covered with verdure, and the white beach on
the bold continent. As they failed up the
Narrows, with a fair wind, the ftrangers
admired the beauty of the country, which
they little expected to find fo well cultivated.
When they were anchored in the harbour,
HENRY requefted a fcull-boat to go on fhore;
upon which an Englifh failor offered his affift-
                                        ance,

ance, rallying him a little; " Why, demme " brother, thefe people can't underftand your " gibberifh; they will fet you in the ftocks " for a Jefuit." They got on fhore, and the failor procured for HENRY's little family a de-cent apartment in Beaver-ftreet. HENRY ex-preffed his acknowledgments to the generous failor, for he really found he fhould never-have been able, in his uncouth broken language, to make the people underftand him.

Here HENRY left his little family while he went to feek a fpot on the vacant lands of this ftate, where he might accommodate them. He failed with a Dutch fkipper to *Albany*, and being informed by him where he might find fuch a place as he wifhed for, he fet off early the morning after his arrival on foot. As he walked along the clovery banks of the *Hudfon*, the long beams of the rifing fun glanced over its crumpled furface, and gilt the oppofite fhores with peculiar beauty; the tall pines of the adjacent foreft waved in folemn grandeur; the thrufh warbled in the thicket; and at every fhort diftance a little fountain caft its filvery waves acrofs the way, and fupplied the thirfty traveller with a feafonable regale. Charmed

L 2   with

with the fcene, HENRY often ftopped. He
furveyed each opening profpect with fingular
pleafure. The bright rays of Hope again
dawned upon his foul, and diffufed its enlivening influence through his late uncheery heart.
" Yes," faid he, " I feel that we fhall, in
" the uncultivated forefts of *America*, enjoy that
" tranquillity which the inhofpitable plains
" of *Europe* denied us." Here he was interrupted by the appearance of a traveller, who
no fooner perceived him than he flew to him.
" O, my HENRY!"----" O, my FREDE-
" RICK!" were all they could fay for fome
time. They clafped each other in their arms.
They wept and fmiled alternately. It was a
fellow foldier of HENRY's, a very dear friend.

After their firft tranfports were over HEN-
RY told him all that had paffed fince they
parted; and the foldier, in return, told him,
that foon after HENRY quitted the army he
lef it too, and in hopes of fettling happily in
the village where he was born, had returned to
it after an abfence of fome years; but upon his
arrival there, finding his parents dead, and the
object of his fincereft affection married to another, in a fit of grief and rage he left his native
country

country and came to *America.* " And here,
" my friend," continued he, " I am happily
" fituated for life ; I have married an amiable
" woman ; my neighbours are all like bro-
" thers ; and the acquifition of your dear fami-
" ly to our little circle will add new pleafure
" to it."

The fun was fetting when they entered the
beautiful village of *Tomhanick.* The farmers
had finifhed their daily tafk, and were fmoaking by their doors, while the younger tribe
gamboled on the green before them : the blufh
of health hung carelefs on every cheek, and
content fmoothed every brow. FREDERICK
invited the cottagers home with him ; and as
they were feated round a table covered with
the fruits of the feafon, he related to them the
hiftory of HENRY's life. The good people
were affected by the recital of his misfortunes,
and promifed to affift him. " You have been
" unfortunate," faid an old man, " but if you
" will live as we do, you fhall be happy."
The next day they affembled, and in the courfe
of two days they finifhed a neat log-houfe for
HENRY, fuch as they themfelves dwelt in.

With

With a heart filled with gratitude and joy, he returned to his ANNE ; he repeated the particulars of his journey and its happy issue, and proposed their removal to their new habitation as soon as possible. To this they all assented with pleasure; and having packed up their little effects, and paid their rent, they set out in a few days for *Tomhanick*. There they were received with the most hearty welcomes ; and as they were much reduced, each of the neighbours contributed something to raise HENRY's stock, and make him happy. There they reside still, beloved and respected by all, and find their industry rewarded by prosperity and contentment.*

* The four last paragraphs of this story were written by Mrs. MARGARETTA V. FAUGERES—indisposition having prevented Mrs. BLEECKER (her mother) from completing it.

LETTERS.

LETTERS.

WHEN I had wrote you my laſt narrative of diſtreſſes, I was afraid I had diſcouraged you, by my complaints, from continuing a correſpondence ſo pleaſing to me. My ſoul was then reſponſive only to the voice of grief, and the whole world ſeemed cheerleſs to me as the fabled region of Cimmeria. The tempeſt of my ſoul has again ſubſided: But, my dear, as you deſire to know how we are circumſtanced, in compliance with your requeſt, I muſt again wound your feelings with a lamentable ſtory: therefore, ſadden your countenance accordingly; and I ſtipulate, that between every paragraph you ſhall pauſe and make a moral reflection.

The tories have viſited many of our neighbours in a hoſtile manner, under the diſguiſe of Indians. This ſtruck a panic over the
ſtouteſt

ſtouteſt of us; but yeſterday they ſeized an old
man, and propoſed the plundering of our houſe
to him; he declined it, though a diſaffected
perſon himſelf, and acquainted us with our
danger; alſo, that the banditti were thirty in
number. You may gueſs (but 'tis likely you
will not) that our diſorder on this exceeded the
confuſion of AGRAMONTA's camp: every
thing topſey-turvy, every one hurrying to ſe-
crete ſome littſe bundle in an unſuſpected va-
cancy, and one dreadful apprehenſion expel-
ling another; for SUSAN and I ventured up in
a loft without light, where ſpectres have been
gamboling for at leaſt a dozen centuries---by
report.

We ſtill remain greatly alarmed, and never
undreſs for bed. However, we have paſſed
the preceding ſeaſon in ſecurity and pleaſure;
we have frequently had ſociable dances, which
by way of eminence we ſtile a ball. The
moſt diſagreeable of our hours are when we
admit politics in our female circle: this never
fails of opening a field of nonſenſical contro-
verſy among our ladies.

I expect ſhortly to remove to *Tomhanick*
again, where converſing with my abſent
friends

friends will be my chief amufement; and as I highly value a fenfible intelligent writer, I wifh I knew how to bribe coufin to favour me with her letters alfo.

You have omitted, my dear, to mention a fyllable of your good mamma and Mrs. B. but even that is a prefumption of their welfare. Pleafe to tender my regards to them, and accept of Mr. BLEECKER's. My little PEGGY begs leave to kifs your hands; and I am, dear girl, with unaffected fincerity, your

ANN ELIZA BLEECKER.

Cojemans, April 12, 1779.

Tomhanick, April 8, 1780.

YOU are to look upon my letters as coming from the ends of the earth, (if a fcriptural phrafe may be allowed) from an abftracted perfon who loves and refpects you, and who contemplates your character with the generous refinement with which we think of our departed friends ; that is, remembering their bright qualities only, while their foibles pafs not under the eye of partial retrofpection.

I believe,

I believe, if ever we meet on this fide eternity, my dear coufin, we fhall mifs fo many
of.our beloved friends-as will effectually damp
all tranfport; we fhall have to mourn over
thofe that are gone, not rejoice over thofe who
are left.--- No, we fhall never-meet; unnum-
bered rivers, hills, and other obftacles arife
and intercept the very idea. But think not I
diflike my fituation here; on the contrary, I
am charmed with the lovely fcene the fpring
opens around me.---Alas! the wildernefs is
within: I mufe fo long on the dead until I am
unfit for the company of the living.

I am very glad to hear that aunt P. is well;
be pleafed to fend my tender regards to her.
Defire your dear mamma and coufin B. to accept of my affection. I receive letters frequently from S. S. he likewife prefents his
refpects to your family. Mr. B. and SUSAN
and PEGGY defire to be remembered.

My dear, may you have happinefs here
equivalent to- your merits, and future blifs
more than a mortal can deferve, is the fincere
prayer of your affured friend,

ANN ELIZA BLEECKER.

I have hinted to PEGGY that· I never receive your letters.

MY

MY DEAR COUSIN,

YOUR letter was more acceptable to me than the fmiles of the returning fpring after this long rigid winter; (and indeed your filence contributed to make it more tedious.) But I wonder what caprice of fortune intercepts all my epiftles: furely fhe owes you feveral voluminous pacquets which I committed to her care. And fince I am in a vein of wondering, I wonder how you could be fo long ignorant of the place of our KITTY's refidence: her ftay with us was fhort; the charming city tempted her away: but fhortly after fhe emigrated to *Halfmoon*, five miles from here, where fhe remains.

As to myfelf, I have but little to inform you, unlefs it fhould be the hiftory of my heart, and even in that there is no novelty. I love the fame perfons, the fame amufements, .the fame opinions I did ten years ago. But my affection is almoft become a painful fenfation to me; for, except my dear little family, all my friends are dead, or far, far abfent. This, the poet obferves, is the perquifite of long life : but my days have been evil and few: I find no
difpofition

difpofition towards new attachments;. and if but a few more of thofe I love drop from me, I fhall be left a wretched individual as I began.

How fhall I apologize, my coufin, for writing in this ftrain to a fair lady who would chufe to hear of none but metaphorical deaths, and innocent murders caufed by her eyes? I will exclude thefe heavy ideas, and be gay to pleafe my fprightly correfpondent.

I believe Hymen likes a fouthern clime; our northern blafts would blow out his torch; but I hope he will return with the Zephyrs, to legitimate feveral premature children in our neighbourhood, which Love has produced in his abfence. I hear of but one marriage round here this winter. Our girls begin to tremble. I believe I muft fend the following advertifement to LOUDON :---

‘ TWO young ladies, poffeffed of many ‘ genteel accomplifhments, amiable qualities, ‘ and every grace of perfon, are willing to ac- ‘ cept of any continental officer as a partner ‘ for life, provided he be a gentleman of birth, ‘ fortune, beauty, and honour.

‘ N. B. None need apply but fuch as have ‘ fignalized themfelves in the prefent conteft.’

Upon

Upon second thoughts I will defer it, as we cannot possibly keep a wedding in taste until the war is concluded.

I can rally no more, our situation is so truly critical as to render levity criminal in us. The savages alarm us daily by sudden eruptions in the country.---Dear girl, my paper obliges me to conclude abruptly: you see I have scarce room to present my love to friends, or stile myself your affectionate

ANN ELIZA BLEECKER.

To Miss V------

DEAR GIRL,

WHILE you are entertaining us with accounts of the brilliant dissipations of the *grande monde*, in return I can only inform you that our trees here are green, that the birds sing, and the rivulets murmur; themes that will not bear expatiating on without degenerating into downright poetry; and I design at present to deliver my sentiments in prose. I find you are making greater lamentations than ever

M   JEREMIAH

JEREMIAH did at the removal of the camp.
Be comforted my dear; as your irrefiftibleneffes
have certainly captured many hearts in it, various will be the pretences of the military
petit maitres for remaining at ———; you
will have a polite circle of invalids to efcort
you about the country, nor be obliged to bend
your ear to the unpolifhed love-tale of a fighing ruftic.

But, my dear, I have been confidering in
what manner you will accommodate your-
felves again to the filent and foft melancholy
of a rural fcene. Major P——, who is here,
obviates this difficulty by obferving, that the
clatter of three young ladies tongues will be
an excellent fubftitute for the thunder of cannon, drums, &c. This I would by no means
admit, affuring him you were a fuperior order
of beings to our common chit-chat females,
wifhing him no greater punifhment for his
rafh judgment than once to be expofed to an
electrical glance from your fine azure eyes.
The Major was convinced, and now fits in
duft and afhes.

As for S****, I know of no one inhabitant
of our foreft fhe can reafonably hope to make
a conqueft

a conqueſt of except our Parſon, who, though paſt his grand climacteric, is ſtill a bachelor, and living within point blank ſhot of her eyes. It is expected he muſt ſoon capitulate or die.

We live perfectly retired, and ſee very little company at preſent, as the ladies in our vicinage are buſy hoeing their corn and planting potatoes. As we are not quite ſo well calculated for this rural employment, we left the ſun-burnt daughters of Labour yeſterday, and went on pilgrimage to the *Half-Moon*, to viſit Mrs. P****s. Though patience is my particular virtue, in our return I was really guilty of ſome unphiloſophic invectives againſt the road: S**** grew captious and ſullen: Mr. BLEECKER contracted his brows; but juſt as he handed us from the carriage, we were preſented with your letters, which, in a few moments, reſtored us to our former complacency and good humour. You ſee what a good effect your epiſtles have: if you have any thing of a generous principle in your compoſition, I am ſure this one motive will induce you to write often, very often. I have encloſed ſome verſes in compliance with your deſire: they were compoſed at the time of our retreat from

M 2 BURGOYNE,

BURGOYNE, the moſt melancholy period of
my life; ſo if they are too ſerious for the vo-
latility of a gay lady's ideas, hand them over to
your good mamma, and I am convinced ſhe
will excuſe their imperfections, in reſpect of
their moral tendency; give my profound re-
ſpects to her: pleaſe to tender my warmeſt affection to Mrs. B. and accept the hand of ſincere friendſhip from your

ANN ELIZA BLEECKER.

Tomhanick, June 12, 17.79.

To Mr. B--------.

Wedneſday Evening, July 12, 1779

MY DEAR,

I Could not ſee the folly and deformity of
my impetuous behaviour this morning, while
blinded by paſſion; but after you was gone,
when I felt loneſome, and had leiſure for reflection, when my fever returned, and I miſ-
ſed that tender ſolicitude which always allevi-
ated my pain when you was near, I cannot de-
ſcribe

scribe how exquisite a compunction seized me; I have been lost the whole day in sorrow, Good God! how inconsistent is the human mind! obstinate in passion, and stormy as the *Caspian*; then again soft and yielding to persuasion, as snow before the warm influence of a summer heaven; and yet perhaps this great agitation of the spirits is meant to keep them from subsiding into a state of insensibility, as strong winds prevent the waters of a lake from stagnating.

I hope health and pleasure will attend you in your journey, and sometimes I hope you will call in my idea to amuse your silent hours when you ride alone through the lofty forest, or along the bank of some placid river, or over some flowery mead, whose glowing gems glitter beneath the crystal globules of morning; these objects inspire love and softness, and it is in such moments I would fain have you think of me. My head aches, I must lie down.

Thursday Evening, July 22.

I HAVE been very sick, and kept my bed all day. Your absence increases my disorder:

M 3   O how

O how folitary am I in this great city! Adieu,
I am too unwell to fit up.

———

Friday Evening, *July* 23.

I FIND myfelf better. Mrs. V. S. paid
us a vifit this afternoon: after tea fhe perfuaded me to walk out; the evening was lovely, the fun fhone with a peculiar foftnefs
through the humid atmofphere, and the glaffy
Hudfon blufhed at the brightnefs of the painted heaven; (pardon my poetical phrenzy;)
but not the blufhing river, nor glowing fkies,
nor fmiling fun could conquer my invincible
melancholy. Here am I returned in as great
a humour for moralizing as ever PLATO was:
however, I fhall quit troubling you to-night
with my reflections, and perhaps to-morrow
a more agreeable fubject may occur. You
fee I continue writing till fome opportunity
bids me clofe the dull journal. Good night.

ANN ELIZA BLEECKER.

———

To Miss V------.

Tomhanick, Oct. 29, 1779.

I Begin to resent your silence, my lovely cousin. I have sent a large paquet to -------, but find no return. I am not skilled in divination, yet I am tempted to interpret your omission into an omen of declining friendship. No, I reject the thought; my P****, my M****, have not such very mutable hearts; my letters have either wandered astray, or my dear girls have been prevented answering as yet.

I can communicate nothing that may prolong this letter agreeably. The glories of summer (my usual topic) languish and lose their lustre; the airy cliffs and deep forests echo nothing but storms; we have not even one bird left with whose warbling I might delight you, nor one shade where I can comfortably recline to describe a lovely landscape to your ladyship. When vernal suns shall again kindle a glow of beauty on the face of Creation, I may possibly entertain you with my Sylvan improvements; till then accept, dear girl, of tea-table news and politics.

We

We are flattered here with an account that General WASHINGTON is preparing to invest *New-York*, that the enemy have evacuated *Rhode-Island* and the Highland forts, and that Count DE ESTAING's squadron is at the Hook. In consequence of this our militia are ordered to garrison the frontier towns. Mr. B. marches to-morrow to *Fort-Edward*, on a three months expedition; S**** and I, in the interim, will be cloistered, shut up, imprisoned, (pray help me to a more emphatical word to express our confinement,) for we have no other passable gallant, and we dare not venture alone through our woods, which are infested at present by wolves and bears, who growl even in our very court-yard. S****, however, depends upon visiting the *Albany* weekly balls with an escort of Majors, Cornets, and other military gentlemen; but she is ill-prepared for such a scene, being, to my knowledge, in the thirty-third page of HOMER's Odyssy, which will utterly disqualify her for such idle company, and I expect send her to the loom with PENELOPE.

ANN ELIZA BLEECKER.

To

To Miss ------------.

YOU aſk me whether I am ſincere? To diſguiſe my ſentiments is an art I have yet to learn. I wiſh, my dear, I had ſome ſpice of the hypocrite; I ſhould then poſſibly attain a better knowledge of this world, which deſerves to be treated with leſs candour. 1 have ſtudied it but ſuperficially; and the more I conſider it, the leſs I like it. You, my dear, have met with rough tempeſts in it; and I, who have encountered rougher, can now ſincerely ſympathize with you. The melancholy vein that ran through your letter wonderfully affected me. SUSAN too has a kind ſuſceptible heart: ſhe feels, ſhe reſents your injuries.

Mr. POPE obſerves, that reſignation is the moſt melancholy of all the virtues; but we can combat Fate with no other weapon than Patience, and it is not ſo hard to effect as we are apt to imagine; the practice is eaſy and full of conſolation. The over-wearied traveller ſits down dejected, benighted, and thinks he can go no farther; but he ſoon finds that very

reſpite

respite which was the result of his despair, has enabled him to proceed cheerly on his journey. Truft in God then my friend, he will make plain the rough path, and the crooked ftraight; your virtues will furvive obloquy and reproach, they will even fhine the brighter for it, and I am fure you have loft no real friend by it.

When will you come to us? we will fhut out the world; we will fhut out every thing but love and joy. My heart tells me we will foon meet, and that is happinefs: Perhaps I may be deceived; but you never will, my dear, in believing me to be your affured and tender friend,

ANN ELIZA BLEECKER.

Tomhanick, Sept. 3, 1779

To Mifs A. M. V------.

WHETHER a fedentary life has a heavy influence on my temper, or that I am verging to a period of life in which we confider things m a moral point of view only, I know not

but

but I find that I often fuffer a constraint when I affect to be gay, and trifle as formerly. But I am under no concern, my dear, of difgufting you by being ferious; your judgment is mature as my years, and puts us on a level: however, I promife to be lively when I can, and expect you will not give me caufe to make the fcriptural complaint, " I have pip-" ed, and ye have not danced; I have mourn-" ed, and ye have not wept."

We have been often alarmed this fummer by unexpected eruptions of the favages on the frontiers, and once in actual flight, when Mr. PARKS was killed at *Fort-Edward*. I never faw fo general a panic as that affair ftruck through the country: but our late fuffering by the rapid approaches of an enemy, is fome apology for the prefent apprehenfions.

I hope the winter will reftore tranquillity to us, when we fhall no more " tremble at the " fhaking of a leaf," but form a happy circle round the fire-fide. Ah, my dear coufin! that circle has been imperfect fince the death of my dear mamma, my dear ABELLA. But let me not repine, I have had my days of more than human happinefs with them; let
me

me alfo fit out my night of affliction content, efpecially fince it admits of much alleviation by the prefence of a few furviving beloved friends. Truly, my coufin, friendſhip is happinefs; diffolve every tender attachment, fet the foul independent of all focial connec-tions, and its exiſtence will become comfort-lefs and burthenfome. A Paradife could not fatisfy ADAM without an EVE. A fine wri-ter elegantly fays, *I fee no funſhine but in the face of a friend.* To trifle a little with the metaphor---I am condemned to moon-light, as I fee your's only by reflection; that is, by your letters.

Dear girl, I admire (in common with the world) your wit and beauty; but it is your good fenfe and amiable qualities have fixed me fo entirely you affectionate friend,

ANN ELIZA BLEECKER.

Tomhanick, Sept. 4, 1779.

To Miſs V------

MY VERY DEAR COUSIN,

IT was but yeſterday I clofed my letter to vou; but an hour before my bleffed huſband

was

was torn (perhaps for ever) from my arms: he was taken by tories in fight of his houfe. O! this cruel difafter has crufhed me to the centre: I am funk deeper than the grave. In the bitternefs of my foul I forget to eat my bread, and mingle my drink with tears. Alas! the man I have loft was too good, too kind; his qualities were fo gentle and amiable; he loved me with too great an excefs of tendernefs; with fo much delicacy and foftnefs, as becomes very painful for me to recollect: And his affection feemed to increafe every day: he was always endeavouring to pleafe me; always anxious about my happinefs. If I looked but a little penfive, he was alarmed. It was but two nights ago that he waked me by putting his hand acrofs my forehead, and finding me in a cold clammy fweat, he ftarted up and got me a glafs of wine. I was not fenfible of any diforder, but was furprifed to find myfelf cold as a corpfe. I fat up, while he, kneeling by the bed fide, grafped my hand in an agony of concern and tendernefs. "Ah! "my beloved, (faid he) we muft quit this "place: you try to hide your diftrefs from "me, but I perceive your mind is filled with

N   "dreadful

" dreadful prefages." Alas! my dear, pray
for me, that the God of all compaffions may
pity him, and reftore him to my bleeding bofom. O! my forrows are fwelled to a de-
luge; they overwhelm me. Almighty God,
I fink, I perifh under the ftroke of thy hand!
fave me from temptation in this my hour of
darknefs and horror! Surely this is a day of
trouble and aftonifhment to me. O that we
all refted in the quiet grave together!

My dear coufin, try (if you pleafe) to
fend the inclofed incoherent lines to my brother. Adieu! adieu! and may the merciful
God fhower his bleffings on your family.

ANN ELIZA BLEECKER.

Auguft, 1781.

To Mifs V------.

MY DEAR PEGGY,

BY a moft wonderful train of furprifing
providences my beloved hufband is reftored to
my arms. I fhall, in the ampleft manner, relate his happy efcape; but your gentle bofom
can beft tell you my happy feelings on this
occafion.

occasion.---He was bufied in the harveft, at a
fmall diftance from the houfe; but having been
previoufly menaced by our inveterate tories,
and my heart prefaging fome heavy calamity,
I preffed him to remain at home, but without
effect. Towards evening, parting from his
labourers, he was returning home with old
MERKEE, a white fervant, and a load of wheat;
when fix men, ftarting from among the bufhes,
prefented their fixed bayonets to his breaft,
bidding him to furrender or he was a dead man.
" I yield myfelf," cried he in furprife, " pro-
" vided you promife to ufe me as a gentle-
" man."---" You fhall be ufed," replied their
leader, " as a prifoner of war commonly is."
Upon this they were taken farther in the wood,
where they pinioned my hufband; a cut-throat
looking Heffian leading him by the rope with
one hand, while the other held a tomahawk,
with which he fwore to difpatch the prifoner
if purfued. But his great anguifh for me made
him infenfible of fear; he begged, in the moft
pathetic terms, that the negro might return to
let me know what was become of him, but all
in vain. MERKEE wept bitterly---" O!"
faid he, " I am an old negro---no matter for

" me;

" me; but my good master is a young man,
" and my dear mistress will break her heart---
" she will die." After a most fatiguing and
rapid march, towards day they encamped in a
deep swamp, where they produced General
St. LEDGER's orders to take my husband and
bring him to *Canada*, but to use him tenderly,
take particular care of his health, and not to
pillage his house. They had watched for him
four days, on a small ascent which commanded a full view of whatever was transacted in
our family; but growing impatient, they had
determined to storm the house that very night;
and swore, had they met with resistance, they
would have sacrified the whole family. The
party consisted of three tories, one Hessian,
and two British; they were afterwards joined
by two more tories. The British were humane, and wept whenever my sad spouse de-
plored the mournful fate of his wife and child.
After three nights march through horrid
woods, (for they slept in the day) my husband's intreaties prevailed on them to let the
boy return with a letter for me. When he
read it to them, most of them shed tears, and
swore it was damned hard a gentleman should
suffer so, but they must obey their orders.

                                        When

When the fourth evening arrived, defpair-
ing of relief, (though he ftill looked up to
God with a hopelefs kind of dependence,)
three Yankees appeared a little way off. One
of whom, advancing, bade them furrender;
but miftaking BLEECKER for the commander
(not obferving his ropes,) he prefented his
piece to fhoot him through the head, when the
tories, feeing a large party coming up, ground-
ed their arms. , They all proceeded to *Bennington*, where the party is laid in irons; while
my fpoufe flew to my arms amid the fhouts
and congratulations of the whole city, which
had feemed wonderfully anxious about his
fate. As to my own wanderings, they were
trifling. I fled inftantly from a place where
every object prefented me with horror. S----,
after weeping for feveral minutes on my neck,
from a noble exertion of fortitude and friendfhip, infifted on remaining there a while to
have an eye to our effects. Our wailings filled
the difmally echoing foreft; even the tory
women melted into tears and compaffion, and
feveral fainted in the hall. You may judge
with what a broken heart I entered *Albany*;
but bleffed be the Saviour of finners, I found
it kind and fympathifing beyond my merits

N 3   How

How my dear lover and myfelf have fupported our trials I know not; but (as MARIA of *Molinions* obferves) " Heaven tempers the " wind to the fhorn lamb." The hand of an Almighty Protector was fo obvious in leading my hufband through his imminent dangers, and " hair breadth efcapes," that on his return home (he told me) he almoft fainted under his gratitude, and had fo firm a truft and reliance on the goodnefs of God, that had he been furprifed by a new party, he would have been affuredly confident of again efcaping. My hour of darknefs and aftonifhment was very great: I prayed with unknown fervency; but, O! I lifted my broken heart in defpair: great God! I will no more diftruft thy love; I will endeavour no more to offend thee. Ah! how infipid, how trifling appear the honours, and riches, and vanities of life, to being held in the fhadow of his hand who is the living God; to having him on our fide who is the Arbiter of all nature! Rejoice with us, my coufin.

We fhall now remain in *Albany*. I am, my beloved coufin, your happy and affectionate

ANN ELIZA BLEECKER.

Albany, Auguft 9, 1781.

To

To Mrs. F. *at Mount-Hope.*

I Sit down, dear BETSEY, to congratulate
you on a new occafion of happinefs to your
family, by the birth of another daughter.
This agreeble event I never was informed of
until this morning, and though you may think
my compliment of the lateft, yet I would
rather be thought impertinent than unfriend-
ly. I fancy you exclaim with LEAH, (in
your exultation) " a troop cometh." Happy
are you, my coufin, enjoying health, peace
and every domeftic blefling. Content hath
limited your defires to your own manfion;
and there every innocent pleafure waits to
gratify them. All that remains is to wifh
you may infure thofe mercies by a grateful difpofition to the giver of them.

Our fituation is more precarious. To-day,
happy in our Sylvan recefs, furrounded by
blooming gardens, orchards, and well cultivated fields; the whole valley echoing with
the bleatings of fheep, &c. and an air of tranquillity and plenty diffufed around our cottages: to-morrow, even this very night, the de-
ftroying favage may change this pleafing profpect

pect into defolation and undiftinguifhed ruin:
and yet I am unwilling to quit my beloved
retreat, the fcene of many recent forrows to
me, but (let me confefs with pleafing recollection) of many, many former bleffings. The
death of my dear mother has produced a dreadful chafm in my family; and though I have
enough round me whofe tender affiduitics
would confole me for a lefs misfortune, fo capital a lofs I fhall mourn through life. I know,
by former obfervation, dear BETSEY, that you
have a very feeling heart: you cannot look
back to the period when your mother and mine
interchanged the moft delicate offices of friendfhip, and fat us an example of the brighteft
virtue, without a fentiment of gratitude and
regret for their lofs; even now their image
rifes to my fancy, pure, lovely and placid as
while among us: ah! how infinitely exalted
and improved by their change! Pardon this
flight, my dear; but let me further infift, that
as our education has given us a fimilarity of
ideas, and an equal bias to friendfhip, fuch
congenial minds ought not to lapfe into a
neglect of each other: permit me, therefore,
my lovely Mrs. F. to renew our obfolete cor-
respondence,

refpondence, and after an interval of many
years, to affure you that I am ftill, with every
fentiment of regard, your

ANN ELIZA BLEECKER.

Tomhanick, Sept. 6.

To *Mifs* M. V------.

I Muft decline your compliments (or rather
oblique flatteries) my lovely coufin; my reafon
will not admit of them, whatever latitude my
vanity might infift on. My ruftic mufe in-
habits too frigid a clime to practice any mufical notes; yet, like all mediocre fingers, fhe
is willing to oblige company, without defer-
ring the favour long, for fear of enhancing
their expectation.

I cannot proceed a fentence farther without
expreffing my abhorrence of that bafe villain
ARNOLD. I think there is wanting in language an appellative, fuitable to his character.
Strange! that for a little money a man would
bear to have his reputation ftigmatized to eternity, and that a hero, as he was ftyled. What
a contraft between him and the heroes of antiquity,

quity, who facrificed every thing, even life,. to their fame! Yet my refentment fubfides into contempt, when I reflect what an abject, vile wretch General ARNOLD is become. The land he has treated with ingratitude, cruelty and perfidy, abhors him, and no doubt the nation he attempted to ferve defpifes him. A traitor is a general object of fcorn; and if his feelings are not quite loft in apathy, furely he may borrow CAIN's exclamation, " My pu- " nifhment is greater than I can bear!" nor fhould I be furprifed to hear he had concluded his villainy by fome act of defperation. In confequence of his infernal treaty, a party of twelve hundred tories, Indians, &c. have made a défcent on our northern frontiers---have fur- prifed *Fort-George* and *Fort-Ann*, and yefter- day demanded the furrender of *Fort-Edward*. Our militia are collecting very faft. *Fort- Stanwix* we hear is likewife invefted. Alas! my dear girl, my heart breaks for the diftreffes around me: The innocent infants, the fimple women perifh unrelifting---fometimes crufh- ed in the flaming ruins of their own houfes--- nothing but countenances of perplexity and horror to be feen, and lamentable wailings to be be heard. We are all prepared for flight upon a nearer approach of the enemy; but fenfible the moment we quit our dwelling, we fubmit them to be plundered. We are determined to remain until to-morrow, when perhaps we may have force enough to repel the favages. Dear girl, wherever I am I fhall acquaint you with our fituation. May heaven defend you from hoftile alarms; and may you forget the clamours of war in the peacable enjoyment of domeftic bleffings. Affure your dear mamma and Mrs. B***** of my fincere regard; and believe me to be, with every fentiment of efteem, dear MARIA, your friend,

ANN ELIZA BLEECKER.

Tomhanick, Oct. 12.

———

October 15.

I HAVE had no opportunity to fend this, fo before I clofe it muft inform you that the above-mentioned party are returned to *Lake-George*. But our fpoufes are gone again this morning to *Ball's-Town*, (fix miles to the weft of this,) where the Indians have burnt feveral houfe, laft night, and carried off a number of prifoners. To add to our apprehenfions, thirty fufpected suspected Indians have come among us, under pretence of hunting, and neither threats nor good words can prevail on them to quit us. The woods are likewise infested with tories, forty having been discovered in one company. Were they not such night destroyers I am sensible we could soon discomfit them; but their irruptions are as unexpected as expeditious.

***

October 16.

SINCE I wrote the above our panic-stricken neighbourhood left their effects and fled several miles; but becoming a little more assured we are returned. All the whig families are convened in my house, but not a man amongst us except my old negro MERKEE, who keeps the horses in readiness for us. Adieu! may God bless you.

***

To Miss V------.

HAPPY, my incomparable girl, is the human mind, in enjoying so great a degree of the benignant heavenly attribute, *Love*. It is this sweet distinction that almost raises us to a

level

level with angels; this immortal magnetifm
by which we are led to exchange feelings; by
which, at this moment, I forget my fears to
rejoice at your fafety---while you, in the midft
of pleafure and fecurity, fadden with generous
concern at the prefumption of my danger.
Bleft be thofe fenfibilities, my dear; and were
they univerfal, the arts of war would yet have
flept in oblivion.

Your very kind letters came to hand laft
night, as SUSAN and I were fitting difconfolate and apprehenfive by the fire-fide; but on
perufing them, we infenfibly forgot our
gloomy fituation, and got fo engaged among
our *R*------ friends, that we paffed the remainder of the evening in merrier chat than
we had many preceding ones.

To-day we have been informed of Governor CLINTON's advantage over the enemy at
Canajohare: no doubt the papers will give you
the particulars before this can reach you: but
rejoice with us, my coufin, at this event, which
will probably put a period to this northern
maffacre. I have wrote M---- a lamentable
epiftle, which I would fupprefs had I time to
write another: but our terrors are not quite

O   fubfided;

fubfided ; and as I lately boafted of our heroifm, I am ready now to write in a ftrain of palinody, and make a formal recantation.

I have forgot many paffages in JOSEPH, and loft the manufcript; but if I can poffibly recollect it, I fhall fubmit it to your criticifm. However, I take the freedom to trouble you with a little hiftory,* written fome time ago for SUSAN, which being altogether a fact, may give you fome idea of favage cruelty, and at the fame time will juftify our fears in your opinion. How this packet in folio will ever arrive to you I know not; it muft be fome very civil perfon who will adventure to take charge of it: whoever it is, I am highly obliged to him ; but really think his trouble will be fully compenfated by the opportunity it will give him of feeing two of the faireft and moft fenfible laffes in R------. Forgive this compliment; it is not flattery; and fince your patience can hold out no longer, I muft, though reluctantly, finifh this paper with giving you leave to write one in return ten times as long, to your fincere and affectionate

ANN ELIZA BLEECKER.

October 19.

* MARIA KITTLE.

T

To Miss V------.

MY DEAR PEGGY,

I AM wholly difcouraged from writing any more to your quarter: our letters, I am fenfible, are loft on the way, as I have not received a line from you or M---- fince early laft fall. This interruption muft certainly be the confequence of an impertinent curiofity in fome people, who break every feal they meet with, and then deftroy the letters for fear of detection. If this fhould fall into fuch hands, I muft obferve to the gentlemen (few ladies being capable of fuch ungenerofity) that fuch a proceeding betrays a want of common honefty and common humanity in them. A period is put to many tender friendfhips by thofe impertinents, each party refenting being neglected by the other.

I hope, my dear, this mild winter prefents you with every elegant pleafure. The army being in your vicinage, muft certainly be productive of entertainment. S---- is at *Albany*, and I believe as fedentary as if fhe was at *Tomhanick*. I expect her with Captains H---- and

O 2   B-------

B------- to-morrow, when we fhall ramble together through our foreſt while the ſnow laſts.---Shall we never fee each other? This unlucky *New-York*---it is almoſt ominous to mention it; but I often think of it with tears, and the longer I am divided from it, the clofer my affections are drawn to it.

I have ſpent the winter quite lonefome, Mr. B------- being always abſent on public buſineſs,.but is now detained in the chimney corner by a broken fhin. I hear no more of K----; we have lately wrote to her, but cannot expect to receive from her ſuch gay communicative letters any more, as ſhe uſed to fend us from *R*------. I hope ſhe finds it agreeable.

I wonder you do not fend off one of your beaus exprefs, with a packet to put me out of pain about you. This undertaking would have a double advantage; it would highly oblige me, and convince you of your adorer's fincerity by his obedience. The beauties of antiquity always made trial of their lovers merits, by urging them on to prodigious exploits; and I defy you to fhew me a fingle knight in hiſtory, enamoured of fome beautiful princeſs, who did not encounter fiery dra-

gons,

gons, kill giants, difenchant miferable ladies, and run innumerable hazards of lofing his life for her fake : and fhall a modern fair one think that her flave would refufe to ride two hundred miles to deliver a letter?

I have fcribbled until you are tired, fo hafte to finifh, and am, with the greateft refpect to all your dear family, (whom I fincerely love) amiable coufin, tenderly your's,

ANN ELIZA BLEECKER.

Tomhanick, January 24.

To Mifs T** E***

December, 1781.

MY DEAREST SUSAN,

OUR mutual fufferings, through a remarkable train of unfortunate events, have fo endeared you to me, that I bear your abfence with forrow and anxiety. After your departure my poor PEGGY was feized with a putrid fever, which almoft fent her into eternity : my feelings on this occafion were exquifitely

O 3 painful;

painful; but bleſſed be God this cloud alſo paſſed over my head, and ſhe recovers finely after two relapſes.

Would you believe it, my dear, we are again at *Tomhanick*, in my old apartment, agreeably ſituated in the neighbourhood of Mr. and Mrs. B-----, who live in the weſt part of my houſe. *Albany* became inſupportable to me; I would rather have lived in ROLANDO's Cavern, than in that unſociable, illiterate, ſtupid town; I prefer ſolitude to ſuch company; but I miſs you, my ſiſter, in every part of this houſe; the hall, the little room, &c. continually remind me of the pleaſant hours we have paſſed together in this unenvied retirement. Will you not return before ſpring? Ah! SUSAN, if you do not I ſhall begin the labours of our flower beds with a heavy heart; your favourite lillies will droop; nor ſhall I have courage to diſengage your pinks from entangling weeds: endeavour, my dear, to come up; I am ſure we ſhall be happy together. I received your obliging preſent, for which I ſincerely thank you, and hope you enjoy all poſſible felicity in *Jerſey*, whoſe preſent gaity is ſuitable to your youth and ſprightlineſs:

fprightlinefs: as foi my difpofition, depreffed by calamities, worn out with forrows, the pensive foftnefs of a rural life accords beft with it.------

Again I am left folitary: Mr. B------- went this morning on an expedition againft the illegitimate Vermonters, (or new claimants) with Col. R---------, from the Manor, who arrived here laft night with his regiment, and eat up all my ducks and faufages. The new claimants are collected at *Sinchoick*, and form a little army: they have miferably mauled poor F---- and R----------, who keep their beds. Our fmall force there increafes daily, and begins to brow-beat the enemy: in fhort, we are all anarchy and confufion: heaven only knows when it will end.

The moft tragical affair has happened here that I ever remember to have heard of. JAMES YATES, (a fon of him at *Pitt's-Town,*) a few nights ago murdered his wife, four children, his horfes and cow, with circumftances of cruelty too horrid to mention: by all appearance he is a religious lunatic.

Dear Sufan, how fhall I conclude? when writing to you my pen infenfibly draws me
beyond

beyond the common limits of a letter; but I know you will be fond of hearing every minute particular refpecting poor *Tomhanick*, where I flatter myfelf you have enjoyed fome hours of pleafure.

Neighbour F--- has had his fhop burnt off yefterday, together with his waggon, fleigh, winter's provifion, and many other articles. Your old friend LETTY B----- is well, and at this moment fparking with your old admirer R----. Let me fee, have I no more news? Alas! alas! nothing but dry politics, and I am willing to fpare you the mortification of them. Indeed, my fweet girl, I am penning a long epiftle; but St. PETER knows whether I fhall ever find conveyance for it: however, I will continue to write on in difcharge of my confcience, and fo good night; to-morrow I refume my pen.------

To-morrow did I fay? three days have intervened fince I have had leifure to think or write. Yefterday morning my fpoufe fent for a horfe, upon which Mr. B----- and myfelf went in a fleigh to fetch him; but, on our arrival at *Sinchoick*, the Yorkers we found had retreated, and the new claimants (reinforced
by

by five hundred Vermonters) had taken poffeffion of the ground. General ALLEN was
barred up in gold-lace, and felt himfelf grand
as the Great Mogul: they had an old fpiked
up field-piece, which, however, looked martial. I fat myfelf down among this formidable fet, and being cold, mildly defired one of
their Captains to fetch a little dry wood. He
obligingly complied, and we foon had a fine
fire. I then began humbly to expoftulate with
thefe wife men of the eaft about the commence-
ment of this civil war; and at length demanded how they could expect to fupport their ju-
rifdiction, in the center of the ftates, who had
not acceded to their claim? They replied,
" The four eaftern ftates were their own peo-
" ple, and would certainly affift them." I
told them I could not fee how they dared
break through the confederacy while they
were fenfible all America's happinefs depend-
ed upon the union. Captain R------ interrupted, " The affiftance of *New-England*
" would not interfere with the union, as this
" was a difpute about land, in which Congrefs
" had no concern;" and then he damned the
Yorkers, and drank fuccefs to *Vermont!* which
extraordinary

extraordinary fpeech and behaviour impofed
filence on fome of us.

I returned home, and to-day vifited the *York*
camp at *Schochticook*, where I took leave of
my dear B------, who is obliged to abfent
himfelf from us while the Vermonters tyran-
nize.

———

January 2, 1782.

I CONCLUDE my journal after a long
interval; but, dear SUSAN, fo many occurrences have intervened, that I have had fcarce
time to breathe; our houfe has been a perfect
garrifon for feveral weeks. Our men intended, laft Sunday, to ftorm JACKSON's
houfe, where the tories were collected; but
they capitulated: however, we are all in arms.
Mr. B------ went plenipo to *Bennington* fome
days ago, where I attended him: we had an
interview with all their great *Sakemakers*;
but the iffue was no way favourable to the
whigs.

We firmly believe thefe commotions will
be fuppreffed before fpring ; when I fhall take
it as an inftance of your affection if you can
relifh our ruftic life, and come up among us;

if

if not, I fhall fubmit and grieve. Dear fifter, I thank you for your letter and prefent, though I never received the latter. CATY's good-will and prefent I regard with affection, and wifh her all health and happinefs.

How fhall I drop my pen! Adieu, dear girl; we have kept your birth-day yefterday, with fome agreeable neighbours, and had a dance in the evening. I am glad you are happy, which is a great and capital fatisfac-tion to your entirely affectionate

ANN ELIZA BLEECKER.

To Mifs S**** T** E***

DEAR SUE,

I Value your affection beyond any acquifi-tion; but my fituation of late has been fo pe-culiarly unfortunate, that I have had no leifure to exprefs mine to you. I am infinitely pleafed that you are happy; but I wifh fome power, partial to me, had prevented your removal by fome very fortunate occurrence. O my fifter! my fifter! every fibre of my heart relaxes

when

when I think of you: the heavieſt ſtorm of life
has not fallen on my ſoul with ſuch a weight
as the loſs of your company. May the gentleſt
ſpirit in-heaven be the cenſor of your actions!
May you be bleſt through the remoteſt ages of
eternity! May---but my heart grows too full
to proceed.

Let us change the ſubject. We have lived
ſeveral weeks in a ſtrange commotion: we
have been often attacked by the Vermonters,
and defended ourſelves with as much reſolution
as ſo many janizaries. Would you believe it,
I have been forced to parade in the line of battle to defend our caſtle: however, the union
was diſſolved, and the new claimants left to
ſhift for themſelves; upon which they were
apprehended by the Yorkers, and carried to
Albany jail: among whom were M-----,
C------, T--------- and his two ſons, JOHN
P-------, W--------, JOHN S--------, and
ſeveral others. The ſame evening I ſent a
meſſage to Mrs. T--------, deſiring her to
return the looking-glaſs ſhe took from us when
BURGOYNE came down, upon which ſhe ci-
vily ſent it. Our neighbourhood looks ſolitary: Mrs. JACKSON, Mrs. CURRY, and many
more

more are all fled with their families in a clan-
deftine manner. This elopement of the tories
gives us new apprehenfions: we fear they will
attempt in the fpring a defcent on this quarter;
and though the fea-coaft is well defended, our
poor frontiers are commonly forgotten.

We have not feen the lads this winter.
M---- P------- was here yefterday with A----
L---------; they have ftolen a wedding. L----
S------- and the Major have likewife conclud-
ed their long courtfhip. J--- H----- is going
to die, and old F--- fends his refpects to you.

Mifs T-- E---, you have all the news, but
I muft add one trifle more:---Your admirer
R---- is no warrior; not all the eloquence of
our *York* party could induce him to face the
enemy: but his fituation admits of fome apology: depreffed with the lofs of you, perhaps
he is become indifferent about character, property, &c. &c.

I fhould not have mentioned this laft mortifying article, but in a late packet I received a
hint as if Mr. R---- was fupplanted in your
efteem by fome R------- *petit maitre*. Beware
of adding to your murders. But, my dear,
you have not entertained me with the fmalleft

P   account

account of your reception in *New-York*, and I claim the favour that you will fill a page on that fubject in your next letter. I alfo infift, that you fhortly make an excurfion this way, and bring our fair coufins with you: the contraft between the gloom of a deep foreft and the brilliancy of a lighted ball-room will make you return to the latter with a double relifh. But the gloom of our foreft has no ill influence on our converfation; we laugh, and fing, and chat in fpite of winter and wars; nor does any thing prompt a momentary figh, but the lofs of our dear SUSAN.

Farewell, my fifter; you have long been fenfible that I am fincerely your

ANN ELIZA BLEECKER.

B------- and the children long to fee you. Don't forget to affure aunt and Mrs. B. of my friendfhip for them. Major G-----, who will deliver this, is a worthy gentleman; I recommend him to your acquaintance. One word more and I finifh: FAN has a fine fon, and has parted with TITUS becaufe fhe took a diflike to his foolifh grinning.---I wifh I was with you one half hour, to chat and borrow a pinch

of

of your perfumed fnuff. Adieu, I fear I fhall
begin again before I clofe this.

The tories are all warned off. P-- T------
will foon be married to J-- P------.

Tomhanick, March 4, 1782.

To *Mifs* T** E***.

MY DEAR SISTER,

THIS day (the anniverfary of an event
fadly important to me) awakes me from a deception I have admitted fince our feparation.
I have been lofing relations, friends, children
and acquaintances many years: but with the
laft farewell falute you gave me, in the bitternefs of grief I reproached Providence it had
not left me one friend: I retired hither, with
my very little family, mourning, and could
not help repeating the words of HEZEKIAH,
" I fhall go foftly all my days."----Your
letters, PEGGY's and MARIA's I have received, often read, and wept over; but, confcious that my gloomy ideas would be unfea-

fonable

fonable in the circle of pleafure, I omitted anfwering as much as poffible.

But this day tells me I have yet a kind companion, who might now have lain fettered in a dungeon, had not Providence interpofed. I have an endearing child, who might have now lain in the dark grave, if the fame mercy had not reftored her. And in fpite of habit, gratitude fhall make me this day cheerful.

Dear SUSAN, you muft perufe the above *alone :* the genuine fentiments of a broken heart appear ridiculous to inexperienced levity : and though your fair companions are fweetly fympathifing, their very fenf bility induces me to conceal from them the hiftory of my feelings.

The news of this place is, that Mifs P----. T------ is married to Mr. J-- P-------; Mr. S---- T--- obliged to abfcond for forgery ; and Mifs S---- C---- is like to take H---- G------- for better for worfe. To defcend a little--- DIANA has loft SHOCK, and is on the verge of marrying with a certain CUFFE; FAN remains a widow, and MERKEE is the moft conftant lover I ever knew: but poor Mrs. F--- was lately delivered of a child who is a
terror

terror to every one that fees it. It feems fhe
was ftruck with fo much horror at the fight of
JAMES YATES's murdered family, that it
made too fatal an impreffion.

I had almoft forgot to mention, that fimple
BETT HERMAN is married to a Heffian: Mr.
B. officiated as prieft, and I gave the happy
couple a wedding-dinner, to which we invited
our moft civilized neighbours. E. and G.
lodge here alternately, to guard Mr. B. and
beg their regards may be prefented you.

To return to myfelf---an unimportant and
almoft forgotten fubject---I have been employed during the winter and fpring in attend-
ing to my health, which has been confiderably
impaired and weather-beaten by the ftorms of
affliction.

> For who to dumb Forgetfulnefs a prey,
> This pleafing, anxious being e'er refign'd;
> Left the warm precincts of the cheerful day,
> Nor caft one longing, ling'ring look behind?
> GRAY'S ELEGY.

Forgive my relapfing into melancholy: I will
make one more exertion to be lively, and if I
cannot fucceed, will conclude my paper.

I have the fineft garden in the country. In
the center of four grafs walks we have erected

P 3   a fpa-

a fpacious arbour, clofely fhaded with annual
vines, where we often drink tea, and enjoy
the profpect of a lovely collection of flowers
on one hand, and a cool fhady orchard on the
other; a luxuriant lot of herbage behind, and
directly oppofite a blufhing vineyard in minia-
ture. Here, often, when perufing THEOCRI-
TUS, TASSO, and VIRGIL, I drop thofe paftoral enthufiafts, to reflect on the hours of
friendfhip I have paffed with my SUSAN: my
cheek then glows with delight, pleafure deli-
cately touches my nerves, and all the fprings
of life move on cheerily. Ah, SUSAN! I
love you more than you imagine. Wherefore
are we feparated? if for your advantage, I am
more than refigned, I am contented.

Do you never hear of SAMMY? does he not
write to you? Though I dwell in the depth
of a vaft foreft, that need not limit his love:
the ftill voice of affection cannot be loft in the
thunder of war. What can be the reafon he
forgets me? I muft either entertain a contempt of my own demerits, or this-----but love
and partiality forbid a decifion.

After all, my SUSAN. I will endeavour to
circumfcribe my happinefs to the little lovely
spot

ſpot I occupy, and try to forget the friends
whoſe abſence is ſo painful to me. O! could
I think (like the inhabitants of *Topinamboo)*
that the mountains which ſurround me were
the limits of the earth, and that the individual
ſpot I dwelt on was the whole world, I might
then truly enjoy the pleaſures it produced.

What ails the lads in your quarter? They
muſt be very inſenſible, or you three fair
nymphs very cruel, or Hymen ſurely would
light his taper at R------. If this vein of
celibacy continues, I would adviſe to erect a
cloiſter, and then your nominal Lady Abbeſs
would have ſomething to do; the Miſs W.'s
would be large contributors, as they have taken
the veil thirty years ago. But leaſt the confinement of a number of beauties in a nunnery
ſhould cauſe an inſurrection in the *beau monde,*
we muſt alſo contrive to ſhut up all the gay,
ſighing, uſeleſs fops in a monaſtery; and to
keep up forms and decencies, Mr. P----
H-----, a ſuperannuated but conſtant adorer
of the widow B. ſhall be appointed *Monſieur
L'Abbé.*

We have lived very quiet this ſummer.
Once a party of five men, headed by ROGER
STEVENS,

STEVENS, lay concealed in the thicket behind
our orchard for three nights; but Mr. B. get-
ting intelligence of it, the neighbours collected
and put them to flight, very indiscreetly, for
they might eafily have furprifed and taken
them. I went to fee the place where they had
ftationed themfelves; they had made a com-
modious bed of dry leaves, and had amufed
themfelves with plaiting grafs and making
true lovers knots. Dear fifter, farewell.

               ANN ELIZA BLEECKER.

Tomhanick, Auguft 6, 1782.

To Mifs T** E***

MY CHARMING SUSAN,

YOUR black eyes feem to have done fome
execution already ; but you, more cruel than
the Princefs of the Steel Caftle, who pitied the
Knight of the Burning Peftle, have difcarded
your STREPHON without a figh. But if you
continue invincible to love fifty years hence,
when your black eyes begin to twinkle through
                        " a pair

" a pair of green fpectacles, with filver rims
and a fhagreen cafe," you may poffibly repent.

Dear Susan, you will eafily diftinguifh
this raillery from the undifguifed fentiments of
my heart: your letter made me feel that I am
indeed your fifter: I love you, my Susan;
and fince your departure there is a chafm in
my family, at my table, at my fire-fide, that
is not filled to my liking by any other; but fo
far I am happy, that you are in a family
where, with proper attention, you will gain
every ufeful, every ornamental accomplifh-
ment.

Now let me tell you the news of thefe parts.
Nanny Bostwick died lately of a confumption. I went to fee the little beauty in her laft
moments; her piety, refignation and fortitude
were very ftriking: fhe fmiled difapprobation
when, to confole her, I hinted fhe might recover. Mrs. P------ too lays very ill. Papa,
who was here yefterday, told me fhe could not
recover to all human appearance: I fhall vifit
her to-morrow, and if this paper is not fealed,
will let you know her true fituation.---I hear
Doctor Brown is dead in *Virginia*; that H----
is very much reduced; and that W------- has
made

made a great fortune in *New-England* by privateering, and improved it by a wealthy marriage. Undoubtedly he omits his ufual queftion, " What do the ladies fay of me?"---- Blefs me, I could fill a volume. S---- C---- has accidentally bleft *Vermont* with a fatherlefs fon, and is gone to *Canada*. We are all well, except JOHNNY. Domine B. dreffes like a very beau. JAMES H----- and MAG S---- traverfe the bufhes on horfeback; and MERKEE thanks you kindly for recollecting him; but FAN refents your neglect. and begs me to let you know that fhe thinks you lofe your manners. I fuppofe you know that MOLLY P------ is married: yes, I recollect I formerly wrote it to you.

All this nonfenfe, my fweet SUSAN, will remind you of the many laughing, indolent hours we have paffed, in the cool of fummer evenings, on our green, where we chatted without referve or impertinent caution, and as the full moon rofe bright in a cloudlefs fky, when the fimple lads and laffes were convened, we fported in the innocency of childifh amufements, and pleafed and fatigued with blind-
man's -

man's-buff, and hide-and-feek, and puſs-in-
the-corner, we went ſweetly to reſt.

Susan, all this little chat is for your own
inſpeɛ́tion. Were you to ſhew this letter to
ſome belle or fop, you would be the leſs eſteem-
ed for converſing with ſuch a very ruſtic, ſuch
a ſtranger to the etiquette of a polite circle.
The well-bred hate ſimplicity: there is a great
gulph between the vulgar adepts of nature,
and the artificial, mechanical ſons of cere-
mony.

To-day is my birth-day: I have made it a
day of thankſgiving to my God, who has often
brought my ſoul out of trouble, and have
made it ſacred to the memory of my beſt loved
friends, by writing them ſeverally long letters.
External rejoicing and feſtivity I care not for:
the ſecret approbation of my conſcience is all
the praiſe I now ſeek after, and more, in my
eſteem, to be valued, than the acclamations
of an empire.

How ſhall I conclude this incoherent epiſtle? When I begin to talk to my Sue, (for,
as Mr. Pope ſays, this is not writing) I know
not how to be ſilent.

Tueſday.

Tuefday.

IT is three days fince I wrote the above. That evening I was feized with a fever; I had a fleeplefs, melancholy night; and the next morning Doctor YOUNGLOVE bled me; but having a dull lancet, he made too large an orifice, by which I loft too much blood: he could hardly ftop it. I was fo weakened that I have lain yefterday and to-day in the hyfterics, and can juft fit up to finifi this for Major V-- B-----, who will take my letters with him to-morrow to *Albany*. However, I have fpirits enough to laugh at my odd figure before company: I fit up in my fhort-gown, a cloak over my fhoulders, no fhoes, no roll on, with my night-cap. I want a deal of indulgence when I am fick; and bleffed be Providence, your brother is the tendereft of nurfes; fo many namelefs affiduities, fuch a winning foftnefs and complacency in his manner, as palliate my diftemper and prevent my complaints. Excufe me; I love to expofe my whole heart to my artlefs SUSAN.

All our prifoners are arrived from *Canada*; they continually pafs our door, and are warmly habited.

habited. Mrs. F---'s fifter is returned, but the favages have murdered two of her children. CHRISTINA F. begs you to remember her. My STREPHON and my little ones infift on your recollecting them affectionately; and I muft make a frequent repetition when I tell you that you are truly beloved by your fifter,

ANN ELIZA BLEECKER.

To Mifs M**** V** W***

I Have been a fad girl, my dear M------, to fufpend writing to my fair one fo long. They tell me you are the prettieft wit about *R*-----, fo that I ought to be cautious how I fcribble; but I will go on in the innocency of my heart, and if you criticife, do it mercifully.

We have had an agreeable jaunt to *New-England*, but in paffing the mountains of *Tawkanok* I think I never faw a more lovely fcene: we had afcended the laft declivity; the vallies below us, interfperfed with farms, and plains, and villages, feemed to be at an incredible depth; when we entered on a level, overfhaded with evergreens, laurel, and hem-

Q   lock,

lock, pine and fpruce, intermixed with red, blue and yellow berries---imitating the fofteft bowers of fummer. Thefe greens naturally ftruck out into long viftas, through which we faw the gildings of the fetting fun long after the mortals below us were funk in darknefs.

We found the people hofpitable and focial; were invited cheerfully into almoft every genteel houfe we chanced to pafs; and return- ed home, like JACOB's fons from *Egypt*, with our money, if not in our fack's mouth, at leaft in our pockets: but tell SUSAN we left little BENJAMIN behind, who is proceeding to the *Nine-Partners*.

I begin to find the winter tedious; my circle of friends here is too fmall; that of my ruftic acquaintance too large: when the heart is not interefted, the mind has little fatisfaction in company: your own feelings will confirm my obfervation. Dear cuz, can't you contrive to vifit us? In vain would the winds beat, and the hail rattle: deep fnows might confine us, and arctic blafts condenfe the atmofphere; ftill our fires fhould fparkle, pleafure and joy and plenty attend us---and friendfhip fhould triumph. Pardon, M------, the tranf-
                                        ports

ports of a foul whofe feelings are too acute:
the diftant idea of an interview with thofe
whom I love elevates me beyond reafon, and
ten times a day I anticipate our happy meeting.

I received yefterday a long letter from Mr.
A-----: he tells me our KITTY is *increafing*:
poffibly I may inclofe a letter for him : I wifh
fhe would write; fhe can (if fhe will) chat
very agreeably. One of thefe days I intend
to tire coufin B. with an epiftle as long and
prolix as an homily: we ufed to be corref-
pondents, but I am afraid fhe grows too proud
to recollect her country friends. A certain
Colonel told me laft week that Mrs. F----
ufed to be a charming and inftructive companion, but that now fhe was grown too fine a
lady for converfation. I told him I never
would believe that the tinfel of fortune could
rob my B----- of the ornaments of humanity :
fo pleafe to inform her of the Colonel's
malignity.

Dear M------, accept Mr. B's. refpects,
and remember me kindly to aunt, and not
lefs kindly to all the reft of my friends in your
houfe: but, by cuftom, I muft write formally

Q 2   and

and with proper diftances what you have long
known, that I am, with every fentiment of
regard, dear girl, your moft affectionate

ANN ELIZA BLEECKER.

To Mifs S**** T** E***

No, I can admit of no excufe; I have
written three letters in folio to my SUSAN,
and have received no anfwer. After various
conjectures about the caufe of fo mortifying
an omiffion, I have come to this conclufion,
that you have commenced a very, very fashion-
able lady---(you fee my penetration)---and
though I am not in poffeffion of JOSEPH's di-
vining cup, I can minutely defcribe how you
paffed the day when my laft letter was handed
you; we will fuppofe it your own journal.

Saturday Morn, Feb. 12

Ten o'clock. WAS difturbed in a very plea-
fant dream by aunt V. W. who told me breakfaft was ready; fell afleep and dreamed again
about Mr. S.

Eleven. Rofe from bed; DINAH handed my
fhoes, wafhed the cream poultice from my
arms,

arms, and unbuckled my curls; drank two dishes of hyson; could not eat any thing.

From twelve to two. Withdrew to my closet; perused the title page of the Pilgrim's Progress: ----- came in, and, with an engaging address, presented me with a small billet-doux from Mr. S. and a monstrous big packet from sister B. Laid the packet aside; mused over the charming note until three o'clock.

Could not read sister's letter, because I must dress, Major ARROGANCE, Colonel BOMBAST, and TOM FUSTIAN being to dine with us; could not suit my colours---fretted---got the vapours: DINE, handing me the salts, let the vial fall and broke it; it was diamond cut crystal, a present from Mr. S. I flew up in a passion---it was enough to vex a saint---and boxed her ears soundly.

Four. Dressed; aunt asked me what sister had wrote. I told her she was well, and had wrote nothing in particular. *Mem.*----I slily broke the seal to give a colour to my assertion.

Between four and five. Dined; TOM FUSTIAN toasted the brightest eyes in company--- I reddened like crimson---was surprised to see M------ blush, and looking round saw P------

bluſh yet deeper than we. I wonder who he meant. Tom is called a lad of judgment. Mr. S. paſſed the window on horſeback.

Six. Viſited at Miſs -----'s: a very formal company: uneaſy in my ſtays---ſcalded my fingers, and ſtained my changeable by ſpilling a diſh of tea; the ladies were exceſſively ſorry for the accident, and Miſs V. Z. obſerved, that juſt ſuch another miſchance had befallen the widow R. three years before the war. Made a party at cards until ſeven in the evening; loſt two piſtoles. *Mem.*---had no ready caſh, but gave an order on -------,

From ſix till three in the morning. Danced with Mr. S.---thought he looked jealous---to puniſh him I coquetted with three or four pretty fellows, whiſpered Colonel Tinsel, who ſmiled and kiſſed my hand; in return I gave him a petulant blow on the ſhoulder. Mr. S. looked like a thunder-guſt; then affected to be calm as a ſtoic; but in ſpite of philoſophy turned as pale as Banquo's ghoſt. M------ ſeemed concerned, and aſked what ailed him? I don't like M------: I wonder what charm makes every body admire her: ſure, if Mr. S. was civil to her, it was enough;

he

he need not be so very affectionate. I flew in a pet to a vacant parlour, and took out sister's letter to read: I laboured through ten lines, contemplated the seal, chewed off three corners, and folding the remains elegantly, put it in my pocket. I suppose it was full of friendship and such like country stuff. However, sister writes out of a good heart to me, and I will answer it. Mr. S. and I were reconciled through the intercession of P——, whose lovely humanity every where commands esteem. We passed the hours very agreeably. On my retiring DINAH attended, and having no paper handy, I gave her sister's letter to put my hair in buckle, while I read these verses, which Colonel TINSEL, with a sigh, gave me:—

> Lofty cretur, wen de sun
> Wantons o'er yu wid his beme,
> Yu smile wid joy—my lukes alone
> Obnoxious ar—woud I war him.

I think the Colonel writes as well as HOMER; I believe he knows as much, what signifies Greek and Hebrew! I hate your starched scholars that talk Latin.

Well SUSAN, you see that in the arctic wilds of *America* your secret actions are brought to light,

light, ſo I hope you will pay more reſpect to this epiſtle.

Mr. B------- begs me, at this very inſtant, to preſent his very humble regards to you, and has made three ſolemn bows to your ladyſhip before I could write a ſentence. POLLY S---- is here, and making ſad execution among our beaus. We live here a merry kind of a laughing, indolent life: we ſuffer no real evils, and are far from regretting the elegant amuſements which attend a city life: all that I want, my ſiſter, is your company. This conſtant repetition you muſt permit (without repining) in all my letters. I never walk in that angle of my garden where your flowers are planted, but I heave a ſigh, as if it were a painted monument to your departed body. Can you never come to us? Were it not for my precarious health, I might even adventure to R------, and kiſs couſin B-----, as my old dear friend, whom I tenderly love, though ſhe forgets me: but I am often ſick; and happy am I that my JACK is ſo good a nurſe; the tenderneſs of his nature and cheerfulneſs of his temper, contribute more to my cure than all the reſtoratives in the diſpenſatory.

Tell

Tell my fweet coufins I love them all ten-
derly; recollect me with affection to aunt
V** W***, and permit my PEG and HAN-
NAH to falute you.

ANN ELIZA BLEECKER.

Tomhanick, March 29, 1783.

This day fourteen years ago, SUSAN, I was
married; repent, and take a hufband.

To *Mr.* S***** S*******.

I Congratulate you, my dear brother, on the
peace; in confequence of which I fincerely
hope you may fee many happy years: as for
me, my bright profpects lie beyond the grave;
I have little to promife myfelf on this fide of
eternity. Affliction has broken my fpirit and
conftitution; I grow daily weaker and more
emaciated, and depreffed with the reflection of
leaving my hufband and child---alas! the only
treafures I have now on earth.

Let me talk freely to you for the laft time,
my brother:---You know your poor BETSEY
was born a folitary orphan: though enjoying
a genteel fortune, yet friendlefs, and a wanderer,

derer, at length I found peace in the company
of a tender hufband. Ah, how foon interrupted! my lovely babes died away like fummer
bloffoms before the froft: ftill I had a kind
mother to complain to; we wept together: but
foon the enemy rufhing upon us like a hurri-
eane, we were fcattered like a flock of frighted
birds: our dear mother fled to *Red-Hook* with
SUSAN; I ftaid awhile at the farm; but a fudden incurfion of fome favages haftened my retreat; I took my beautiful ABELLA on my
arm, and PEGGY by the hand, and wandered
folitary through the dark woods, expecting
every moment to meet the bloody ally of *Britain:* however, we arrived fafe at *Arabia,* where
I met my hufband, who had been to *Albany;* he
procured a chaife, and took us to the city; the
alarm increafing, we got a paffage in a floop
with fifter SWITS and family; twelve miles
below *Albany* my ABELLA died of a dyfentery;
we went afhore, had one of my mahogany
dining-tables cut up to make her coffin, and
buried the little angel on the bank. I was
feized with the diftemper; and when we came
to *Red-Hook,* found my dear mamma wafted to
a fhadow: fhe mourned over the ruins of her
family,

family, and carried me to uncle H------'s, who received us very reluctantly. Soon after my dear mother died, and I returned to *Albany*, where, in a few days, I faw poor fifter CATY* expire. We retired again to *Tomhanick*, where we lived fometime bleft in domeftic tranquillity, though under perpetual alarms from the favages: at length, one afternoon, a fmall party from *Canada*, who had unperceivedly penetrated the country, carried off Mr. BLEECKER with his two fervants. This fhock I could not fupport. My little PEGGY and I went to *Albany*, where we wept inceffantly for five days, when God was pleafed to reftore him to our arms. Soon after I fell into premature labour, and was delivered of a dead child. Since that I have been declining; and though we often fled from the enemy fince, been cruelly plundered, and often fuffered for very neceffaries, yet your filence, my brother, hurts me more than thefe.

Mr. BLEECKER talks of taking me to *New-York* this fpring, but I believe I fhall never reach it; my health is fo precarious that I dare not, even here, venture an afternoon's vifit. I could

* Mrs. SWITS.

could wiſh to ſee you before I died; but I am uſed to diſappointments. I have given you my little hiſtory that you may ſee I die of a broken heart. Farewell, my only brother; may God preſerve your family, and continue all your bleſſings. When you ſee my poor little PEGGY, and my poor little HANNAH SWITS, think of your friends who have periſhed before you, and love and pity them for their ſakes. Give my kindeſt love to BETSEY, and accept of your brother's. I am, dear SAMMY, your very affectionate ſiſter,

ANN ELIZA BLEECKER.
Tomhanick, May 8, 1783.

To *Miſs* S**** T** E***.

MY DEAR SUSAN,

INDISPOSITION has of late ſo diſpirited me that I have omitted to write to any of my friends; but within theſe few days I am ſenſibly better, and feel this evening in a chatty humour. ·Let me firſt of all give you the news---LYDIA S------ is married to Mr.

JOHN

JOHN B--------, and Mifs POLLY S--- to Lieutenant G----- (fon of ENNIS G----- the taylor;) moreover, NATJE L------ (your old enemy) is likewife become fomebody's ef- poufed wife. Lord STERLING died laft night, and (I am quite a gazette) beau T--- is gone to *Canada.* The lads lodge with us, and we have endeavoured to pafs the winter as gleefully as plenty and fimplicity can make us---E---- kiffes your hands; JAMES is a profefs'd flave to PEGGY S----; and POLLY will join us to- morrow, when Mr. B. and his fpoufe intend to leave the merry circle at *Tomhanick,* and take a ramble to *New-England.* I have been informed that MRS. A----- has bleft the Doctor with a fon and daughter; if fo, I give you joy. Did you ever fee fo incoherent an epiftle? however, you muft confefs, did I reduce fo much news to order, and tell every thing elegantly, it would fwell my paper be- yond the common limit; befides, I do not mean to fet up for " the complete letter-wri- ter." My PEG is quite difappointed at your filence, and regrets that fhe ever fent her fcrawl to *R------:* and indeed, SUSAN, (now I think on it) you have correfponded with me

R   rather

rather like a formal acquaintance than a warm
friend; with every post you might have sent
me some scribble; sometimes a half a quire,
sometimes a half a line; the dawnings of
friendship, emotions of humanity, sentiments
of piety, or impressions of love, ought to have
been candidly confided in the bosom of your
own ELIZA: they would have brightened my
moments of solitude, and have made me forget my oblivious situation. SAMMY too has
helped to embitter my cup of life; he has contracted his affection within the orb of his little family, and cannot shoot out a ray of love
at this distance, to enlighten and bless a forlorn sister: I love him sincerely; may he and
his be forever happy. My sister, I shall grow
too dull if I proceed; I had better conclude;
but I am fond of talking to you. Let me
drop into news again---POLLY P------ (Mrs.
L.) has a fine son; and I had like to have forgot to mention that *Vermont* intends again to
renew the cast and western claims. Upon a
late resolve of Congress, (handed particularly
to them) they have assumed an insulting arrogance of behaviour, threaten Congress, and
imprecate

imprecate *New-York*. In fhort, I fancy we fhall have all our perfecutions to go over again.

But what have your black eyes been doing all this while? have you captured no heart worth retaining? I am afraid the gentlemen are fo feverely attracted by the charms of three fair ones, that (like Mahomet's fhrine) they cannot attach themfelves to either. Pray be feen feparate.

We have here a ruftic beauty come into our foreft, that would be much admired (I mean for perfon, not manners) by all the beaus of *R------:* the fymmetry of her form, glitter of her eyes, and leffening fhades of vermilion on her cheek, which lofe themfelves imperceptibly in a complexion of the moft delicate whitenefs; thefe, when improved in the *beau monde* by artificial graces, would make her an irrefiftible toaft; fhe has the romantic name of MELANESSA; but being of a tender conftitution, not able to work, has no declared admirer.

> Full many a gem of pureft ray ferene,
> The dark unfathom'd caves of ocean bear;
> Full many a flower is born to blufh unfeen,
> And wafte its fweetnefs on the defert air.
>
> GRAY.

R 2   Dear

Dear girl, you are tired with my imperti-
nence, but I hafte to relieve you. Your brother begs you to remember him with tendernefs; the children love you; even FAN and
MARKEE folicit your remembrance of them;
and O, my fifter! might you but really feel
how much I am your affectionate
                          ANN ELIZA BLEECKER.
Tomhanick, Dec. 10, 1783.

POETICS.

POETICS.

JOSEPH.

—

WITH many children was the Patriarch
    bleft,
Yet *Jofeph* he preferr'd before the reft:
To tend his flock was all the youth's employ
To ferve his God and Sire his only joy:
Jacob of his lov'd confort now depriv'd,
Beheld her graces in the fon reviv'd;
And all the love he had to *Rachel* gone,
Was by degrees transferr'd unto her fon.
A filken veft, that caft a various fhade,
He fondly to the boy a prefent made:
Here vivid fcarlet ftrove with lively green, ⎫
The purple, blended with the white, was feen, ⎬
And azure fpots were interfpers'd between. ⎭
    This gaudy robe (the bafis of his woe,
The fource from which his future forrows flow)
Kindled his elder brethren's wakeful pride:
(When envy mounts, affection will fubfide)
Their dawning hate in vain to hide they ftrove,
Each look too plain confefs'd expiring love.

The fun obliquely fhot his humid beams,
When *Jofeph* wak'd, one morn, and told his
    dreams:
' My brethren, we, methought, were on a plain,
' And binding into fheaves the yellow grain;
' When mine arofe; your's form'd a circle round,
' And reverently bow'd low to the ground.'
At this each faee the innate rage exprefs'd:
And *Jofeph* thus, indignant, they addrefs'd.
' Shalt thou indeed a fov'reign to us be?
' And fhall we fall as fuppliants on the knee?
' Vain boy! renounce thofe hopes---hence to
    the field
' A fhepherd's crook, not fceptre, fhalt thou
    wield.'
Again, when flumbers ftole upon his eyes,
And active Fancy bade the vifion rife,
To him th' eleven ftars, the orb of day,
And cryftal moon refpectful homage pay.
This on the morn the wond'ring youth difclos'd
When *Jacob* the prediction thus oppos'd:
' Shall I, thine aged fire, whofe filver hairs
' And arms unnerv'd proclaim my length of
    years,
' Proftrate on earth myfelf thy vaffel own?
' And fhall thy mother bow before her fon?
                  ' Ambition,

' Ambition, *Joseph*, has thy heart poſſeſs'd,
' And dreams illuſive riſe from ſuch a gueſt.'
But yet he wonder'd what might be deſign'd,
And the preſaging viſions treaſur'd in his mind.

It chanc'd his elder ſons at early dawn
Led their fair flocks to *Dothen*'s verdant lawn:
There, while the kids and lambs crop off the
 flow'rs,
In cloſe converſe they paſs th' eloping hours:
Beneath a cedar's boughs, whoſe awful ſhade
Extended o'er the plain, was *Levi* laid:
What rais'd the tears that trembled in his eyes?
Iſſacher aſk'd; and *Levi* thus replies:

' *Jacob* was once impartial in his love;
' To pleaſe us all, and we to pleaſe him ſtrove.
' Have we not toil'd beneath the burning ray
' Of yon bright orb, who riſing we ſurvey;
' And when the lamp of night illumes the ſkies,
' When dews deſcend and noxious miſts ariſe,
' In ſilent vales a careful watch we keep,
' And from the rav'ning wolves protect the
 ſheep?
' Is this the kind return for all our care?---
' We aſk but equally his love to ſhare;
' And that denied, to aggravate the ſmart,
' A ſimpering boy engroſſes all his heart:
        ' What

' What can entitle him to fuch a claim,
' Domeftic labours, or a martial fame?
' In *Mamre*'s groves his hours flide foft away,
' In reft at night, in indolence all day:
' With lies of us he fills the cred'lous ear,
' Too horrid to repeat, or you to hear.
' For this a fuperb robe adorns his limbs,
' And partial heav'n for this in myftic dreams
' Prefages a reward.   But words are vain.'
Here *Levi* ceas'd, and *Iffacher* began.

 ' Ah! 'tis too plain, too obvious to the fight, ⎫
' That *Jofeph* is our parent's chief delight, ⎬
' Although a bafe ufurper of our right: .⎭
' You fee ambition rifing in his foul;
' And when his years mature to manhood roll,
' Elated with the hopes of fway, he'll try
' On us, my friends, his dreams to verify.'

 He ended: but his cheeks with anger glows:
When bloody *Simeon* from the ground arofe.
Awhile he paus'd; at length his lips impart
The black defign corroding at his heart.

 ' Brethren, this war of words and coward rage
' Suits not our youth, but meets impotent age;
' Let one decifive ftroke remove our fears,
' Obftruct the fates, and calm inteftine wars.'
         Reuben

Reuben at *Simeon* glanc'd a frown, and fpoke:
' The fentence yet in embrio I revoke:
' The *Sechemites*, (who, murder'd on the plain,
' Sad monuments of cruelty remain)
' Have they to death inur'd your gloomy eyes,
' That for a childifh dream your brother dies?
' Would you in guiltlefs blood your jav'lins
  ftain,
' And Nature's law by fuch a deed profane?
' My foul fhrinks at the thought: loud found-
  ing fame
' Would through the world the fratricide pro-
  claim.
' Brethren, regard his youth---our father's age;
, One fatal ftroke deftroys both child and fage:
' Congenial fouls: the union of the heart
' Death can't divide, nor living can we part.
' Ah! tell me, *Simeon*, is the action brave
' To fink a fage and infant in the grave?
' Miftaken valor, and inhuman deed,
' For one man's fault to make a nation bleed!
' Much more inhuman this: the fon confpires
' A harmlefs brother's death, and aged fire's.
' Think not with their laft breath your fears
  are fled;
' God's vengeance ftill purfues the guilty head!
        And

' And why abridge his days? Ah! brethren,
    know,
By fhort'ning his, you fill your own with
    woe.'
He ended unapplauded, and beheld
The object of their conteft on the field,
Far as the eye could reach: his gloffy hair
Curl'd on his neck; his robe wav'd light in air,
Clafp'd by a plate of gold, that as he run
In brightnefs feem'd to emulate the fun.

Hate, ftifled by reproof, flam'd in each eye,
When at a diftance they perceiv'd the boy;
In ev'ry look black difcontent was fpread,
And *Judah*, pale with envy, rofe and faid:
 ' Vain fophiftry! how do our joys fubfide,
' While that prophetic dreamer fwells with
    pride?
' No; let him die: his veft we'll ftain with
    blood,
' And tell his fire we found it in the wood:
' Some beaft, I'll cry, and deep affliction feign,
' Oh *Jacob*, has thy fon, thy *Jofeph* flain!
' If *Reuben* new objections here create,
' Then let him bear our juft, immortal hate.'
  When *Reuben* found his death was now de-
    creed,
Refolv'd to fave the youth, or with him bleed,
                   He

He loud exclaim'd---' At leaſt with this com-
ply,
' (Since by our hand the innocent muſt die)
' I am his brother, give me not the pain
' To ſee his blood guſh from the purple vein,
' To ſee his ſoul part from his quiv'ring lip,
' And hear the groan which uſhers in his ſleep.
' Where yonder cedars raiſe their lofty heads,
' And round the rocky place a horror ſpreads,
' There is a pit, to water long unknown,
' Dark its acceſs, with brambles overgrown :
' Here be the child immur'd : the ſides are ſteep,
' Of ſtone cemented, and profoundly deep ;
' A certain and concealed death his fate ;
' Guiltleſs of blood we gratify our hate.'
He heſitated---by real ſorrow mov'd,
While his propoſal all the ſwains approv'd.
  But *Reuben* hop'd, when ſleep had clos'd
their eyes,
With the lov'd youth his father to ſurpriſe ;
Then lead him where he might ſecurely wait
The period when he ſhould ſurvive their hate.
  Joſeph, ſoon as his brethren he deſcries,
A placid ſweetneſs triumph'd in his eyes,
Joy ting'd his blooming cheeks with deeper red,
He innocently ſmil'd, advanc'd, and ſaid:
                                        To

‘ To *Sechem*’s vale our fire bade me repair,
‘ If you were well, folicitous to hear:
‘ I rov’d o’er meads enamel’d with gay flow’rs,
‘ I rang’d the forefts and explor’d the bow’rs;
‘ At length my erring fteps a ftranger led
‘ To *Dothen*, where he faid your flocks were fed
‘ But why this gen’ral gloom on ev’ry face,
‘ This ftupid grief which faddens all the place?
‘ O tell me! quick difpel each rifing fear,
‘ Or let me drop the fympathetic tear.’---
He pleads, impatient for the truth to gain;
But dazzling virtue aw’d the filent train.
The confcious blood revolting from each cheek,
Rufh to the guilty heart and refuge feek:
Now vice prepares the formidable blow,
Yet fhrinks, encountering a defencelefs foe:
She fummons all her forces to her aid,
And big with death, now hovers o’er his head.

　　Rapid as lightnings thro’ the æther glance,
So fwift they to th’ aftonifh’d youth advance;
Trembling with rage they flew; they feiz’d
　　his hair,
And bade him inftantly for death prepare.

　　Aghaft he gaz’d; he ftiffen’d with furprife,
His blood congeals, he fcarce believes his eyes;
A fudden horror thrills thro’ ev’ry vein,
He cafts an anxious look back o’er the plain;

He

He fees no hope ; then finking on his knees,
He thus effay'd their anger to appeafe :
  ' What have I done, my brethren, that your
     rage
' United fhould againft a child engage?
' Alas! what heavy crime demands my death?'
Here rifing tears fupprefs'd his lab'ring breath ;
Thefe when difcharg'd, again the fhepherd
     pleads :---
' Is there no friend, not one who intercedes?
' With guiltlefs blood pollute not Nature's laws.
' Tell me my fault, and let me plead my caufe :
' If innocent, acquit; if guilty found,
' In public then let juftice give the wound.'
  He ceas'd to fpeak, and their decifion wait ;
When *Nepthali* exclaim'd, ' Our will is fate.'
Then with a cord his trembling hands they
     bound,
And rais'd him pale and fainting from the
     ground :
His terror power of utterance denies,
But yet he weeps and lifts his fpeaking eyes.
They lead him to the grove, whofe folemn fhade
The wind and folar ray could fcarce pervade ;
The dark abyfs they found, and op'd a way
By which defcending *Jofeph* left the day :

       S   The

The hollow fides re-echo back his moan,
And diftant rocks reflect the doubled groan;
In deeper notes his plaintive cries return'd,
While low excluded from the light he mourn'd.

Th' inhuman ruftics foon depart the place
Where confcious Vice now flufh'd each guilty
    face:
The fun fhone hot; impervious to his ray
A grove of palms the fainting fwains' furvey:
Beneath their fhade a filver current ftole,
Whofe lucid waves o'er moffy carpets roll.
Here they repair, and feated on the ground,
With rofeate wine the fhining goblet crown'd;
The viands on the velvet grafs they fpread, ⎫
The grape luxuriant and the milk-white   ⎪
    bread;   ⎬
When thoughtful *Reuben*, fighing, rofe and ⎪
    faid: ⎭
'While you the feftive banquet here prepare,
'To feek the ftraying lambs fhall be my care.'

Scarce was he gone, when from a neigh-
    bouring vale
The fragrant fmells of fpicery exhale;
The aromatic loads by camels borne,
From *Geliad* fent, to *Egypt* now return:
Thefe were proceeded by a num'rous train
Of trafficers, who from fair *Midian* came.
                            Th' in-

Th' inviting fhade, where cool the fhepherds
    lay,
Allur'd the merchants from their tirefome way;
They join the fwains, and prefs the verdant
    ground,
While the replenifh'd goblet paffes round.
    But pale remorfe, from cool reflection fprung,
On half-repenting *Judah*'s brow was hung;
His brother's groans reverb'rate on his ear,
But yet his envy *Jofeph*'s merits fear.
While thefe contending paffions rend his breaft
Apart the lift'ning fhepherds he addrefs'd:
   ‘ My friends, the eldeft curfe of righteous
      heaven
‘ Was to the murderer of a brother given;
‘ Tho' *Jofeph*'s crimes would juftify his death,
‘ We can be juft, and yet prolong his breath.
‘ Let us redeem the victim from the grave,
‘ And fend him to *Egyptia* as a flave;
‘ From thofe far plains he never can return,
‘ But muft repent his faults, fubmit and mourn:
‘ No black reflection then will give us pain,
‘ And ufeful gold, my brethren, too we gain.’
    The mercenary fhepherds all agree,
And fet him from his gloomy prifon free:

                He

He fmites his breaft, wet with inceffant tears;
His languid eyes to heav'n he pleading rears,
Whofe filent eloquence reveal'd his fears.
But when he faw the ftrangers in the fhade,
Diffufive hope thro' all his features fpread;
He wip'd away the pendant tears, and fmil'd,
When by the hand proud *Afhur* took the child;
His fordid foul from all foft ties eftrang'd,
Jofeph, without remorfe, for gold exchang'd:
The youth's fimplicity and early bloom,
Each ftranger with attractive force o'ercome:
They paid the fhining ore, and journey'd on,
For in the weft funk the declining fun.
  Meanwhile, o'er diftant hills, and mofs-
        grown rocks,
The penfive fwain purfues the timid flocks.
Now late returning, and o'ercome with heat,
Secures his charge and feeks a cool retreat;
Beneath a cedar's length'ned fhadow laid,
The vaft expanfe, admiring, he furvey'd,
In vivid tints, by fetting fol array'd
Magnificently gay. Here ftreak'd with gold,
The purple clouds their borrow'd paints unfold;
The blufhing weft with deep carnation glows,
And o'er the fkies a bright reflection throws.
---Now imperceptibly on clofing flow'rs
The filent dews defcend in filver fhow'rs,

                                    Th' ap-

Th' appearing ſtars exert a feeble light,
And *Reuben* welcomes the approach of night:
He riſes and explores the diſmal ſhade,
And ſtooping o'er the cavern's verge he ſaid:
' *Joſeph!* my brother *Joſeph!* I am come,
' Impatient to reverſe thy cruel doom;
' Forgive thy *Reuben*'s part in this black deed,
' 'Tis ſtratagem alone thy life has freed:
' Oh *Joſeph* ſpeak! ſurely thou doſt ſurvive:
' Oh ſpeak my brother, if thou art alive!
' Alas! no voice but echo's hollow ſound,
' No voice but mine remurmers o'er the
        ground!
' Where ſhall I flee, to what dark diſtant ſhore,
' To ſhun reproach? for *Joſeph* is no more.
' Why did my lips (conſenting to his death)
' When they pronounc'd his doom, not loſe
        their breath?'---
Again he calls, and raging in deſpair,
From his ſwoln breaſt the folding garment tears.
Now wild with grief, and wand ring thro' the
        gloom,
He met the *Hebrews* all returning home:
A kid they'd kill'd, and in the ſanguine gore
Had dipt the robe which blameleſs *Joſeph* wore.
Soon they appear'd on *Mamre*'s peaceful plain,
And enter'd *Iſrael*'s tent, a guilty train;

S 3   Each

Each feign'd to be with anxious care oppreſt,
And *Simeon*, weeping, thus his fire addreſt :
' Oh canſt thou recollect this bloody veſt !'
    Old *Jacob* view'd it with a pauſing eye ;
He trembled, groan'd, and ſcarce could make
    reply ;
An univerſal horror ſeiz'd his frame,
At length burſt forth th' ungovernable flame :
' It is my ſon's ! (he cry'd) my ſon is ſlain !
' Curſt be the hour that rent him from my ſide !
' What baneful planet did my actions guide ?
' Come, death, convey me to the peaceful urn ;
' *Joſeph* is dead ! why ſhould I live to mourn ?'
    In vain they try to calm his ſwelling grief ;
He cheriſh'd ſorrow, and refus'd relief.

On *Mrs.* JOHANNA LUPTON.

HER ſoul, unfetter'd from the bands of clay,
With ſwift-wing'd haſte to heaven takes its
    way ;
She tow'rs the æriel ſpace on wings divine,
While weeping friends ſurround the bloodleſs
    ſhrine :
                 The

The soften'd heart there breathes a tender figh,
And grief fits penfive in each moiften'd eye:
Supprefs the rifing tear, and with her fing,
‘ Death, where's thy vict'ry? Grave, where
        is thy fting?'
Sing how with God fhe refts in endlefs day,
All tears of forrow ever wip'd away ;
‘ Sing how by tortures heav'n her faith has
        try'd ;
‘ The faint endur'd it, tho' the woman dy'd!'
    Ah, nature will prevail! 'tis all in vain:
Say, facred mufe, what lofs do we fuftain?
She wip'd the eye of grief---it ceas'd to flow;
Her pitying heart ftill felt another's woe;
Indigent virtue fhar'd her earthly ftore ;
She call'd herfelf God's fteward for the poor:
A duteous child; a faithful, loving wife ;
Serene in death, as tranquil was her life :
A pious mother---mother now no more ;
Her foft folicitude and cares are o'er :
Sifter and friend, each tender name in one.
And is fhe gone? but heav'n's great will be
        done !
Like *Noah's* dove, the wand'rer found no reft,
Till in his ark her Saviour took the gueft.
Oh may we meet her on the eternal fhore,
Where death fhall never feparate us more !

                                To

To Mr. L*****.

THE sun that gilds the weſtern ſky
　　And makes the orient red,
Whoſe gladſome rays delight the eye
　　And cheer the lonely ſhade,

Withdraws his vegetative heat,
　　To ſouthern climes retires ;
While abſent, we ſupply his ſeat
　　With groſs, material fires.

'Tis new-year's morn ; each ruſtic ſwain
　　Ambroſial cordials take ;
And round the fire the feſtive train
　　A ſemi-circle make :

While clouds aſcend, of ſable ſmoke,
　　From pipes of ebon hue,
With inharmonick ſong and joke
　　They paſs the morning through.

You tell me this is ſolitude,
　　This Contemplation's ſeat ;
Ah no ! the moſt impervious wood
　　Affords me no retreat.

　　　　　　　　　　　　But

But let me recollect : 'tis said,
  When *Orpheus* tun'd his lyre
The Fauns and Satyrs left the shade,
  Warm'd by celestial fire.

His vocal lays and lyra made
  Inanimated marble weep ;
Swift-footed Time then paus'd, 'tis said,
  And sea-born monsters left the deep:

Impatient trees, to hear his strain
  Rent from the ground their roots?---
Such is my fate, as his was then,
  Surrounded here---by brutes.

<hr>

To the fame

D EAR Sir, when late in town you chose
To correspond no more in prose,
My viscious muse---(but 'tis in vain
Of her abuses to complain)---
Neglects to aid, as I expected,
And so I must be self-directed.
  You've broke th' agreement, Sir, I find ;
(Excuse me, I must speak my mind)
It seems, in your poetic fit,

                                      You

You mind not jingling, when there's wit;
And so to write like *Donne* you chose,
Whose prose was verse, and verse was prose:
From common tracts of rhyming stray,
And versify another way.
Indeed it suits, I must aver,
A *genius* to be singular.

On *F------r* kept in durance vile,
Did once more erring fortune smile:
Again he would extend his ray,
And shine his riches all away.
Birch said, (and what he said I sing)
' A shilling is a serious thing;'
But like *Icarus*, *F------r* springs,
Where suns dissolv'd his waxen wings:
No more the wings his weight sustain,
He plunges headlong in the main:
The shades of death steal o'er his eyes;
And to black *Styx* the spirit flies.

Life is a grand vicissitude
Of pain and health, of ill and good:
Your goose now mourns a murder'd mate,
(Attend while I the fact relate)
He chanc'd upon a cloudless morn,
To wander in our neighbour's corn;
Perhaps he thought all lands were free,
And none had private property;

Or

Or sure he ne'er had trod the plain,
And pick'd, like *Eve*, forbidden grain:
Careless he fed, in graceful ease
And sweet simplicity of geese.
Ill-fated bird! he there was kill'd
By man, the tyrant of the field.
  His widow's wing, Oh dire relation!
Next underwent sad amputation:
Weep not, dear Sir, at this abuse;
She bears it like a patient goose:
I fear the widow is a prude,
Or matters sooner would conclude;
Or else you have a coward heart,
And fear to act the suitor's part.
Of all the things beneath the sun, you know,
Faint heart fair lady never won.   Adieu.

To the same.

FROM plains and peaceful cots I send
The humble wishes of a friend:
May love still spread his silken wing,
And life to you be ever spring:
May virtue guide you with her clue,
Life's mazy path to wander thro';
And may your offspring the blest tract pursue:

On

On you may Heav'n benignly fmile,
And inward peace external cares beguile;
Long may you live fupremely bleft,
Then die, and be a Saviour's gueft.
The wifh is o'er, permit me to defcend
To the familiar converfe of a friend.
Well, you've done right to get a wife,
For change the comfort is of life;
Befides, I've read in ancient ftory,
A virtuous wife's a crown of glory:
And yet 'tis true that fome adorn
Their hufband's brows with crown of horn:
The wifeft man on earth we find
Was partial to the female kind,
Till he was trick'd a thoufand ways,
(But men are wifer now-a-days)
Which made the honeft Jew exclaim,
They were all vanities, and vain:
His father, you remember *David*,
Who tore *Saul*'s fkirt, and ran away with't,
He alfo had, (tho' lov'd of God)
Plurality of wives allow'd:
But fince polygamy's abolifh'd,
The wives are chafte, the hufbands polifh'd
Since with plagiary you've tax'd me,
And never fince for pardon afk'd me,

                                        To

To prove my falfe accufer guilty,
Repeat his borrow'd lines I will t'ye:
" No goofe that fwims, but foon or late
" Will find fome gander for a mate."
You'll find this couplet, I'll engage,
In *Wife of Bath*, the hundredth page,
Volume the fecond,---works of *Pope*---
Brother, you're now convinc'd, I hope.

However, what you prophefied
About the goofe, is verified ;
She's flipt her neck in marriage noofe,
And owns a fov'reign Lord, and *goofe*.
Adieu, *Mon Cher Ami* ; the Mufe
Begs you her freedom will excufe.

To the fame.

DEAR brother, to thefe happy fhades repair,
And leave, Oh leave the city's noxious air:
I'll try defcription, friend---methinks I fee
'Twill influence your curiofity.

Before our door a meadow flies the eye,
Circled by hills, whofe fummits croud the fky;
The filver lily there exalts her head,
And op'ning rofes balmy odours fpread,
While golden tulips flame beneath the fhade.

T   In

In short, not *Iris* with her painted bow,
Nor varied tints an evening sun can show,
Can the gay colours of the flow'rs exceed,
Whose glowing leaves diversify this mead:
And when the blooms of *Flora* disappear,
The weighty fruits adorn the satiate year:
Here vivid cherries bloom in scarlet pride,
And purple plums blush by the cherries side;
The sable berries bend the pliant vines,
And smiling apples glow in crimson rinds;
Ceres well pleas'd, beholds the furrow'd plain,
And show'rs her blessings on th' industrious
　　　swain;
Plenty sits laughing in each humble cot;
None wish for that which heaven gives them not.
But sweet Contentment still with sober charms,
Encircles us within her blissful arms;
Birds unmolested chaunt their early notes,
And on the dewy spray expand their throats;
Before the eastern skies are streak'd with light,
Or from the arch of Heaven retreats the night,
The musical inhabitants of air,
To praise their Maker, tuneful lays prepre.
Here by a spring, whose glassy surface moves
At ev'ry kiss from Zephyr of the groves,
While passing clouds look brighter in the
　　　stream,
Your poet sits and paints the rural scene.

To

To Mr. BLEECKER.

YES, I invok'd the Mufes' aid
To help me write, for 'tis their trade;
But only think, ungrateful Mufes,
They fent dame *Iris* with excufes,
They'd other bufinefs for to follow,
Beg'd I'd apply to God *Apollo*.
    The God faid, as heav'n's charioteer,
He had no time to mind us here;
Said if we rac'd round earth like *Phœbus*
One day, it fadly would fatigue us;
Yet we expect, when tir'd at night,
He'd ftay from bed to help us write:
Nor need we afk his fifter *Phœbe*,
For turning round had made her giddy;
Her infpiration would confufe us,
So counfell'd us to coax the Mufes.
Quite difappointed at this lecture
I left his worfhip fipping nectar;
But, pettifhly as I left his dome,
It chanc'd I met the Goddefs *Wifdom*.
No wonder fhe is wife, 'tis faid
She was the product of *Jove*'s head.

T 2

'Bright

‘ Bright Queen,’ faid I, ‘ in thefe abodes
‘ I beg’d a favour of the Gods:
‘ They wifh’d the poets at the devil,
‘ And the nine ladies were uncivil:
‘ *Apollo* told me he was lazy,
‘ And call’d his fifter *Phœbe* crazy.
‘ Permit me then your kind protection;
‘ From you I cannot fear rejection.’
   Tritonia gave me fmiles and nods,
(The unfual compliments of Gods,)
And look’d benign as rifing fun,
Which gave me courage to go on.
‘ ---Oh Goddefs! let your powerful arms
‘ Keep young *Ulyffus* from all harms;
‘ Attend him in each ftrange adventure,
‘ And be, in human form, his *mentor:*
‘ Oh bid him fhun *Circean* feafts,
‘ Whofe magic pow’r turns men to beafts;
‘ Nor let him touch the fatal tree,
‘ Left he forget *Penelope:*
‘ Keep him from a *Calypfo*’s arms,
‘ And all the treacherous *Syren*’s charms:
‘ In *Cyclop* cells let him not enter;
‘ Permit him not at games to venture;
‘ Sure as he does, he is undone,
‘ Each fharper is a *leftrigon;*
                ‘ Nor

' Nor city luxury inure him,.
' To be a modern epicurian;
' (For *Temperance*, celeftial maid,
' Is ftill a virtue of the fhade:)
' And dire difeafes burn each vein
' Of thofe who *Temperance* prophane,
' And kill her facred beeves in vain.
' The *Grecians* once to *Pluto's* glooms
' So funk for flaughter'd hecatombs.
' If men believ'd in tranfmigration,
' How would it fpare the brute creation?
' But, Goddefs! let him foon return,
' Nor twice ten years in abfence mourn;
' To thofe who love, a month appears
' As long as twenty tedious years.'
  Minerva rais'd her ægis high,
That blaz'd effulgence thro' the fky,
And, fmiling took the common oath,
To be immenfely kind to both;.
Then down from heaven's pure æther flew
Swifter than light---in fearch of you.

On the IMMENSITY of CREATION..

OH! could I borrow fome celeftial plume,
This narrow globe fhould not confine me long

T 3   In

In its contracted fphere---the vaft expanfe,
Beyond where thought can reach, or eye can
           glance,
My curious fpirit, charm'd fhould traverfe o'er,
New worlds to find, new fyftems to explore:
When thefe appear'd, again I'd urge my flight
Till all creation open'd to my fight.

  Ah! unavailing wifh, abfurd and vain,
Fancy return and drop thy wing again;
Could'ft thou more fwift than light move ⎫
           fteady on,   ⎪
Thy fight as broad, and piercing as the fun, ⎬
And *Gabriel's* years too added to thy own; ⎪
Nor *Gabriel's* fight, nor thought, nor rapid wing, ⎭
Can pafs the immenfe domains of th' eternal
           King;
The greateft feraph in his bright abode
Can't comprehend the labours of a God.
Proud reafon fails, and is confounded here;
---Man how contemptible thou doft appear!
What art thou in this fcene?---Alas! no more
Than a fmall atom to the fandy fhore,
A drop of water to a boundlefs fea,
A fingle moment to eternity.

                                A THOUGHT

A THOUGHT on DEATH.

ALAS! my thoughts, how faint they rife,
   Their pinions clogg'd with dirt;
They cannot gain the diftant fkies,
   But gravitate to earth.

No angel meets them on the way,
   To guide them to new fpheres;
And for to light them, not a ray
   Of heavenly gace appears.

Return then to thy native ground,
   And fink into the tombs;
There take a difmal journey round
   The melancholy rooms:

There level'd equal king and fwain,
   The vicious and the juft;
The turf ignoble limbs contain,
   One rots beneath a buft.

What heaps of human bones appear
   Pil'd up along the walls!
Thefe are *Death*'s trophies---furniture
   Of his tremendous halls;

                    The

The water oozing thro' the ſtones,
   Still drops a mould'ring tear ;
Rots the gilt çoffin from the bones,
   And lays the carcaſe bare.

This is *Cleora*---come, let's ſee
   Once more the blooming fair ;
Take off the lid---ah ! 'tis not ſhe,
   A vile impoſtor there.

Is this the charmer poets ſung,
   And vainly deified,
The envy of the maiden throng ?·
   (How humbling to our pride !)

Unhappy man, of tranſient breath,
   Juſt born to view the day,
Drop in the grave---and after death
   To filth and duſt decay.

Methinks the vault, at ev'ry tread,
   Sounds deeply in my ear,
‘ Thou too ſhalt join the ſilent dead,
   ‘ Thy final ſcene is here.'

Thy final ſcene ! no, I retract,
   Not till the clarion's ſound
Demands the ſleeping priſ'ners back
   From the refunding ground :

                    Not

Not till that audit shall I hear
  Th' immutable decree,
Decide the solemn question, where
  I pass eternity.

Death is the conqueror of clay,
  And can but clay detain;
The soul, superior, springs away,
  And scorns his servile chain.

The just arise, and shrink no more
  At graves, and shrouds, and worms,
Conscious they shall (when time is o'er)
  Inhabit angel forms.

ELEGY on the Death of CLEORA.

NO more of Zephyr's airy robe I'll sing,
Or balmy odours dropping from his wing,
Or how his spicy breath revives the lands,
And curls the waves which roll o'er crystal
  sands.
No more I'll paint the glowing hemisphere,
Or rocks ambitious, piercing upper air;
The subjects of the grave demand my lay,
Spectator now, I soon shall be as they.

Cleora,

Cleora, art thou gone? thou doft not hear
The voice of grief, nor fee the dropping tear;
And yet, it foothes my forrows while I mourn
In artlefs verfe, and weep upon thy urn.
-----Tho' bright from thee the rays of beauty
   ftream'd,
Thy mind irradiate, ftronger graces beam'd;
The meteor fhone fo permanent and fair,
Who'd not miftook the vapour for a ftar?
----E'en then----when lying poets flattering
   breath
Pronounc'd fo fair a form exempt from death;
The icy angel met her on the plain,
And bade our friend adorn his ghaftly train;
The vital heat forfakes her loitering blood;
The blood ftands ftill---the fprings of life all
   ftood;
Down funk the fair, while nature gave a groan,
To fee her nobleft ftructure fall fo foon.

 But fay, fome pow'r, where is the fpirit fled,
To wait the time when it fhall join the dead?
Say, fprings her active foul beyond the fkies,
Or ftill around the clay enamour'd flies?
Or fits exalted on th' empyreal height,
'Midft deluges of primogenial light?
Or elfe expatiates, with enlarged pow'rs,
Where mortal man's conception never foars?
      ---Ah!

---Ah ! when the brittle bands of life are burſt,
To meet her on the ſhores of bliſs. I truſt;
Sure I ſhall know her in the realms above,
By thoſe ſweet eyes which beam inceſſant love:
There we'll renew the friendſhip here begun,
But which ſhall laſt thro' th' eternal noon :
Till then ſuſpend my fond enquiries, where,
And with what ſouls ſhe breathes immortal air;
Meanwhile, with imitative art I'll try,
Nobly like her to live---like her to die!

Written in the Retreat from BURGOYNE.

WAS it for this, with thee a pleaſing load,
I ſadly wander'd thro' the hoſtile wood;
When I thought fortune's ſpite could do no
  more,
To ſee thee periſh on a foreign ſhore?
 Oh my lov'd babe! my treaſure's left behind,
Ne'er ſunk a cloud of grief upon my mind;
Rich in my children---on my arms I bore
My living treaſures from the ſcalper's pow'r:
When I ſat down to reſt beneath ſome ſhade,
On the ſoft graſs how innocent ſhe play'd,
       While

While her sweet sister, from the fragrant wild,
Collects the flow'rs to please my precious child;
Unconscious of her danger, laughing roves,
Nor dreads the painted savage in the groves.

Soon as the spires of *Albany* appear'd,
With fallacies my rising grief I cheer'd;
'Resign'd I bear,' said I, 'heaven's just reproof,
'Content to dwell beneath a stranger's roof;
'Content my babes should eat dependent bread,
'Or by the labour of my hands be fed:
'What tho' my houses, lands, and goods are gone,
'My babes remain---these I can call my own.'
But soon my lov'd *Abella* hung her head,
From her soft cheek the bright carnation fled;
Her smooth transparent skin too plainly shew'd
How fierce thro' every vein the fever glow'd.
---In bitter anguish o'er her limbs I hung,
I wept and sigh'd, but sorrow chain'd my tongue;
At length her languid eyes clos'd from the day, ⎫
The idol of my soul was torn away; ⎬
Her spirit fled and left me ghastly clay! ⎭

Then---then my soul rejected all relief,
Comfort I wish'd not for, I lov'd my grief:
'Hear, my *Abella!*' cried I, 'hear me mourn,
'For one short moment, oh! my child return;
'Let my complaint detain thee from the skies,
'Though troops of angels urge thee on to rise.'

                                    Al!

All night I mourn'd---and when the rifing day
Gilt her fad cheft with his benigneft ray,
My friends prefs round me with officious care,
Bid me fupprefs my fighs, nor drop a tear;
Of refignation talk'd---paffions fubdu'd,
Of fouls ferene and chriftian fortitude;
Bade me be calm, nor murmur at my lofs,
But unrepining bear each heavy crofs.
   ' Go!' cried I raging, ' ftoick bofoms go!
' Whofe hearts vibrate not to the found of woe;
' Go from the fweet fociety of men,
' Seek fome unfeeling tyger's favage den,
' There calm---alone---of refignation preach,
' My Chrift's examples better precepts teach.'
Where the cold limbs of gentle _Laz'rus_ lay
I find him weeping o'er the humid clay;
His fpirit groan'd, while the beholders faid
(With gufhing eyes) ' fee how he lov'd the dead!'
And when his thoughts on great _Jerus'lem_
        turn'd,
Oh! how pathetic o'er her fall he mourn'd!
And fad _Gethfemene_'s nocturnal fhade
The anguifh of my weeping Lord furvey'd:
Yes, 'tis my boaft to harbour in my breaft
The fenfibilities by God expreft;
Nor fhall the mollifying hand of time,
Which wipes off common forrows, cancel mine.
       U   _A COM-_

A COMPLAINT.

TELL me thou all pervading mind,
  When I this life forsake,
Must ev'ry tender tie unbind,
  Each sweet connection break?

How shall I leave thee, oh! my love,
  And blooming progeny?
If I without thee mount above,
  'Twill be no heav'n to me.

Ah! when beneath the arching vault
  My lifeless form's remov'd,
Let not oblivion sink the thought,
  How much, how long I lov'd.

Come oft my grassy tomb to see,
  And drop thy sorrows there;
No balmy dews of heav'n shall be
  Refreshing as thy tear.

There give thy griefs full vent to flow
  O'er the unconscious dead,
With no spectator to thy woe
  But my attendant shade.

ANOTHER.

ANOTHER.

STILL apprehending death and pain,
To whom great God shall I complain?
 To whom pour out my tears
But to the pow'r that gave me breath,
The arbiter of life and death,
 The ruler of the spheres?

Soon to the grave's Cimmerian shade
I must descend without thine aid,
 To stop my spirit's flight;
Leave my dear partner here behind,
And blooming babe, whose op'ning mind
 Just lets in Reason's light.

When she, solicitous to know
Why I indulge my silent woe,
 Clings fondly round my neck,
My passions then know no commands,
My heart with swelling grief expands,
 Its tender fibres break.

Father of the creation wide,
Why hast thou not to man deny'd
 The silken tye of love?

Why

Why food celeftial let him tafte,
Then tear him from the rich repaft,
    Real miferies to prove?

A PROSPECT of DEATH.

DEATH! thou real friend of innocence,
Tho' dreadful unto fhivering fenfe,
I feel my nature tottering o'er
Thy gloomy waves, which loudly roar:
Immenfe the fcene, yet dark the view,
Nor *Reafon* darts her vifion thro'..
Virtue! fupreme of earthly good,
Oh let thy rays illume the road;
And when dafh'd from the precipice,
Keep me from finking in the feas:
Thy radient wings, then wide expand,
And bear me to celeftial land.

To *Mifs* CATHARINE TEN EYCK.

COME and fee our habitation,
    Condefcend to be our gueft;
Tho' the veins of warring nations
    Bleed, yet here fecure we reft.

                                By

By the light of *Cynthia*'s crefcent,
　Playing thro' the waving trees ;
When we walk, we wifh you prefent
　To participate our blifs.

Late indeed, the cruel favage
　Here with looks ferocious ftood ;
Here the ruftic's cot did ravage,
　Stain'd the grafs with human blood.

Late their hands fent conflagration
　Rolling thro' the blooming wild,
Siez'd with death, the brute creation
　Mourn'd, while defolation fmil'd.

Spiral flames from talleft cedar
　Struck to heav'n a heat intenfe ;
They cancell'd thus with impious labour,
　Wonders of Omnipotence.

But when *Conqueft* rear'd her ftandard,
　And th' *Aborigines* were fied,
Peace, who long an exile wander'd,
　Now return'd to blefs the fhade.

Now *Æolus* blows the afhes
　From fad *Terra*'s black'ned brow,
While the whift'ling fwain with rufhes
　Roofs his cot, late levell'd low.

U 3　　　　　　　　From

From the teeming womb of Nature
 Burſting flow'rs exhale perfume;
Shady oaks, of ample ſtature,
 Caſt again a cooling gloom.

Waves from each reflecting fountain,
 Roll again unmix'd with gore,
And verging from the lofty mountain,
 Fall beneath with ſolemn roar.

Here, emboſom'd in this *Eden*,
 Cheerful all our hours are ſpent;
Here no pleaſures are forbidden,
 Sylvan joys are innocent.

THE STORM.

COME let us ſing how when the Judge
 Supreme
Mounts the black tempeſt, arm'd with point-
 ed flame,
What cluſt'ring horrors form his awful train:
 Columns of ſmoke obſcure the cryſtal ſkies,
The whirlwind howls, the livid lightning flies,
The burſting thunder ſounds from ſhore to ſhore,
Earth trembles at the loud prolonged roar:
                                    Down

Down on the mountain forefts rufh the hail,
Th' afpiring pines fall headlong in the vale;
The riv'lets, fwell'd with deluges of rain,
Rife o'er their banks and overflow the plain.

Th' affrighted peafant ope's his humble door,
While from his roof the clatt'ring torrents pour,
He fees his barns all red with conflagration,
His flocks borne off by fudden inundation;
His teeming fields, robb'd of their wavy pride,
By cat'rects tumbling down the mountain's fide.
The fhock fufpends his pow'rs, he ftands
        diftreft,
To fee his toil of years at once revers'd.
His tender mate, of philofophic foul,
Reproves his grief, and thus her accents roll:
' Exert thy fortitude, for grief is vain,
' Our bread by labour we can yet obtain:
' If riches were the teft of virtue, then
' Pale *Poverty* were infamy to men;
' But fince we find the virtuous often dwells
' In public odium, or in lonely cells,
' While thofe whofe crimes blot Nature's af-
        pect o'er,
' Who burn whole towns, and quench the
        flames in gore;
                                ' In

' In *Pleasure*'s lap supine their moments spend,
' Yet with annihilation when they end;
' The laws of retribution then require,
' Our joys begin with death---when their's
  expire;
' Reason allows no scepticism here,
' The *good* must hope, the *bad* have much to
  fear:
' And take a retrospect of thy past years,
' What placid scenes on every hand appears!
' To call the tears of black *Remorse* no crime,
' Can now suffuse thy cheek or cloud thy mind.
' Grieve not that *Fate*, with elemental strife
' Has torn away our hopes of mortal joys;
' To put our virtues but in exercise
' Are the misfortunes that arise in life.'

 The rustic heard his sorrows all away,
Sweet Peace broke on him with a bright'ning
  ray;
Calmness and Hope their empire repossest,
Amidst the storm he feels serenely blest;
Amidst the wreck of all his earthly store
He feels more grateful than he did before.

DESPONDENCY

DESPONDENCY.

COME *Grief*, and fing a folemn dirge
  Beneath this midnight fhade;
From central darknefs now emerge,
  And tread the lonely glade.

Attend each mourning pow'r around,
  While tears inceffant flow;
Strike all your ftrings with doleful found,
  Till *Grief* melodious grow.

This is the cheerlefs hour of night,
  For forrow only made,
When no intrufive ray of light
  The filent glooms pervade.

Tho' fuch the darknefs of my foul,
  Not fuch the calmnefs there,
But waves of guilt tumultuous roll
  'Midft billows of defpair.

Fallacious *Pleafure*'s tinfel train
  My foul rejects with fcorn;
If higher joys fhe can't attain,
  She'd rather chufe to mourn

For

For blifs fuperior fhe was made,
  Or for extreme defpair:
If pain awaits her paft the dead
  Why fhould fhe triumph here?

Tho' *Reafon* points at good fupreme,
  Yet *Grace* muft lead us thence;
Muft wake us from this pleafing dream,
  The idle joys of *Senfe*.

Surely I wifh the blackeft night
  Of Nature to remain,
'Till Chrift arife with healing light,
  Then welcome day again.

ELEGY on the death of Gen. MONTGOMERY.

MELPOMENE, now ftrike a mournful
    ftring,
Montgomery's fate affifting me to fing!
Thou faw him fall upon the hoftile plain
Yet ting'd with blood that gufh'd from *Mon-
    calm*'s veins,
Where gallant *Wolfe* for conqueft gave his
    breath,
Where num'rous heroes met the angel Death.
                              Ah!

Ah! while the loud reiterated roar
Of cannon echoed on from fhore to fhore,
Benigner *Peace*, retiring to the fhade,
Had gather'd laurel to adorn his head:
The laurel yet fhall grace his buft; but, oh!
America muft wear fad cyprefs now.
Dauntlefs he led her armies to the war,
Invulnerable was his foul to fear:
When they explor'd their way o'er tracklefs
      fnows,
Where Life's warm tide thro' every channel
      froze,
His eloquence made the chill'd bofom glow,
And animated them to meet the foe;
Nor flam'd this bright confpicuous grace alone,
The fofter virtues in his bofom fhone;
It bled with every foldier's recent wound;
He rais'd the fallen vet'ran from the ground;
He wip'd the eye of grief, it ceas'd to flow;
His heart vibrated to each found of woe:
His heart too good his country to betray
For fplendid pofts or mercenary pay,
Too great to fee a virtuous land oppreft,
Nor ftrive to have her injuries redrefs'd.
Oh had but *Carleton* fuffer'd in his ftead!
Had half idolitrous *Canadia* bled!

                 'Tis

'Tis not for him but for ourfelves we grieve,
Like him to die is better than to live;
His urn by a whole nation's tears bedew'd,
His mem'ry bleft by all the great and good:
O'er his pale corfe the marble* foon fhall rife,
And the tall column fhoot into the fkies;
There long his praife by freemen fhall be read,
As foftly o'er the hero's duft they tread.

* In St. Paul's Church, in the city of New-York, is a
beautiful monument raifed to his memory, by order of Congrefs, 1783.

THAUMANTIA and FAME.

Go *Thaumantia*,' faid *Jove*, ' and defcend
    from the fky,
  ' For *Fame*'s golden clarion I hear;
' Go learn what great mortal's defert is fo high
  ' As to afk notes fo loud, fweet, and clear.
The goddefs in hafte met the ftarry wing'd dame,
  And demands why her notes fhe does raife?
' For the greateft of patriots and heroes,' faid
    Fame,
  ' Tell *Jove* it is WASHINGTON'S praife!'

RECOLLECTION.

RECOLLECTION.

SOON as the gilded clouds of evening fly,
And *Luna* lights her taper in the fky,
The filent thought infpiring folemn fcene
Awakes my foul to all that it has been.
I was the parent of the fofteft fair
Who ere refpir'd in wide *Columbia*'s air;
A tranfient glance of her love beaming eyes
Convey'd into the foul a paradife.
How has my cheek with rapture been fuffus'd,
When funk upon my bofom fhe repos'd?
I envied not the ermin'd prince of earth,
Nor the gay fpirit of æriel birth;
Nor the bright angel circumfus'd with light,
While the fweet charmer liv'd to blefs my fight.
   What art thou now, my love!---a few dry
         bones,
Unconfcious of my unavailing moans:
Oh! my *Abella!* oh! my burfting heart
Shall never from thy dear idea part!
Thro' *Death*'s cold gates thine image will I bear,
And mount to heav'n, and ever love thee there.

X   *On*

On Reading DRYDEN's VIRGIL.

NOW ceafe *thefe* tears, lay gentle *Vigil* by,
Let *recent* forrows dim the paufing eye :
Shall *Æneas* for loft *Creufa* mourn,
And tears be wanting on *Abella*'s urn ?
Like him I loft my fair one in my flight
From cruel foes---and in the dead of night.
Shall *he* lament the fall of *Illion*'s tow'rs,
And *we* not mourn the fudden ruin of *our's* ?
See *York* on fire---while borne by winds each
          flame
Projects its glowing fheet o'er half the main :
Th' affrighted favage, yelling with amaze,
From *Allegany* fees the rolling blaze.
Far from thefe fcenes of horror, in the fhade
I faw my *aged parent* fafe convey'd ;
Then fadly follow'd to the friendly land,
With my *furviving infant* by the hand.
No cumb'rous houfhold gods had I indeed
To load my fhoulders, and my flight impede ;
The hero's idols fav'd by *him* remain ;
My gods took care of *me*---not *I* of *them !*
The Trojan faw *Anchifes* breathe his laft,
When all domeftic dangers he had pafs'd :

                                        So

So my lov'd *parent*, after fhe had fled,
Lamented, perifh'd on a ftranger's bed.
---*He* held his way o'er the Cerulian Main,
But *I* return'd to hoftile fields again.

To Mifs TEN EYCK.*

DEAR *Kitty*, while you rove thro' fylvan
  bow'rs,
Inhaling fragrance from falubrious flow'rs,
Or view your blufhes mant'ling in the ftream,
When *Luna* gilds it with her amber beam ;
The brazen voice of war awakes our fears,
Impearling every damafk cheek with tears.

The favage, rufhing down the echoing vales,
Frights the poor hind with ill portending yells ;
A livid white his confort's cheeks inveft ;
She drops her blooming infant from her breaft ;
She tries to fly, but quick recoiling fees
The painted Indian iffuing from the trees ;
Then life fufpenfive finks her on the plain,
Till dire explofions wake her up again.
Oh horrid fight ! her partner is no more ;
Pale is his corfe, or only ting'd with gore ;

    X 2   Her

* NOW MRS. BRIDGEN.

Her playful babe is dafh'd againft the ftones,
Its fcalp torn off, and fractur'd all its bones.
Where are the dimpling fmiles it lately wore?
Ghaftly in agony it fmiles no more!
Dumb with amaze, and ftupify'd with grief,
The captur'd wretch muft now attend her chief:
Reluctantly fhe quits the fcene of blood,
When lo! a fudden light illumes the wood:
She turns, and fees the rifing fires expand,
And conflagration roll thro' half the land;
The weftern flames to orient fkies are driv'n,
And change the azure to a fable heav'n.

Such are our woes, my dear, and be it known
Many ftill fuffer what I tell of one:
No more *Albania*'s fons in flumber lie,
When *Cynthia*'s crefcent gleams along the fky;
But every ftreet patrole, and thro' the night
Their beamy arms reflect a dreadful light.

Excufe, dear girl, for once this plaintive ftrain;
I muft conclude, left I tranfgrefs again.

To Mr. BLEECKER, *on his paffage to New-York.*

SHALL Fancy ftill purfue th' expanding fails,
Calm *Neptune*'s brow, or raife impelling gales?
Or with her *Bleecker*, ply the lab'ring oar,
When pleafing fcenes invite him to the fhore,

                                            There

There with him thro' the fading vallies rove,
Bleft in idea with the man I love?
Methinks I fee the broad majeftic fheet
Swell to the wind; the flying fhores retreat:
I fee the banks, with varied foliage gay,
Inhale the mifty fun's reluctant ray;
The lofty groves, ftript of their verdure, rife
To the inclemence of autumnal fkies.

Rough mountains now appear, while pen-
    dant woods
Hang o'er the gloomy fteep and fhade the floods;
Slow moves the veffel, while each diftant found
The cavern'd echos doubly loud rebound:
A placid ftream meanders on the fteep,
'Till tumbling from the cliff, divides the frown-
    ing deep.

Oh tempt not Fate on thofe ftupendous rocks,
Where never fhepherd led his timid flocks;
But fhagged bears in thofe wild deferts ftray,
And wolves, who howl againft the lunar ray:
There builds the rav'nous hawk her lofty neft,
And there the foaring eagle takes her reft;
The folitary deer recoils to hear
The torrent thundering in the mid-way air.
Ah! let me intercede---Ah! fpare her breath,
Nor aim the tube charg'd with a leaden death.

But

But now advancing to the op'ning fe a,
The wind fprings up, the lefs'ning mountains
      flee ;
The eaftern banks are crown'd with rural feats,
And Nature's work, the hand of Art completes.
Here *Philips*'s villa,* where *Pomona* joins
At once the product of a hundred climes ;
Here, ting'd by *Flora*, *Afian* flow'rs unfold
Their burnifh'd leaves of vegetable gold.
When fnows defcend, and clouds tumultuous fly
Thro' the blue medium of the cryftal fky,
Beneath his *painted mimic heav'n* he roves
Amidft the *glafs-encircled* citron groves ;
The grape and lucious fig his tafte invite,
Hefperian apples glow upon his fight ;
The fweet auriculas their bells difplay,
And *Philips* finds in *January*, *May*.
    But on the other fide the cliffs arife,
Charybdis like, and feem to prop the fkies :
How oft with admiration have we view'd
Thofe adamantine barriers of the flood ?
Yet ftill the veffel cleaves the liquid mead,
The profpect dies, th' afpiring rocks recede ;
New objects rufh upon the wond'ring fight,⎫
Till *Phœbus* rolls from heav'n his car of ⎬
      light, ⎭
And *Cynthia*'s filver crefcent gilds the night.

                                    I hear
                * The SEAT of Colonel PHILIPS.

I hear the melting flute's melodious sound,
Which dying zephyrs waft alternate round,
The rocks in notes refponfive foft complain,
And think *Amphian* ftrikes his lyre again.
Ah ! 'tis my *Bleecker* breathes our mutual loves,
And fends the trembling airs thro' vocal groves.

Thus having led you to the happy ifle
Where waves circumfluent wafh the fertile foil,
Where *Hudfon*, meeting the *Atlantic*, roars,
The parting lands difmifs him from their fhores;
Indulge th' enthufiaft mufe her fav'rite ftrain
Of panegyric, due to *Eboracia*'s plain.

There is no land where heav'n her bleffings
    pours
In fuch abundance, as upon thefe fhores;
With influence benign the planets rife;
Pure is the æther, and ferene the fkies;
With annual gold kind Ceres decks the ground,
And gufhing fprings difpenfe bland health
    around.

No lucid gems are here, or flaming ore,
To tempt the hand of Avarice and Pow'r;
But fun-burnt Labour, with diurnal toil,
Bids treafures rife from the obedient foil,
And Commerce calls the fhips acrofs the main,
For gold exchanging her fuperfluous grain;
While Concord, Liberty, and jocund Health
Sport with young Pleafure 'mid the rural wealth.

A SHORT

A SHORT PASTORAL DIALOGUE.*

LUCIA.

COME, my *Delia*, by this spring
Nature's bounties let us sing,
While the popler's silver shade
O'er our lambkins is display'd.

DELIA.

See how she has deck'd the ground
Op'ning flow'rets blush around;
Cryſtals glitter on each hill,
Poliſh'd by the falling rill.

LUCIA.

Here the berries bend the vine,
Lucid grapes at diſtance shine;
Here the velvet peach, and there
Apples, and the pendant pear.

DELIA.

View this maple, from whoſe wound
Honey trickles on the ground:
Who theſe luxuries can taſte
Thankleſs of the rich repaſt?

LUCIA.

* Deſigned for the uſe of her daughter and niece when very young.

LUCIA.

Delia, I could fit all day
Lift'ning to your grateful lay;
But now folar beams invade,
Let us feek a clofer fh de.

HOPE arifing from RETROSPECTION.

ALAS! my fond enquiring foul,
   Doom'd in fufpence to mourn;
Now let thy moments calmly roll,
   Now let thy peace return.

Why fhould'ft thou let a doubt difturb
   Thy hopes, which daily rife,
And urge thee on to truft his word
   Who built and rules the fkies?

Look back thro' what intricate ways
   He led thy unfriended feet;
Oft mourning in the cheerlefs maze,
   He ne'er forfook thee yet.

When thunder from heav'n's arch did break,
   And cleft the finking *fhip*,
His mercy fnatch'd thee from the wreck,
   And from the rolling deep:

And

And when *Difeafe*, with threat'ning mein,
    Aim'd at thy trembling heart,
Again his mercy interven'd,
    And turn'd afide the dart.

When *Murder* fent her hopelefs cries
    More dreadful thro' the gloom,
And kindling flames did round thee rife,
    Deep harvefts to confume;

Who was it led thee thro' the wood
    And o'er th' enfanguin'd plain,
Unfeen by ambufh'd fons of blood,
    Who track'd thy fteps in vain?

'Twas pitying heav'n that check'd my tears,
    And bade my infants play,
To give an opiate to my fears,
    And cheer the lonely way.

And in the *doubly dreadful night*
    When my *Abella* died,
When horror ftruck---detefting light!
    I funk down by her fide:

When wing'd for flight my fpirit ftood,
    With this fond thought beguil'd,
To lead my charmer to her God,
    And there to claim my child;

                                    Again

Again his mercy o'er my breaſt
　Effus'd the breath of peace;
Subſiding paſſions ſunk to reſt,
　He bade the tempeſt ceaſe.

Oh! let me ever, ever praiſe
　Such undeſerved care :
Tho' languid may appear my lays,
　At leaſt they are ſincere.

I never will diſtruſt thee more,
　Tho' hell ſhould aim her dart;
Innoxious is infernal pow'r,
　If thou Protector art.

It is my joy that thou art God,
　Eternal, and ſupreme---
Riſe Nature! hail the power aloud,
　From whom creation came.

On ſeeing Miſs S. T. E. *croſſing the Hudſon.*

TIS ſhe, upon the ſapphire flood,
　Whoſe charms the world ſurpriſe,
Whoſe praiſes, chanted in the wood,
　Are wafted to the ſkies.

To

To view the heaven of her eyes,
    Where'er the light barque moves,
The green hair'd fifters, fmiling, rife
    From out their fea-girt groves.

E'en *Neptune* quits his glaffy caves,
    And calls out from afar,
' So *Venus* look'd, when o'er the waves
    ' She drove her pearly car.'

He bids the winds to caves retreat,
    And there confin'd to roar:
' But here,' faid he, ' forbear to breathe,
    ' 'Till *Sufan* comes on fhore.'

To Mifs M. V. W.

PEGGY, amidft domeftic cares to rhyme
I find no pleafure, and I find no time;
But then, a Poetefs, you may fuppofe,
Can better tell her mind in verfe than profe:
True---when ferenely all our moments roll,
Then numbers flow fpontaneous from the foul:
Not when the mind is harraffed by cares,
Or ftunn'd with thunders of inteftine wars,
Or circled by a noify, vulgar throng,
(Noife ever was an enemy to fong.)
                      What

What tho' the fpiral pines around us rife,
And airy mountains intercept the fkies,
Faction has chac'd away the warbling Mufe,
And Echo only learns to tattle news,
Each clown commences politician here,
And calculates th' expences of the year;
He quits his plow, and throws afide his fpade,
To talk with *fquire* about decreafe of trade:
His tedious fpoufe detains me in her turn,
Condemns our meafures and neglects her
    churn.
Scarce can I fteal a moment from the wars
To read my Bible, or to fay my pray'rs:
Oh! how I long to fee thofe halcyon days
When Peace again extends to us her rays,
When each, beneath his vine, and far from
    fear,
Shall beat his fword into a lab'ring fhare.
   Then fhall the rural arts again revive,
Ceres fhall bid the famifh'd ruftic live:
Where now the yells of painted fons of blood
With long vibrations fhake the lonely wood,
All defolate, *Pomona* fhall behold
The branches fhoot with vegetable gold;
Beyond the peafant's fight the fpringing grain
Shall wave around him o'er the ample plain;

      Y   No

No engines then shall bellow o'er the waves,
And fright blue *Thetis* in her coral caves,
But commerce gliding o'er the curling seas,
Shall bind the sever'd shores in ties of peace.
   Then WASHINGTON, reclining on his spear,
Shall take a respite from laborious war,
While *Glory* on his brows with awful grace
Binds a tiara of resplendent rays.
How faint the lustre of imperial gems
To *this immortal wreath* his merit claims!
See from the north, where icy mountains rise,
Down to the placid climes of southern skies,
All hail the day that bids stern discord cease,
All hail the day which gives the warrior peace:
Hark! the glad nations make a joyful noise!
And the loud shouts are answer'd from the skies;
Fame swells the sound wrapt in her hero's
       praise,
And darts his splendors down to latest days.

To Mrs. D------.

DEAR *Betsey* now *Pleasure* the woodland
     has left,
  Nor more in the water she laves,
Since winter the trees of their bloom has bereft,
  And stiffen'd to crystal the waves.
                                        Now

Now clad all in fur our gueſt ſhe appears,
  By the fire-ſide a merry young grig ;
She pours out the wine, our penſiveneſs cheers,.
  And at night leads us out to a jig.

Then venture among the tall pines if you dare,
  Encounter the keen arctic wind ;
Dare this for to meet with affection ſincere,
  And *Pleaſure* untainted you'll find.

I know you have *Pleaſure*, my ſiſter, by whiles,
  But then ſhe appears in great ſtate ;
She is hard of acceſs, and lofty her ſmiles,
  While *Envy* and *Pride* on her wait.

Thro' *drawing rooms*, *Betſey*, you'll chaſe her
    in vain,
  The Colonel may ſeek her in *blood* ;
The Poets agree (and they cannot all feign)
  That ſhe's *born* and *reſides* in the *wood*.

On a great COXCOMB *recovering from an Indiſpoſition.*

NARCISSUS (as *Ovid* informs us) expir'd,
Conſum'd by the flames his own beauty had fir'd;

Y 2   But

But *N---o* (who like him is charm'd with his
　　face,
And fighs for his other fair-felf in the glafs)
Loves to greater excefs than *Narciſſus*---for
　　why?
He loves himfelf *too much* to let himfelf die.

An EVENING PROSPECT.

COME my *Sufan*, quit your chamber,
　　Greet the op'ning bloom of *May*,
Let us on yon hillock clamber,
　　And around the fcene furvey.

See the fun is now defcending,
　　And projects his fhadows far,
And the bee her courfe is bending
　　Homeward thro' the humid air.

Mark the *lizard* juft before us,
　　Singing her unvaried ftrain,
While the *frog*, abrupt in chorus,
　　Deepens thro' the marfhy plain.

From yon grove the *woodcock* rifes,
　　Mark her progrefs by her notes,
High in air her wings fhe poifes,
　　Then like lightning down fhe fhoots.

　　　　　　　　　　　　　　Now

Now the *whip-o-well* beginning,
  Clam'rous on a pointed rail,
Drowns the more melodious finging
  Of the *cat-bird, thrufh,* and *quail.*

Penfive *Echo,* from the mountain,
  Still repeats the fylvan founds,
And the crocus border'd fountain,
  With the fplendid fly abounds.

There the honeyfuckle blooming,
  Reddens the capricious wave;
Richer fweets---the air perfuming,
  Spicy *Ceylon* never gave.

Caft your eyes beyond this meadow,
  Painted by a hand divine,
And obferve the ample fhadow
  Of that folemn ridge of pine.

Here a trickling rill depending,
  Glitters thro' the artlefs bow'r;
And the filver dew defcending,
  Doubly radiates every flow'r.

While I fpeak, the fun is vanifh'd,
  All the gilded clouds are fled,
Mufic from the groves is banifh'd,
  Noxious vapours round us fpread.

Rural

Rural toil is now fufpended,
  Sleep invades the peafant's eyes,
Each diurnal tafk is ended,
  While foft *Luna* climbs the fkies.

Queen of reft and meditation,
  Thro' thy medium I adore
Him---the Author of Creation,
  Infinite, and boundlefs pow'r.

'Tis he who fills thy urn with glory,
  Tranfcript of immortal light;
Lord! my fpirit bows before thee,
  Loft in wonder and delight.

A HYMN.

OMNICIENT and eternal God,
  Who hear'ft the fainteft pray'r
Diftinct as Hallelujahs loud,
  Which round thee hymned are.

Here, far from all the world retir'd,
  I humbly bow the knee,
And wifh, (as I have long defir'd,)
  An intereft in thee.

                                    But

But my revolting heart recedes
  And rushes to the croud ;
My paffions ftop their ears and lead,
  Tho' confcience warns aloud.

How deeply finful is my mind?
  To every ill how prone?
How ftubborn my dead heart I find
  Infenfible as ftone?

The hardeft *marble* yet will break,
  Nor will refift the *fteel* ;
But neither *wrath* nor *love* can make
  My flinty bofom feel.

My paffions like a torrent roar,
  And tumbling to hell's glooms
Sweep me away from Reafon's fhore,
  To " where *Hope* never comes."

By labour turn'd the ufelefs ftream
  Thro' fertile vales has play'd ;
But for to change the courfe of fin
  Demands immortal aid.

All nature pays the homage due
  To the fupremely bleft ;
All but the favour'd being who
  Was plac'd above the reft.

He

He bids the teeming earth to bear,
  The blufhing flow'rs arife;
At his command the fun appears
  And warms the orient fkies.

Oh! was I but fome plant or ftar,
  I might obey him too;
Nor longer with the Being war,
  From whom my breath I drew.

Change me, oh God! with ardent cries
  I'll venture to thy feat;
And if I perifh; *hell* muft rife
  And tear me from thy feet.

To *Mifs* BRINCKERHOFF, *on her quitting
New-York.*

ELIZA, when the fouthern gale
Expands the broad majeftic fail,
While Friendfhip breathes the parting figh,
And forrow glitters in each eye,
The veffel leaves the flying fhores,
Receding fpires and lefs'ning tow'rs;
And as it cleaves the lucid fea,
The. diftant tumult dies away:

Then

Then penſive as the deck you quit,
Careſſing ſable rob'd regret,
Indulging every riſing fear,
And urging on the pendant tear,
While Recollection's flatt'ring eye
Your former pleaſures magnify ;
Then ſhall your guardian ſpirit ſmile,
Rejoic'd that Fate rewards his toil ;
And as he mounts on ærial wing,
Thus to his kindred angels ſing :
' Hail, happy hour that ſnatch'd my fair
' To æther pure, from *city air*,
' Where *Vice* triumphant lifts her head
' And hiſſes *Virtue* to the ſhade ;
' Where *Temperance* vacates each feaſt ;
' Where *Piety* is grown a jeſt ;
' Where *Flatt'ry*, dreſs'd in robes of truth,
' Inculcates pride in heedleſs youth ;
' Where oft with folded wings I ſpy
' The torpid ſoul inactive lie,
' Shut up in ſenſe, forbid to rear
' Her plume beyond our atmoſphere.
  ' How bleſs'd my charge, whom gentler fate
' Leads early to the *green retreat*,
' Where every object thoughts inſpire
' Exalted to ſeraphic fire ;

' And

' And where the speculative mind
' Expatiates free and unconfin'd;
' There surely I shall find accefs
' To cherish ev'ry budding grace,
' Enlarging still each nobler pow'r,
' Till active, like myself they soar.
  ' And when my pupil learns her worth,
' She'll feel a just contempt for earth,
' And fix her elevated sight
' Alone on primogenial light:
' Nor shall her *charms external* fade,
' But bloom and brighten in the shade;
' While innate graces still shall rise,
' And dart their radiance thro' her eyes.'

To *JULIA AMANDA*.

F AIR *Julia Amanda*, now since it is peace,
Methinks your hostilities also should cease;
The shafts from your eyes, and the snares of
     your smile,
Should cease---or at least be suspended awhile:
'Tis cruel to point your artillery of charms
Against the poor lads who have laid down their
    arms.

                    The

The fons of *Bellona* who *Britain* defies,
Altho' bullet proof, muft they fall by your eyes?
In vain have they bled, they have conquer'd in
         vain,
If returning in triumph, they yield to your chain.
For fhame! in the olive's falubrious fhade
Your murders reftrain, and let peace be obey'd;
Since *Europe* negociates, alter *your* carriage,
While they treat of *peace*, make a treaty of
         marriage.

PEACE.

—

ALL hail vernal *Phœbus!* all hail ye foft
         breezes!
Announcing the vifit of fpring;
How green are the meadows! the air how it
         pleafes!
How gleefully all the birds fing!

Begone ye rude tempefts, nor trouble the æther,
Nor let blufhing *Flora* complain,
While her pencil was tinging the tulip, bad
         weather
Had blafted the promifing gem.

                                 From

From its verdant unfoldings, the timid narciſſus
  Now ſhoots out a diffident bud ;
Begone ye rude tempeſts, for ſure as it freezes
  Ye kill this bright child of the wood :

And *Peace* gives new charms to the bright
      beaming ſeaſon ;
  The groves we now ſafely explore
Where murd'ring banditti, the dark ſons of
      treaſon,
    Were ſhelter'd and aw'd as before.

The ſwain with his oxen proceeds to the valley
  Whoſe ſeven years ſabbath concludes,
And bleſſes kind heaven, that *Britain*'s black ally
  Is chas'd to *Canadia*'s deep woods.

And *Echo* no longer is plaintively mourning,
  But laughs and is jocund as we ;
And the turtle ey'd nymphs, to their cots all
      returning,
    Carve ' WASHINGTON,' on every tree.

I'll wander along by the ſide of yon fountain,
  And drop in its current the line,
To capture the glittering fiſh that there wanton ;
  Ah, no ! 'tis an evil deſign.

                                    Sport

Sport on little fishes, your lives are a treasure
  Which I can *destroy*, but not *give*;
Methinks it's at best a malevolent pleasure
  To bid a poor being *not live*.

How lucid the water! its soft undulations
  Are changeably ting'd by the light;
It reflects the green banks, and by fair imitations
  Presents a new heaven to sight.

The *butterfly* skims o'er its surface, all gilded
  With plumage just dipt in rich dies;
But yon infant has seiz'd the poor insect, ah!
    yield it;
  There, see the freed bird how it flies!

But whither am I and my little dog straying?
  Too far from our cottage we roam;
The dews are already exhal'd; cease your
    playing,
  Come, *Daphne*, come let us go home.

A PASTORAL DIALOGUE.

SCENE---TOMHANICK.   1780.

SUSANNA.

ELIZA, rise, the orient glows with day,
Already *Phosphor* darts his amber ray;

Z   The

The fainting planets vanifh from the fkies,
Diftinct already all the profpects rife ;
Begin our walk, but cheer the lonely way
With mufic, previous to the fwallow's lay.

ELIZA.

My fifter, ceafe, thefe hoftile fhades refufe
Admiffion to the lute or peaceful Mufe ;
Lo ! the broad ftandard fhades the flow'ry plain,
Nor crooks (but mufquets) arm the awkward
          fwain ;
Death's heavy engines thunder thro' the vale,
And *Echo* but retorts the favage yell ;
From undiffembled grief my numbers flow,
And few the graces that attend on woe.

SUSANNA.

Yet fing---e'en woe a pleafure can impart,
When fweetly warbled, or if told with art.

ELIZA.

Columbia refcued from barbaric pow'rs,
Drew all the fons of want unto her fhores ;
The indigent, th' oppreft, a fighing hoft,
And wretches exil'd from their native coaft ;
For whom European affluence could not fpare
A frugal morfel, pining Want to cheer ;
Hither repair'd, and with inceffant toil
Fell'd the tall trees from the incumber'd foil :
                              From

From the low cottage now recede the oaks,
The foreſt anſwers to the woodman's ſtrokes;
Hard was the toil, but amply (ſoon) repaid
By golden harveſts, which the valleys ſhade;
Vertumnes added to his native ſtores
Exotic fruits, and *Flora* planted flow'rs:
Then temples roſe, the harbours open'd wide,
And wealthy ſhips flow'd in with every tide.

Thus rich and happy, virtue made them gay,
And hard got Freedom bleſt each cheerful day;
By induſtry thoſe bleſſings they obtain'd,
And learn'd to value what they dearly gain'd.
---Americans! ye thought your labours o'er,
Ah no! the hydra Envy brings you more.
Now caſt thine eyes o'er the Cerulian Main,
See *George* conſpicuous by his bloody reign;
Hard by *Oppreſſion's* iron chair is ſeen,
Where menacing ſhe ſits with threat'ning mein;
Still as the monarch ſmiles, and to her turns,
Sad *Freedom* trembles---all the people mourns.
' Art thou indeed a king,' the fury cries,
' And ſee'ſt thy *ſubjects* all like rivals riſe?
' A land of princes, opulent and proud,
' Scarce thou thyſelf diſtinguiſh'd from the
          croud:

Z 2   ' Reduce

' Reduce their fumlefs ftores, their pow'r with-
 ftand,
' Kings were not made to *afk*, but to *command:*
' See the licentious land by riot rent,
' Say, what but fear can keep the flaves content?
' Soon thy rich rival on th' Atlantic fhore
' Will fcorn to afk thy aid, or own thy pow'r:
' Then bow thy fceptre heavy o'er the waves,
' Thy fafety urges, and they muft be flaves;
' Reftrict their trade, feverer laws invent,
' And to inforce them be thy armies fent.
Ah fimple prince! learn but the eafier arts,
With mildeft fway to rule thy people's hearts;
Firm as the centre then thy throne fhould ftand,
Rever'd and guarded by a grateful land.

 Columbia weeps, fhe kneels before the throne,
But plaints, and tears, and fighs, avail her none;
One fad alternative alone remains,
The woes of war, or elfe the tyrant's chains.
 This, *Virtue* from the weftern mountains
  heard,
' Be calm, my fons,' fhe cried, ' I am your
 guard;
' But if th' ambitious homocide fhall dare
' To pour acrofs the feas the tide of war,
       ' Arm,

' Arm, arm in hafte! 'tis heav'n's and free-
  dom's caufe!'
Confenting nations echoed loud applaufe.
  Now Britain's marine thunders fhake the
    ground,
New Albian's ftructures fall in ruins round;
The mournful fires extend along the ftrand,
And ocean blufhes as the fires expand;
The flames ftill rife, till quench'd with human
    blood,
The fanguine ftream commixes with the flood;
Then ocean blufhes deeper ftill with gore,
And *Defolation* fhrieks along the fhore:
Nor do her coafts alone the fury feel,
Deep in her forefts gleams the deadly fteel;
Britannia's ally, from his dark recefs,
With fell intent invades the fhades of Peace.
See the low cot with ivy cover'd o'er,
Where age and youth fit fmiling at the door;
The virgin carols on the dufty road,
And fprightly mufic fills the vocal wood:
Calm are the fkies, the dewy poppies blow,
Nor man, nor beaft is confcious of a foe:
Swift, like a hurricane deftruction flies,
The cottage blazes, and its owner dies.

Z 3

Look from this point, where op'ning glades
    reveal
The glaffy *Hudfon* fhining 'twixt the hills;
There many a ftructure drefs'd the fteepy fhore,
And all beyond were daily rifing more:
The bending trees with annual fruit did fmile,
Each harveft fure, for fertile is the foil:
Nor need the peafant immolate his ox,
Nor hunger prefs him to decreafe his flocks;
The ftately ftag a richer feaft fupplies,
The river brings him fifh of various fize;
With water fowl his filver lakes abound,
And honey gufhes from the maple's wound.

    Autumnal fhow'rs attemper'd *Phœbus'* ray,
The blooming meads with deep'ning green
    were gay,
The birds were cheerful, nor the ruftic lefs,
Joy on his cheek, and in his bofom peace;
Down rufh'd the *tawny natives* from the hill,
And every place with fire and murder fill;
Arm'd with the hatchet and a flaming brand,
They foon reverfe the afpect of the land:
Obferve, *Sufanna*, not a bird is there,
The tall burnt trees rife mournful in the air,
Nor man nor beaft the fmoking ruins explores,
And *Hudfon* flows more folemn by thofe fhores.

                     But

But ah! I fee thee turn away and mourn,
Thy feeling heart with filent anguifh torn;
Cheer up, tho' long and dark has been our night,
The deepeft fhades precede the morning light;
And when I recollect our heavenly aid,
Hope fluihes round and diffipates the fhade;
He who reveng'd the blood of *Abel* fpilt
Has thunders fure for more extenfive guilt;
Nor can we doubt, when horrors round us clos'd
His obvious arm how lately interpos'd,
To render Britain's *northern phalanx** vain,
To blaft the *traitor,†* and defeat his plan.

For what conteft we? is it thirft of gain,
Or thirft of blood that fills the land with flain?
Ah, no! tenacious of the gift of God
We would defend our *Freedom* with our blood;
She arms our fons, *fhe* bids them nobly dare,
And calls on *Conqueft* to decide the war:
What tho' the *Goddefs* ftill defers the blow,
Her arm fhall foon repel th' invading foe;
Her arm unfurl our ftarry ftandard wide,
For *Conqueft* loves to be on *Freedom*'s fide.
Then let the difappointed navy fly,
Curfing the winds and inaufpicious fky,
While acclamations fill the region round,
And from their hollow fhips loud fhouts rebound.

* BURGOYNE's army.　　† ARNOLD.

RETURN

RETURN TO TOMHANICK.

HAIL, happy fhades! tho' clad with heavy
    fnows,
At fight of you with joy my bofom glows;
Ye arching *pines*, that bow with every breeze,
Ye *poplars*, *elms*, all hail my well-known trees!
And now my peaceful *manfion* ftrikes my eye,
And now the tinkling *rivulet* I fpy;
My *little garden* Flora haft thou kept,
And watch'd my *pinks* and *lilies* while I wept?
Or has the grubbing *fwine*, by furies led,
Th' inclofure broke, and on my flowrets fed?
    Ah me! that fpot with blooms fo lately
        grac'd,
With ftorms and driving fnows is now defac'd;
Sharp icicles from ev'ry bufh depend,
And frofts all dazzling o'er the beds extend:
Yet foon fair *Spring* fhall give another fcene,
And yellow *cowflips* gild the level green;
My little *orchard* fprouting at each bough,
Fragrant with cluft'ring blofloms deep fhall
        glow:
                                    Ah!

Ah! then 'tis fweet the *tufted grafs* to tread,
But fweeter flumb'ring in the balmy fhade;
The rapid *humming bird*, with ruby breaft,
Seeks the parterre with early *blue bells* dreft,
Drinks deep the *honeyfuckle dew*, or drives
The lab'ring bee to her domeftic hives:
Then fhines the *lupin* bright with morning gems,
And fleepy *poppies* nod upon their ftems;
The humble *violet* and the dulcet *rofe*,
The ftately *lily* then, and *tulip* blows.

   Farewell my *Plutarch!* farewell pen and
      Mufe!
Nature exults---fhall I her call refufe?
Apollo fervid glitters in my face,
And threatens with his beam each feeble grace:
Yet ftill around the lovely plants I toil,
And draw obnoxious herbage from the foil;
Or with the lime-twigs *little birds* furprife,
Or angle for the *trout* of many dyes.

   But when the vernal breezes pafs away,
And loftier *Phœbus* darts a fiercer ray,
The fpiky corn then rattles all around,
And dafhing cafcades give a pleafing found;
Shrill fings the locuft with prolonged note,
The cricket chirps familiar in each cot,

                 The

The village children, rambling o er yon hill,
With berries all their painted baſkets fill,
They rob the ſqirrels little walnut ſtore,
And climb the half exhauſted tree for more;
Or elſe to fields of maize nocturnal hie,
Where hid, th' eluſive water-melons lie;
Sportive, they make inciſions in the rind,
The riper from the immature to find;
Then load their tender ſhoulders with the prey,
And laughing bear the bulky fruit away.

ESSAYS,

IN

PROSE AND VERSE.

BY

MARGARETTA V. FAUGERES.

ESSAYS.

BENEFITS OF SCOLDING.

1790.

I HAVE often wondered that amongſt the numbers who write for the edification of the public, no one has ever thought fit to expatiate upon the *Benefits of Scolding*; nor can I conceive why an art, whoſe origin we may trace in years before the flood, and which is ſo much in uſe among the moderns, ſhould be diſregarded by writers.

It is an ancient art, and I am perſuaded a very beneficial one, not only to individuals, ſuch as huſbands, wives, children, and ſervants, but to the community at large. Schools, in particular, are much indebted to it; and though they may not acknowledge it, nor think it merits an eulogy from their pens, yet the flouriſhing ſtate of many of our ſeminaries ſpeaks loudly in its favour. People in general would rather ſuffer corporeal puniſhment than

A a be

be lectured upon their faults; and I have known many who did not mind the rod to be deterred from a continuance of their follies, merely by the lashes of the tongue.

A scolding officer has often made his subalterns as angry as hornets in an engagement; and a coward, when enraged, will fight most courageously. Perhaps he might have called them cowards in his ill-humour, and they, out of spite, have exerted themselves and performed wonders, which, had their leader been a tame, peaceable creature, they would have looked upon as impracticable: and we know an able politician, when a motion was made in the house of which he was a member, prejudicial to the state which he lived in, who not only scolded the house out of countenance, but out of the motion too, and made them lay it by for years.

The spouse of SOCRATES was of a turbulent temper, which made his friends pity him much; but SOCRATES was a wise man, and well knowing the utility of scolding, told them, that she taught him patiently to put up with the humours of other men.

Scolding

Scolding is not only good for the mind but the body too. It makes refpiration more free, and cures colds ; and by promoting perfpiration, has been known to remove complaints of long ftanding. Let the following account fpeak for it :---

A lady of my acquaintance was in a very ill ftate of health fome time ago, as every body thought in a confumption ; but one day (as the Doctors were fitting by her) luckily fomething went wrong, and the poor invalid forgetting her reduced fituation, gave vent to her feelings, and fcolded moft eloquently, and difplayed her talents in fuch a manner as rectified the miftake, brought on a profufe perfpiration, and greatly relieved her. The benefits arifing from fuch proceedings were more than fhe could have expected; fhe, however, repeated it with the fame fuccefs, and is now a hearty woman.

But fome may be apt to inquire, " If this is true, might not people live for ever were they to keep on fcolding ?" No one, I believe, has ever yet made the experiment, nor fhould I dare with to propagate fuch an opinion ; but this I know, that almoft all fcolds live to be

A a 2   pretty

pretty old, nor do I remember ever to have heard of a perfon who died fcolding.

My fcolding abilities are at prefent very flender, but there is room for improvement; and it is probable, if I fhould make any confiderable proficiency in that fcience, I may favour the public with a fpecimen.

FINE FEELINGS
Exemplified in the Conduct of a Negro Slave.

1791.

NOTWITHSTANDING what the learned Mr. JEFFERSON has faid refpecting the want of finer feelings in the blacks, I cannot help thinking that their fenfations, mental and external, are as acute as thofe of the people whofe fkin may be of a different colour; fuch an affertion may feem bold, but facts are ftubborn things, and had I not *them* to fupport me, it is probable I fhould not attempt to oppofe the opinions of fuch an eminent reafoner.

In the interior parts of this ftate lived (a few years ago) a man of property, who owned a number of blacks; but formed in Nature's
most

moſt ſavage mould, his chief employment was inventing puniſhments for his unfortunate dependants, and his principal delight in practiſing the tortures he had invented. Among the number of his ſlaves was an old Negro, who, in his younger days, had been a faithful ſervant; but captivity and ſorrow had at length broken his ſpirit, and deſtroyed that ambition which actuates the free, and gives energy and life to all they perform. This was a proper ſubject for the cruelty of Mr. A------- to act upon. Upon the commiſſion of the ſmalleſt fault, or the moſt trifling neglect, he would himſelf tie MINGO, (as butchers do ſheep intended for ſlaughter) and after having beaten him till the blood followed every ſtroke of the whip, he would retire, leaving the wretch weltering in his gore, expoſed to the burning rays of ſummer or the gelid gales of winter. When reſted he would return, and after a repetition of his amuſement, would releaſe the ſufferer, leſt a few more minutes of ſuch extreme agonies ſhould ſhorten the period of MINGO's woes, and his maſter's felicity. However, this mode of puniſhment becoming a little troubleſome to Mr. A----, he thought

A a 3

of

of another which he believed would anfwer
nearly as well: he caufed a large ox-chain to
be made, and putting it about MINGO's waift,
he brought it round his neck, and there faftened
it again, leaving an end of about four yards,
to which he nailed a piece of wood weighing
upwards of forty weight. With this clog the
flave was obliged to work---and this at night
was placed in the mafter's chamber, (the chain
paffing through a hole in the door) while
MINGO flept on the ground out fide of the
houfe, from which uncomfortable couch nothing but the moft bitter cold excufed him.

Seven long years did the miferable being
groan under this load, when the captain of a
veffel, hearing of his hard fate, out of pity
bought him.

After having paid the money he went home,
and fending for MINGO, told him he was
free:---" You are your own mafter," faid the
humane failor; " but you are old, and help-
" lefs---I will take care of you."---Over-
powered with joy, the old man clafped the
captain's knees; he wept aloud---he raifed his
fwimming eyes to heaven---he would have
fpoken his thanks;---but his frame was too
feeble for the mighty conflict of his foul---he
expired at his benefactor's feet!

A FRAGMENT.

A FRAGMENT.

1792.

THE darkening ftorms of *Winter* are fled--- his icy honours are diffolved---and the hoarfe gale that fported on the foaming bofom of the ocean, and bent the tall pines of the defert, lies hufh'd in the cell of Tranquillity---At the enchanting call of *Spring*, the timid *Snowdrop* unfolds her filvery beauties, and the fair *Hyacinth* diffufes abroad her delicate perfume; the green blade raifes its tender ftem, and *Nature*, wiping away her tears, puts on the fmile of lovelinefs---But, alas! O *Spring!* thy charms delight not the forrowful foul of JACINTA; in vain doft thou fport around *her* whofe heart is the dwelling of woe---Solitary as *Night* fhe wanders among the tombs---for ALDELLO, the youth of her love, fleeps the deep flumber of death---Yes, he is gone, he is fallen to *dumb Forgetfulnefs* an early prey---Clofed are thofe animated eyes which beamed love, and unfeeling is that *heart* which could once melt at the tale of diftrefs---Alas! it no longer refponds to

the

the light airs of *Festivity*, nor heeds the mellow warblings of *Melancholy*; but imprisoned within the narrow precincts of the grave, it is cold--- cold as the clod that conceals it.---

Flow on my tears---bathe the clayey couch of ALDELLO, and let the sighs of my breast mingle with the sounds of night, for the friend of my heart is no more---I sigh unpitied---I moan unheard---and when my tears fall, they fall not on the bosom of *Compassion*---Nightly will I visit the place of thy repose, my love--- I will think of thy departed virtues, and weep to their memory---and *this* shall be the solace of my griefs: the hand of *Spring* shall re-decorate thy turf with verdure---and the leafless willow that nods o'er thine urn, shall she again attire---*Here*, fragrant *Evening* shall shed her sweetest tears---and *here*, the *white clover*, nightly lifting its moist odours to the winds, shall blossom to adorn thy grave.---.

The THRUSH shall desert the dark forest, to swell
 O'er thy tomb, my ALDELLO, her sorrowful song;
While the light blowing gales in the mountains that dwell,
 O'er the flow rolling HUDSON the note shall prolong.

＊　＊　＊　＊　＊　＊　＊　＊　＊

THE

THE CHINA ASTER.

1792.

I PLANTED it with my own hand,' faid my little fifter, holding up a withered *China after*, plucked up by the roots---' I covered it from the fun---I watered it night and morning, and *after all*---(wiping her eyes with the corner of her frock)---*after all, it is dead!'*---

Alas! how many are the occurrences in life, thought I, which refemble MARY's flower. Too eafily believing what we wifh, we adopt fome pretty trifle, and laying it as it were in our bofom, love it ' as a daughter.'--- *Fancy* paints it in gay colours; increafing in beauty we fee its little leaves expand, and trace its progrefs with anxious folicitude from the *fwelling bud* to the *full blow*; and then, when we fondly expect to enjoy it, *reality* tells us--- *after all, it is dead!*----

How often does an *only fon* engrofs all the cares of his parents, and wind himfelf round every fibre of their heart---To cherifh the idol is every wifh on the ftretch---to indulge it are all the rarities of art and nature procured;

fleeplefs

fleeplefs nights and anxious days are *their* lot ;
and lo ! when they hope to fee the end of their
labours, ftruck by the hand of *Difeafe*, or de-
bafed by the contaminating touch of *Vice*, the
agonizing parents find, *after all, it is dead!* ---

And how fanguine are the expectations of
thofe relatives and friends, who poffefs a lovely
girl, endowed with all the charms of *beauty*
and *goodnefs!* how do they exult in her very
idea! fhe is the folace of their calamities, and
the ftaff of dependence for their declining
years---*Friendfhip* rifes in her defence like a
wall---and *Affection* nourifhes her as the mild
dews of Spring---Ah! to how little purpofe!
the canker worm of *Love* preys upon the delicate
root of this fweet *fenfitive*; and the fcorching
winds of Difappointment drink up its moifture
---it fades; the hands of Friendfhip and Affection are united to fupport it in vain; for,

> The deep drawn oft repeated figh
> Hath caus'd Health's blufhes to decay;
> The tear that moiften'd Beauty's eye
> Hath worn its luftre quite away.

It languifhes and dies---and *Regret*, bitterly
weeping, raves round the *lovely fallen*, and
exclaims, *after all, it is dead!* * * * * * *
* * * * * * * * * * * * *

POEMS

POEMS.

A DREAM.

March, 1789.

WHEN drowfy Sleep had clos'd my weary
    eyes
Fancy convey'd me to a fandy fhore,
Where the fteep cliffs, wet with the midnight
    dews,
    Re-echo'd to the furge's hollow roar;

Night had methought put on her foberft
    charms,
    The filvery ftars a feeble glimmer gave,
The winds rung mournful through the elm s
    green arms,
    And the wan moon-beams trembled on the
    wave;

When from among the rocks the voice of Grief
    I heard, it fadly warbled in the air;
Wond'ring, I turn'd to view from whence it
    came,
    And lo! a *form* appear'd divinely fair:

                    Her

Her auburn hair hung crelefs round her neck,
  Sorrow fat weeping in her beauteous eye;
The rofe had faded in her downy cheek,
  And from her beating bofom fled a figh:

Grief from her frame the bloom of health had
    chas'd,
  The flood fhe approach'd with tott'ring
    pace and flow;
To the blue vault of heav'n her eyes fhe rais'd,
  And, fighing, thus began a tale of woe:

' Still as the eve returns, my penfive foul
  ' O'er the *Atlantic* cafts a mournful glance,
' And o'er the fwelling furges, as they roll,
  ' Purfues my BELMONT to the fhores of
    France.

' When he departed tears refus'd to flow,
  ' Seal'd were the fountains of my aching eyes,
' And my big heart fwell'd with oppreffive woe,
  ' Juft breath'd a wifh to yonder beaming
    fkies.

' *Ye winds be profperous, and ye fapphire fkies*
  ' *Let no black tempeft o'er your bofom move;*
' *Be calm ye feas, nor let your billows rife*
  ' *To agitate the mind of him I love.*

                   ' No

' No *angel* wafted to the fkies my pray'r;
  ' Vain was the wifh, it funk upon the fhore;
' BELMONT was gone! the part'ner of my care
  ' Was gone forever, to return no more!

' By winds tempeftuous was the veffel driv'n
  ' O'er the *broad wafte* where lonely waters
      roll;
' Darknefs hung awful round the low'ring
      heav'n,
  ' And heavy thunders groan'd from pole to
      pole.

' All round the fhip the clam'rous billows dafh'd,
  ' *Here* mountains rofe, there funk to yawn-
      ing graves;
' From heaven's wide gates a mighty torrent
      rufh'd,
  ' And plung'd them headlong in the foaming
      waves.

' There funk forever all my hopes of blifs---
' I bade a long farewell to happinefs;
' From that fad moment when the ruthlefs deep
' On its cold bofom laid my LOVE to fleep.

' Low my fond BELMONT, low now lies thy
      head;
  ' Rude furges wafh acrofs thy peaceful
      breaft;

        B b   ' Forgot

' Forgot are all thy *cares*, thy *fears* are fled,
  ' And all thy *griefs* in blifsful flumbers reft !' '

She paus'd; fhe ceas'd, check'd by a flood of
    tears;
  When from the waters rofe her BELMONT'S
    fhade;
Serene his afpect as the night was clear;
  Thus fpake the angel to the forrowing maid :

' CALISTA, give thy fruitlefs forrows o'er,
  ' Oh wipe thofe riv'lets from thy beauteous
    eyes,
  ' Weep for thy faithful, long-loft LOVE no
    more,
    ' Nor fwell thy bofom with heart-rending
    fighs.

' Why fhouldft thou grieve ? why forrow for
    the dead?
  ' Doft thou not know thy plaints are all in
    vain?
  ' When low in death the humid corfe is laid,
    ' Nor *fighs* nor *tears* fhall bring it life again.

' When awful thunders rattled round the fkies,
  ' Mixt with the fhriekings of the *hopelefs*
    crew;
                              ' When

' When lived lightnings dim'd our lifted eyes,
  ' And *Death* itself prefented to our view!

' Amid this foul-affrighting difmal fcene,
  ' Upon the ROCK OF AGES ftanding firm,
' *My* happy fpirit refted all ferene,
  ' Nor trembled at the roarings of the ftorm.

' When gloomy waters rank'd me with the dead,
  ' Quick to the deep my guardian *feraphs* flew,
' And on their glittering pinnions me convey'd
  ' Far, far beyond where fhines the ethereal
    blue.

' There on the bofom of *unfading* Blifs
  ' I reft, while ages after ages roll;
' Each paffing age fhall fee my joys increafe,
  ' And ftill enlarging my capacious foul:

' Yet thence my watchful fpirit hies,
  ' With pleafing cares, and hovers round my
    fair,
' To footh corroding forrows that arife,
  ' And mitigate the pangs of anxious care.

' Adieu much lov'd CALISTA! weep no more,
  ' Banifh fad thoughts, prepare to meet thy
    love;

B b 2   ' Soon

Soon will this hasty strife of life be o'er;
   Adieu, CALISTA, we shall meet above!'

The VISION gently faded from mine eyes;
   Scarce did his form the yielding waters cleave,
And the soft *echo* of his tuneful voice
   Died on the dashings of the distant wave.

A VERSION of the LORD's PRAYER.

Nov. 1790.

OMNICIENT God! great Ruler of the
      earth!
   Parent of man! exuberent source of good!
Whose hand hath spread the south and frigid
      north,
   Whose throne from all eternity hath stood.

Upborne on Contemplation's lofty wing,
   We bring our supplications to the throne
Of *him* from whom our choicest blessings spring,
   Whose being ne'er hath a beginning known.

Thou who with dazzling glory art array'd,
   Forever hallow'd be thy sacred name;
Nor may the creature which thy hand hath
      made
   Presume his Maker's awful name profane.
                  But

But haften on the bleft important hour,
　　When all creation *thee* her Lord fhall know,
When all fhall feel and own thy mighty pow'r,
　　And ev'ry knee and ev'ry heart fhall bow.

As by the orders which furround thy hill,
　　And chaunt their hymns round thy effulgent
　　　　throne,
And thy commands with tirelefs fpeed fulfil;
　　So let thy will, oh GOD! on earth be done.

Each day convenient food let us receive,
　　And what thou fee'ft we lack do thou beftow;
And oh! may heav'n the kind forbearance give
　　Which daily we our fellow mortals fhew.

Ah let not Pleafure's facinating baits
　　Allure us to the flipp'ry paths of Sin!
Nor let her gently lead us to thofe gates
　　Which fhe, alas! will never enter in:

But fhield us, Lord, beneath thy potent wing;
　　Wide o'er the earth thy peaceful banner
　　　　fpread,
And there let ev'ry way-worn pilgrim bring
　　His cares, and reft beneath its ample fhade.

Bb 3　　　　　　　　　　Oh

Oh earth ! come worfhip at JEHOVAH's throne !
  Ye habitants of heav'n your anthems raife,
Omnipotence and glory are his own,
  HE but is worthy of eternal praife !

To ALFRED, in Anfwer to a Complaint.

October, 1790.

MY friend 'tis true, I own it is,
  The world's a cheat, as is believ'd ;
And thofe who look for folid peace
  On earth, will find themfelves deceiv'd ;
There are no pure fubftantial joys
To be poffefs'd below the fkies.

But I believe, beneath the fun,
  No pow'r exifts, by Reafon fway'd,
Who has not had, in Life's gay run,
  His fhare of happinefs difplay'd ;
A fhare of that which fills the breaft,
And lulls the foul perturb'd to reft.

O Youth ! what blifs in thee is found !
  Bleft time of gambol, fport and joy,
When mufic rolls in ev'ry found,
  And ev'ry object charms the eye ;

                 When

When few our cares, and foon forgot,
Each pleas'd, delighted with its lot.

When riper years fteal o'er our head,
 They often come replete with good;
But we, by erring Fancy led,
 Reject the benefits beftow'd,
Some empty flitt'ring form purfue,
And lofe the fhade and fubftance too:

Yet are there not of that poffeft
 Which makes their lives glide on with eafe,
Something which makes one mortal bleft
 But would deftroy another's peace,
Which reconciles him, foon or late,
To the moft adverfe turn of Fate?

The ragged grey mifanthropê,
 Difgufted, from the world withdraws,
Yet looks with pitying eye to fee
 Mankind deride his fapient laws;
Humanely drops a tear and cries,
" O that mankind like me were wife!"

The flave hard labouring at the oar,
 Believes his lord's condition worfe,
(The gouty, tortur'd epicure,)
 And breathes his pity in a curfe;

Nor

Nor would the wretch exchange his chain
For all the glutton's wealth and pain.

E'en he you think oppreſt with care,
    The idle beggar at your door,
Who only wants a little ſhare,
    A cruſt, a drink, he aſks no more!
He thanks the pow'rs who have not ſaid,
By labour he ſhould earn his bread.

Whatever garments Bliſs aſſumes,
    She is to time nor place confin'd,
Nor ſtraw thatch'd cot, nor ſtately rooms,
    But dwells in the contented mind:
She holds her empire in the breaſt---
The cheerful mind is ever bleſt.

We mar our peace by pond'ring o'er
    The evils incident to man;
Sorrows to come, ills yet in ſtore,
    " We wont be happy when we can."
Let man not then condemn the fates
For evils he himſelf creates.

LINES

LINES
Written on a blank Leaf of Col. Humphrey's Poems.

October, 1790.

WHEN firſt the ſavage voice of WAR
We heard, Death bellowing from *afar*
   Acroſs the ſurging ſeas,
Thy tuneful lyra, hadſt thou ſtrung,
And *Liberty*'s enchantments ſung,
The muſic floating from thy tongue
   Had bid the tumult ceaſe:
Soon had it quell'd the fierce alarms,
The *foes*, footh'd by its ſoft'ning charms,
Had gladly thrown aſide their arms,
   And ſued for ſmiling PEACE.

To ARIBERT.

October, 1790.

OFT' pleas'd my ſoul looks forward to that
   day-
  When ſtruggling to aſcend the hills of light,
My ſpirit burſting from theſe walls of clay,
   Through heav'n's broad arch ſhall bend its
   ſteady flight:
               While

While a few friends attend the lifeleſs ſorm,
  And place it in the boſom of the earth ;
Cov'ring it cloſe, to ſhield it from the ſtorm
  And the cold bluſters of the whiſtling north.

Near the ſea ſhore the corſe ſhall be convey'd ;
  A ſmall white urn the poliſh'd ſtone ſhall
      grace,
And a few lines, to tell who there is laid,
  Shall *Friendſhip*'s hand engrave upon the face.

The dark green willow, waving o'er my head,
  Shall caſt a ſadder ſhade upon the waves ;
And many a widow'd ſwain, and ſlighted maid,
  Shall wear a garland of its weeping leaves :

Far ſpreads its ſhadow o'er the pathleſs vale---
  Through its lank boughs the zephyrs ſighing
      paſs,
And the low branches, ſhaken by the gale,
  Bend ſlowly down and kiſs the fading graſs.

To this lone place the bird of night ſhall come ;
  To me ſhall hie the widow'd turtle too,
And as ſhe perches on the chilly tomb,
  Warble her woes in many a plaintive coo.

There too the trav'ller who hath loſt his way,
  By the dim glimmer of the moon's pale beam,
                                    Shall

Shall ſpy the marble which conceals my clay,
　And reſt his weary feet to read the name.

When o'er our world Night's auburn veil is caſt,
　Oh! ſhould'ſt thou ever wander near theſe
　　ſhores,
Pond'ring the cheerful hours which fled ſo faſt,
　With thoſe who were---but are, alas! no
　　more:

To this lone valley let thy footſteps turn---
　·Here, for a moment reſt tny pauſing eye;
Juſt bruſh the wither'd leaves from off my urn,
　And yield the tribute of a friendly ſigh.

With thee perhaps *Matilda* too may ſtray,
　To ſee where lies the friend once held ſo dear,
And (as ſhe wipes the gath'ring duſt away)
　May to my mem'ry drop perhaps a tear:

And ſhould ſome artleſs, undeſigning friend
　Enquire ' whoſe head reſts here?' him you
　　may tell,
As ſlowly o'er the ſod your ſteps you bend,
　' 'Tis *Ella* reſts within this humble cell.'

　　　　　　　　　　　　　　To

To the Memory of ALEON, who died at Sea
in the Year 1790.

February, 1791.

ALEON is dead!---The sullen trump of
    fame
  Blew the sad tidings to the western shore :
The scythe of Time, the wasting hand of Pain
    Hath lodg'd him with the myriads gone be-
    fore.

How late he wept his brother-warriors dead !
  Cut off untimely in Life's early day:
Alas ! the kindred spirit too is fled ;
  We now to him the same sad tribute pay.

He, like themselves, ' the creature of a day,'
  Beneath the frigid arm of Death hath bow'd:
Yes, *Aleon* lies---the valiant and the gay,
  Deep in the bosom of the stormy flood.

Thus courage, beauty, sentiment, and wit
  Bloom in an hour, and bloom but to decay:
Life quits its suppliants, as the airy sprite
  Before the morning gale fleets fast away.

                  Yet

Yet to his mem'ry fhall a pile be rear'd,
  And each paft fervice meet a kind return;
Still fhall his name by freemen be rever'd,
  And laurels fpring and bloffom round his
    urn.

‘ But penfive poetefs,’ fome one may fay,
  ‘ When thefe memorials of the *good* fhall
    fade,
‘ Will not his worth to time become a prey,
‘ And fink into Oblivion's darkeft fhade ?’

Ah! furely no---the triumph ends not here,
  Beyond the tomb his brighteft profpects rife;
Sublime he foars above this *vale of tears*---
  He gains a life eternal when he dies.

An ADDRESS *to a* PROFILE.

1791.

BEAUTIFUL profile, much, too much
    belov'd,
  By her whofe artlefs heart dictates this lay;
Why is thy dear original remov'd
    From my impatient eyes fo far away?

C c

Thou

Thou dear refemblance of that noble youth,
    Why art thou all that I can call my own
Of him? why not his heart, that feat of truth!
    Why are my tender cares to him *unknown?*

Ah! rather why did I my heart permit
    Fondly to roam o'er Hope's illufive plain?
Why for a ftranger did its pulfes beat,
    While flutt'ring paffions throb'd through
        ev'1y vein?

While I complain, perhaps he gaily roves,
    From cruel doubts and difappointments free;
And (fick'ning thought!) perhaps he fondly
        loves,
    Nor knows there lives a haplefs maid like
        me!

Deceitful Hope! thy flow'ry courts I'll quit,
    Nor more prefent my off'rings at thy fhrine,
But fcorning cenfure, weep my wayward fate,
    For L**** never---never can be mine.

ELEGY

ELEGY *to Miʃs* ANNA DUNDASS.

'O ELLA! tune thy lyra,' didſt thou ſay?
　And art thou, ANNA, pleas'd with notes like
　　　mine,
Which chord but with the flow ton'd dirge-
　　　like lay,
　Which ſad and plaintive weep at ev'ry line?

Let others aſk refulgent Sol for aid,
　When glows the orient with pervading day;
Or court the Muſes in the balmy ſhade,
　Where vi'lets bloom and dimpling foun-
　　　tains play.

I wait not Phoſphor's nor Apollo's beam,
　Nor the warm ſmiles of joy inſpiring Spring,
To rouſe my Muſe---woe is a ready theme,
　And drowſy night the ſeaſon when I ſing.

Such nights, when Luna faintly gilds the
　　　waves,
　And ſhad'wy forms fleet o'er the wat'ry
　　　waſte;
When reſtleſs ſpirits leave their turfy graves,
　And ſtalking ſlow, moan to the hollow blaſt.

　　　　　C c 2　　　　　　　'Tis

'Tis then, amidft the univerfal gloom,
  My penfive foul purfues her fav'rite plan,
Weeps o'er my friends defcended to the tomb,
And mourns the melancholy ftate of man.

" Child of a day,"---the being of an hour,
  He hurries fwiftly through Life's troublous
      fcene ;
Treads the fame round which thoufands trod
      before,
  Then dies, and is as tho' he ne'er had been.

Yes, he muft die, the neareft friends muft part,
  The victor Death accepts not of a claim ;
And though the ftroke may crufh a kindred
      heart,
  He heeds it not---to fupplicate is vain..

But oh! 'tis fad to fee an infant pour
  Its plaints round one juft ready to depart ;
This burfts the heart confign'd to Death before,
  And adds a fting to his acuteft dart.

This, Ann Eliza, on a dying bed,
  Severely felt---fhe fondly wept for me ;
She ftrain'd me in her arms, and weeping faid,
  " When I am gone---ah! who will care
      for thee ?
                              " What

" What tender friend will guide thy infant
    thought
  " When cares fhall call thy father far away?
" By whom wilt thou to act aright be taught?
  " Ah! who, my ELLA! who will care for
    thee?"

Oh! 'twas a bitter pang---I feel it yet!
  My bofom fwells with every figh fhe gave;
And the foft drops with which her cheeks
    were wet
  Wound the full heart they dropt but to-re-
    lieve.

But ANNA, left my forrows give thee pain,
  While thus the tear of fond affection flows,
I'll hufh my plaints---and clofe the mourning
    ftrain,
  And bid adieu awhile---to all my woes.

MORNING.

1791.

THE fpicy morn, with purple ray,
  Faintly illumes the eaftern fkies,
While from each dew befprinkled fpray
  Ambrofial odours gently rife;

Silence ſtill holds the wide domain,
  The Zephyrs ſlumber in the ſhade ;
The ſtream that creeps along the plain,
  Scarce murmurs to the liſt'ning glade:

No ſongſtreſs breathes her artleſs lay,
  No footſteps print the dewy vale,
O'er the broad lawn no lambkins ſtray,
  For ſleep ſtill nods o'er hill and dale,

Where penſive Grief forgets to ſigh,
  There Morpheus ſtill thy ſtation keep,
And with thy ſignet ſeal the eye,
  The eye which only wakes to weep.

But while I ſpeak, the proſpects change,
  The warblers dance upon the air,
The fleecy tribe the paſtures range,
  Refreſh'd with ſleep, and free from care :

All nature bows---all nature ſings,
  And to its author homage pays ;
Each part a grateful tribute brings,
  The whole creation gives him praiſe.

Be thou not, oh ! my languid ſoul,
  An indolent ſpectator here,
While clouds of cheerful incenſe roll
  To him who rules above our ſphere :

Before

Before him pour the lay fincere,
　　When Morning's beams thine eyes fhall blefs,
And let the fhades of Ev'ning hear
　　That ftill thou doft his name confefs.

EVENING

1791.

SOL's golden chariot down the weftern fky
　　Has roll'd, clos'd are the pearly gates of light;
The varied profpects, *fading*, leave the eye
　　Wrapt in the *fhroud* of *folitary night*.

Hudfon, in filence, laves the moon-gilt fhores,
　　The winds hum fullen o'er the lucid plain,
And *Grief* her plaints in penfive mufic pours,
　　While *Echo*, *fad*, repeats the melting ftrain.

Ah! what a tone arrefts my raptur'd ear,
　　Sweet as the *thrufh*'s note at clofe of day,
While balmy breezes, thro' the humid air,
　　On gilded plumes waft the foft founds away.

'Tis *Artha* fings, the mournful voice I know,
　　I know the broken figh which checks the
　　　　fong,
　　　　　　　　　　　　　　　　While

While accents foft of unaffected woe,
　Warm from the heart, drop from her artlefs
　　tongue.---

" O *chilly moon!* O *paler lamp* of *heav'n!*
　" The joys I've known by thy fair light
　　are o'er,
" And thefe fad eyes, which hail'd returning
　　ev'n,
　" See beauty in thy *filver ray* no more:

" For fince my *brother* flumbers with the dead,
　" Each once-lov'd object wears a cheerlefs
　　gloom ;
" Each jocund thought, each happier view is
　　fled,
　" Is with my *Orlin* funk into the tomb.

" *Five* years had feen me tafte unmingled joys,
　" When *War's* trump blew---I heard the
　　folemn fwell ;
" My *father* heard his ftruggling *country's* voice,
　" He felt *her* wrongs---he rufh'd to war---
　　he fell !

" With pious hand my *Orlin* wip'd the tear
　" From the *pale cheek* of *her* who gave us
　　breath ;
　　　　　　　　　　　　　　　" But

" But vain to foothe her anguifh was his care,
" She *pining* funk, *cropt* by the *hand of Death !*

" *One* yet remain'd my heedlefs fteps to guide,
" To feel *my* forrows he forgot his own ;
" Bleft with his care, I had no wifh befide ;
" But *he*---oh, bitter thought !---*he* too is
    gone !

" O life ! how complicated are thy woes !
" Fain from thy realm of forrow would I fly,
" Forgot the goods and ills thou canft beftow,
" And pafs thy *clofing gates* without a figh.

" Peace ! peace, my heart ! thy achings foon
    will ceafe,
" Forbear thy pantings, I fhall foon rejoin
" The happy fpirits of my *loves* in peace,
" And tafte with them the blifs which is
    divine.

" *Silent* as *Death* the moments ftole along,
" Laft night, as late thro' *mould'ring ruins* I
    paft ;
" The *bird* of *eve* had clos'd her *darkling* fong,
" Nor hung an *echo* on the dying blaft :

                                    " When

" When lo! in *fleeplefs unremitted* calls
 "The *death-watch* beat the flying hours away,
" And *fighing ghofts* bent thro' the *broken walls*,
    " And flowly whifp'ring, chid my ling'ring
      ftay.

" O grant me refignation! power fupreme!
   " 'Till thou in love fhalt fummon me away,
" 'Till *Death* fhall wake me from this troub-
      lous dream,
   " And mine eyes open on eternal day."

So be' it love---may *Peace* her pinions fpread
 Around the weary couch by *Artha* preft;
May *angels* warble fonnets round her head,
 To lull her melancholy foul to reft.

And oh! may heav'n, in pity to her woes,
 Soothe her fad heart, to many a pang a prey,
And in *religion* grant her fweet repofe,
 'Till *angels* waft her to the realms of day.

NIGHT.

1791.

H AIL TWILIGHT! hail thou fober pleaf-
      ing form,
Who now approacheft us in fair array,
                                    Thou

Thou offspring of the *Sun*, where'er thy light
Is fhewn, thou giv'ft new life to all around;
The weary *peafant* from the gilded mount,
With joyous heart, defcries thee from afar,
And haftening homeward, whiftles through
     the field
His thanks to thee for bringing him relief.

The *horfe* and *oxen* now forfake the plough,
Or quit the heavy yoke, and feek the fhade,
Where in fome rolling ftream they quench
     their thirft,
Or on the bank repofe their weary limbs
In fleep; enjoy the *prefent* hour, nor fee
Their *future* ills, nor recollect the *paft*.

But fee the EVENING folemnly draws near;
All Nature welcomes her; the *fleecy tribe*
Bleat forth their thanks to him who gave them
     breath,
As flowly to their fold they bend their way,
And their *conductor* lifts his heart and eyes
In filent awe, and gives his Maker praife:
The *feather'd choir* now warble foftlieft notes,
And every hill refponds to Mufic's voice;
While wandering breezes through the dewy
     wood
On their light plumes, the whifpering *echos*
     bear:

            And

And shall I hold my peace when all around
Invite me to partake with them the rich,
The sweet, the great repast of *gratitude?*
No! I'll break forth and mingle with the
          throng,
And thus address my *Author* and my *End:*
' LORD, what is *man*, or what his mighty deeds,
' That thou from thine eternal throne should'st
          stoop
' To pity him, and grant him *happiness*,
' To be his guest, and *health* to be his friend?
' Where'er we turn we see thy mighty love,
' Thy matchless goodness, and unequall'd pow'r:
' Make us to love thee, FATHER, as we aught
' And make our ev'ry action, word and thought
: To speak thy goodness, and to give thee
          praise."
     The *queen* of night, with her resplendant
          train,
Shines from behind the hills ; her golden lamps
Hung high in heaven, bedeck the dark blue sky,
And grace the *earth*, and scatter wonted light.
Ye wond'rous worlds who now to us appear
Like little orbs, *inferior* to our own,
Still sparkle bright, and glitter on through time,
And shew to all the nations round, that HE
Who built your spheres, is powerful and great!
                              How

How calm the night! how filent and ferene!
No dreadful whirlwinds blow, nor thunders
 roar,
Nor earthquake fhakes the ground, but all is
 hufh'd,
The Zephyrs foftly fteal through the deep grove,
Fanning the flumbering birds, while *Cynthia's*
 beam
Quivers in filence o'er the glaffy ftream,
Mov'd by the breathings of the paffing gale.
 Not fuch the eve when BERTRAND left
 thefe fhores,
Deep howl'd the ftorm, heav'n's windows
 open'd wide,
And rain, hail, fleet and fnow came rufhing
 down
In many a fiery blaft, on furious wing :
Then fulphur mixt with ice, and flame with
 fnow,
Black thunders roll'd acrofs the angry heav'n,
And forked lightnings thro' the fable fkies
Hurl'd fwift deftruction on the world beneath ;
Old *Ocean* roar'd, and from his loweft caves
Sent forth his darkening waves, which round
 the fhip
With force impetuous long dafh'd to and fro ;
  D d   But

But ere the rifing of another fun
Oerwhelm'd the paffengers with " watry
          death."
     Oh ! what a night of forrow and defpair !
BOREAS and NEPTUNE, and ÆOLUS fought;
The weeping NAIADS left their oozy beds
And fled for fuccour to the diftant fhores,
While frighted THETIS ftiff'ning with amaze,
Forgot the pow'r to flee !
Long held the conteft, till the pitying SUN
Look'd down, and faw how in confufion wild
The wat'ry empire lay ; he interpos'd,
And fumm'd up all his fhining rays, a hoft
Of glittering warriors, whofe refulgent fpears
Difpers'd the fluttering clouds, and calm'd the
          air.
Now Midnight's mournful veil is drawn around,
While the wan moon gleams fainter through
          the trees,
Vapours opaque the fhadowy mountains fhroud,
And fhrieking ghofts fleet faft along the plain.
   . Now is the mournful time ! the hour of woe,
When Poverty's forfaken aged fons
Tofs on their thorny couch in deep diftrefs,
And Sorrow's ancient weeping daughters now
Reflect on all their woes, their former griefs,
Their miferies, and dread futurity :
                              Hark !

Hark! how that groan, wrung from the heart
    of woe,
In bitter agonies arrests my ear!
Dismally plaintive rolls the feeble sound,
And calls for succour from some pitying hand:
Ah! the dread *King* of Terrors e'en they call
To hurl with speed the long expected dart!
Perhaps he strikes! perhaps just now the soul
Sprung from its bands into eternity!
Dark seems the passage---all the lights are
    clos'd,
And the dim eyes of my affected soul
Open upon the doleful scene, in vain:
How feels the soul just stepping from its barque,
Upon those boundless shores, dreary and dark,
Where ends all space and time, a stranger
    there?
She knows not where to turn her wondering
    form
Till some kind *Spirit*, sent from the abode
Of Jesus, takes her to the land of peace,
Or from the realms of sorrow, some black
    fiend
Seizes her pale, and trembling as she stands,
And plunges her into the gulph of woe!
How silent, O how peaceful is the GRAVE!
Silent and dark as thee, O much lov'd *Night!*

        There

There neither *Pride* nor *Difcontent* can come,
Nor penfive *Melancholy*, no, nor is
The mournful voice of *Sorrow* heard to weep!
There are our griefs in fweet oblivion loft,
When every avenue of life is clos'd;
And though our friends may moan around our
      couch,
We ftill fleep on regardlefs of their plaints:
There finds the weary traveller a reft,
And *there* the child of Poverty a home;
The bofom that with fharp affliction throbb'd,
And the fad heart that fwell'd with many a
      figh,
There reft in filence, and the fad tongue which
In piteous accents told its miferies
And woes, ceafes for ever to complain!
  Oh thou repofitory of the dead!
Thou afylum of many a broken heart!
Clofe lock'd within thy cold unfeeling arms
ELIZA's body fleeps! duft finks to duft!
And the flow *worm*, unconfcious of her worth,
Crawl o'er my parent's confecrated breaft,
That breaft fo lately fill'd with every grace,
With every virtue which could charm the foul:
But their meridian foon, too foon they reach'd;
For while gay *Beauty* mantled on her cheek,
               And

And jocund *Youth* fat fmiling in her eyes,
E'en then the King of Horrors rais'd his dart
And chill'd her blood, and bid her trembling
  heart
With fond maternal love to beat no more.

 Mine was the lofs, but fure it was her gain,
Death could but conquer clay, the reft was free.
Methinks I fee her leaving mortal life,
Her fpirit fluttering to attend the calls
Of waiting angels, whofe melodious voice
Wear out the pangs of death, and hail her fafe;
While the big foul, burft from its narrow fhell,
Expanding flies: the fcene grows brighter ftill;
Some lofty feraphim appears her guide;
With joyful fmiles his radiant footfteps fhine,
And fcatter day and glory from the fkies:
They reach the gates where " Blifs forever
  reigns,"
Where griefs and carking cares no more fhall
  be,
But loft in wondering at the SAVIOUR's love,
Each *fpirit* fpends eternity in blifs,
In filent rapture, namelefs extacy!

 Oh thou *pure effence!* could I follow thee
Still farther on, how would my foul rejoice!
But *Nature* bids me ftop, nor urge my flight
(Eagerly ftretch'd) to where I cannot fee.

   Dd 3   Forever

Forever fled from earth!---my heart ftill
    bleeds
At the remembrance, when in agonies
I faw her lay, when the cold chills of Death
Ran through her frame, and every drop of life
Within its clofing channel lay congeal'd!
Fresh in my mind the uncheery fcenes arife,
Each *groan* again I hear! each piercing *cry!*
Each *languid look* I fee! the *dawn* of *death*,
And the fad beatings of the death bell ftill
Hum flow and difmal in my frighted ear!
    Alas! O God! wilt thou not hear the pray'r
Sent from a heart fincere, robb'd of a fond
Indulgent parent, whofe *oft-heard* advice
By thine affiftance me hath brought thus far.
    O bow thy mighty ear! ftill be my God,
Protector, and my Guide thro' Life's fad
    ways!
That when my foul fhall fever from its clay,
And I *unmourn'd* flide gently in the grave,
My happy fpirit, purified, may join
Eliza, on the fhores where *Rapture* dwells,
And thro' Eternity's exhauftlefs round
Praife and adore the Sov'reign Lord of
    all.

To

To MORTIMER
Embarking for the West-Indies.

1791.

FAREWELL, my friend, the steady gale
  Invites the anxious crew away,
Rolls up the waves, swells ev'ry sail,
  And ling'ring chides thy long delay.

And yet, methinks, with falt'ring voice,
  A something bids me wish thee stay;
'Tis *Friendship* waits to give advice,
  Just hear her speak, and then away.

While wand'ring o'er the stormy deep,
  Resign thyself to *Virtue*'s sway;
Let *Rectitude* thy bosom keep,
  And *Peace* shall gild each fleeting day.

And oft as with reverted eyes
  You sighing look towards your home,
Remember, that benignant skies
  Protect you wheresoe'er you roam.

Let gratitude dictate a lay
  To *him* who brought thee o'er the main,
Where the fair islands greet thine eye,
  Where spring and autumn jointly reign.

Tho'

Tho' fplendid *Vice* with dauntlefs hand,
    There flights the mafk fhe puts on *here*;
Where thoufands court her lov'd command,
    And worfhip her with zeal fincere.

Yet when her gay, her frantic train
    Would tempt thee to the rounds they run,
Remember, that *thou* art a man,
    That *thou* art *Eboracia*'s fon.

Nor let the fenfelefs, daring proud,
    Who flock around unwary youth,
Perfuade thee to the impious croud
    Who mock at God, and hate the truth.

But all thy days to *Wifdom* give,
    Improve the moments as they fly;
So fhalt thou like the righteous *live*;
    So fhalt thou like the righteous *die*.

A VERSION of part of the 7th Chapter of JOB.

1791.

As fighs the lab'rer for the cooling fhade,
When *glowing* fun-beams fcorch the verdant
        blade,
Or as the hireling waits the fcanty fum,
By the hard hand of painful labour won;

So.

So waits my ſpirit, with anxiety,
Death's calm approach, from woe to ſet me
    free ;
For oh ! my days are ſpent in vanity,
And nights of ſorrow are appointed me.

    I love not life---it is a burden grown---
Diſtreſs and *Care* have claim'd me for thei
    own,
And pale *Diſeaſe,* with unrelenting hand,
Sports with my ſighs, and caſts them to the
    wind.

    In vain doth night return to bleſs theſe eyes ;
Sighing, I ſay, " Oh when ſhall I ariſe ?
" When will the night be gone !" Convuls'd
    with pain,
I raiſe my eyes to heav'n for aid in vain ;
My heart grows faint---and toſſing *to and fro,*
I waſte the lonely hours in ſullen woe.

    Or if indeed my eyes ſhould chance to cloſe,
And weary nature gain a ſlight repoſe,
Then am I *ſcar'd* with terrifying dreams ;
Wild ſhrieks I hear, and melancholy ſcreams,
While hideous ſhapes croud on my troubled
    ſight,
Adding new horrors to the glooms of night.
                     Oh !

Oh! I'm forlorn---in bitternefs of foul
My cries burft forth---like floods my forrows
        roll---
Forgot---abandon'd---deftitute---alone---
No pitying ear inhales the *heart-wrung* groan,
No friendly converfe my fad fpirit cheers,
No feeling breaft receives my bitter tears;
Gone is each comfort---hope itfelf is fled;
O that I refted with the quiet dead!
No glimpfe of good mine eyes again fhall fee,
Let me alone---my days are vanity.

But foft my griefs, my life is but as wind,
Soon will it pafs and leave no trace behind;
Soon will my aching heart a refpite have,
Lodg'd in the mould'ring chambers of the grave.
As fleets the cloud before the northern blaft,
So doth the life of mortal beings hafte;
And I fhall fleep in duft---there weary pain
Shall never vex my anguifh'd frame again:
Then tho' *adverfity*, with *iron hand*,
Shall crufh the *rifing honours* of the *land*;
Tho' *war* may wafte--and *ficknefs* blaft in
        death,
The foul that *murder* fpar'd upon the heath,
Yet fhall I flumber, 'midft the awful roar,
For he that fleeps in death fhall wake no more.
                              A SALUTE.

A SALUTE to the Fourteenth Anniverfary of AMERICAN INDEPENDENCE..

1791.

ALL hail to thy return,
O! ever bleft aufpicious morn,
　By mercy's author giv'n:
See! to greet the happy day
Sol expands his brighteft ray,
And not a cloud obfcures his way,
　Nor fhades the face of heav'n.
More fweet *this* day, the cannons martial roar,
Than all the dulcet founds which mufic's foul
　can pour;
　For ev'ry gale that o'er *Columbia* flies
Bids on its balmy wings fome Pæan rife,
　Some fong of *Liberty*;
And ev'ry peal that mounts the fkies,
In folemn tones of grandeur cries,
　"AMERICA IS FREE!"
Sound, O Fame! thy ciarion ftrong,
Bear the golden notes along,
　Let *Gallia* hear the fong;
Beat each heart with pleafure high,
　　　　　　　　　Flufh

Flufh each cheek with pureft joy,
Let rapture glitter in each eye,
    And tune each grateful tongue.
Hail! O *land!*---long may old time behold
Freedom o'er thee her ftandard wide unfold,
    While ages fhall roll on,
'Till to a *chaos* finks again this ball,
'Till worlds to primogenial *nothing* fall,
    And quench'd thy blaze, O fun!

WINTER.

November, 1791.

OFT times the wand'ring Mufe by filence led,
When penfive Night hath wrapt the world in fleep,
By dewy lawns and warbling rills hath ftray'd,
    Trod the green flope, or climb'd the craggy fteep ;

Or, by the margin of fome weeping ftream,
    Where fpreads the *fenfitive* its leafage fair,
Watch'd the *faint quiv'rings* of the *lunar beam,*
    Or *feeble glimmerings* of fome *diftant ftar* ;

Or,

Or, where some ragged cliff, with low'ring
  brow,
Blackens the surface of the swelling deep,
Where billows dash, and howling tempests Llow,
Where *wizard shapes* their nightly revels k ep;

Or on the shelly shores, where *spirits* roam,
 Sounding their sorrows to the midnight gale,
While round their steps the restless waters foam,
 And hollow caves respond the dismal wail.

There (as upon the flood floats the moon's rays,
 And rolling planets shed their silv'ry light;)
There, wrapt in musings deep, and stedfast gaze,
 In solemn rapture hath she past the night.

But now the frighted Muse these scenes forsakes,
 Quits the gay forest and enamel'd plain,
The shadowy vales, the smooth pellucid lakes,
 For *Winter* comes with all his blustering
  train---

He rolls his rapid storms along the skies;
 With tumult fraught, the raving tempest
  roars;
O'er the broad beach the heaving surges rise,
 Groan in the winds, and foam along the shores.

With hasty wing the *vernal season* flies,
  Some *happier clime*, with smiles benign to
    charm,
While the *keen arctic* whistles round *our* skies,
  And the tall forest nods before the storm.

Despotic *Time*, who guides the changing year,
  Blasts the fair scenes that rose at his command,
And weeping *Nature*, desolate and drear,
  Owns the sad traces of his spoiling hand:

And yet, *again* shall *this same* hand unfold
  Winter's cold gates, and bid the fountains
    flow;
Make *rosy Spring* profusely pour her gold,
  And bid her blossoms wear a richer glow.

The *lark* shall quit the solitary bush,
  Smooth her soft plumes, and tune her warb-
    ling tongue,
While from some copse the late dejected *thrush*
  Cheers the glad vallies with a sprightly song.

Cease then, O Muse! to drop the useless tear,
  Ah! touch no more the melancholy string,
Since *Earth* again the blooms of life shall wear,
  And *wintry glooms* give place to *smiling Spring*.

FRIENDSHIP

FRIENDSHIP.

January, 1792.

FRIENDSHIP! I hate thy name---my
 rancled heart,
 ' Forever wounded by thy *treacherous* hand,
' Bleeding afrefh defies the pow'r of art,
' Its pangs to foften, or extract the fmart;
' For who, ah who can draw the bitter dart
 ' Implanted by a *chofen, bofom friend?*
 ' Too long I harbour'd thee within my breaft,
 ' Thou bafe deftroyer of my reft;
' Too long thy galling yoke did bear:
' For while I cherifh'd thee with foftering care,
' Thou didft thy pois'nous fting prepare,
 ' And wrung the heart that fondly thee careft.
 ' But *now* adieu, thy reign is o'er,
  ' For thee that heart no longer fighs;-
 ' And at thy voice fhall joy no more
  ' Suffufe this cheek, nor grace thefe eyes.
 ' Thy ev'ry tranfport I'll forego,
  ' Thy fov'reignty difclaim;
 ' And if no more thy *fweets* I know,
  ' I know no more thy *pain.*

' Tranquil my hours fhall glide away,
    ' No more a prey to poignant woes ;
' *Content* fhall blefs each rifing day,
    ' And charm each night with calm re-
        pofe.
' No more fhall *tears* ftray down my cheek,
    ' Wak'd by thy fympathetic voice,
' Nor *griefs*, too big for utterance, break
    An injur'd heart that venerates thy ties ;
'Nor *fighs* all eloquent a language teach,
    ' That mocks the idle power of fpeech.'
Thus, once in anguifh'd mood I *wept* and *fung* ;
Warm from the heart th' unfeeling accents
    fprung ;
    For *Perfidy's cold touch* had chill'd
    Each fofter, gentler motion there,
And ev'ry painful *chafm* had fill'd
    With *weak miftruft* and *fretful care.*
But vain I fought thofe fcenes of blifs,
    Which *Fancy's* flatt'ring pencil drew ;
When the delights of fmiling Peace.
    Each hour fhould brighten as it flew :
With *Friendfhip* ev'ry joy had fled,
    With *her* each rapture took its flight ;
Nor longer charm'd the *branching fhade,*
    Nor *fragrant morn,* nor *fpangled night.*

                        In

In vain for me the fongfter fwell'd its throat,
In vain the buds their moiften'd fweets dif-
    clofe ;
Nor *cheer'd* their glowing tints, nor *footh'd* the
    note ;
Alas ! the felfifh heart no pleafure knows.
Ah, *Hope!*' figh'd I, ' are *thefe* thy proffer'd
    joys ?
' Are *thefe* the hours of blifs that fhould be
    mine ?
' Few have I known fince loos'd from Friend,
    fhip's ties.'
Again my vows I offer'd at her fhrine.
Sudden, as from *Caftalia*'s favour'd fpring,
    As fweet, as foft a tone I hear,
As ever floated on mild *Ev'ning*'s wing,
    Or footh'd *pale Echo*'s ear.
Caught by the *ftrain,* each tear forgot to flow,
    Each bitter rifing murmur ftraight repreft ;
When, with enchanting air and placid brow,
    The lovely fair *Califta* ftood confeft.
In feelings loft, tumultuoufly fweet,
    Exultingly I own'd her gentle fway,
And bleft the *heart* whofe fympathetic beat
    Hail'd the young dawn of *Friendfhip*'s rifing
    day.

 To

To the Reverend J*** N*****

January, 1792.

HERE, *late*, where *Ruin*'s standard was un-
      furl'd,
And bloody *war* laid waste our *western* world,
The mildest beams of *Peace* benign are shed,
And *Piety* exalts her conquering head ;
Age finds her flow'ry path, and heedless youth
Submissive kneels the advocate of truth !
With *spirits* chang'd we think of feuds no
      more,
But greet our *seniors* on a distant shore ;
Tho' barren wilds and mountains intervene,
And the *Atlantic* rolls her floods between.

Will then fair *Olney's aged bard* excuse
The weak exertions of a youthful muse ?
The genuine wishes of whose heart sincere,
All *glowing* breathe to *heaven* for him a pray'r.

Long may'st thou to thy land a blessing be,
And *many* fruits of thy kind labours see ;
May *Patience* soothe thee in thy worldly cares,
And a bright *faith* light thy declining years ;
'Till *late* our GOD shall call the *Wanderer*
      home,
And bid the longing, hoping *exile*, " come."
                                    Then

Then may thy *soul*, upborne on angel's wing,
Fleet to the realms of everlasting love;
With raptur'd myriads *Mercy*'s fource to fing,
And *all* the fullnefs of *Emanuel* prove.

To the MOON.

April, 179?.

WHILE wand'ring through the dark blue
    vault of heav'n,
  Thy tracklefs fteps purfue their filent way,
And from among the ftarry hoft of ev'n,
  Thou fhed'ft o'er *flumbering earth* a milder
    day ;
And when thou pour'ft abroad thy fhadowy
    light
  Acrofs the ridgy circles of the ftream,
With raptur'd eyes, O changeful nymph of
    night !
  I gaze upon thy beam.

GREAT was the *hand* that form'd thy round,
    O Moon !
  That mark'd the precincts of thy fteady
    wheel,

                    That

That bade thee fmile on *Night*'s oblivious
    noon,
And rule old *Ocean* s folemn fwell;
GREAT was the POWER, that fill'd with ra-
    diant light
Thofe *Worlds* unnumber'd, which from
    pole to pole
Hang out their golden lamps to deck thy flight,
Or gild the *Planets* which around thee roll.

From realms of Love, beyond where moves
    the *Sun*,
    Whofe diftant beams create our brighteft day,
Beyond where *Stars* their ceafelefs circles run,
Or *lurid Night* emits his opaque ray;
    Mounted on the dark'ning ftorm,
On the ftrong whirlwind's ragged pinions
    borne,
With *glory* circumfus'd, the *Source of Blifs*
Sublime, came flying o'er the vaft *abyfs*.

His voice was heard---in dire difmay
    Chaotic Darknefs fled away,
While burfting waves of *Light* the flight be-
    held,
And all the fpacious void triumphant fill'd.

                                    Without

Without delay, *this* reftlefs ball
Uprofe, obedient to his call;
But that he fpake it into light,
It ftill had flumber'd in eternal night:
The *mountains* rear'd their verdant head,
The *hills* their deftin'd places found,
And as the *fountains* pour'd their waters round,
Ocean fubmiffive wander'd to her bed;
The *Sun* arofe---with beam benign he fhone,
And *terra* cheer'd with fplendours all his own.

" Go gild the morn," his maker faid.
Impatient to obey,
O'er half the globe his rays he fpread,
And blaz'd along the day.

Then waft *thou* form'd with all the ftarry train
That decorate the ev'ning fkies;
Some made to travel through the fapphire plain,
And fome forbid to fet or rife.

Long haft thou reign'd, and from thine amber
throne
The various changes of *this world* haft known;
Haft feen its *myriads* into being rife,
Shine their fhort hour, and then their *life*
refign;

New generations feize the fickle *prize*,
    And like their fires, but ftrengthen to decline:
Yet be not vain, (though fince thy natal day
    Some thoufand years their circling courfe
        have made)
For lo! the *æra* haftens on apace,
    When all thy glory fhall for ever fade.
Earth fhall the *revolution* feel,
    The *change* of feafons fhall be o'er,
Time fhall forget to guide his wheel,
And *thou*, O Moon, fhalt *fet* to *rife* no more!

SILENCE.

Philadelphia, 1792.

DAY flow retreats on fhowery wing,
    And Evening climbs the eaftern fkies;
    The hovering vapours round the fhores arife,
Or to the tall rock's frowzy fummit cling:
        The hum of bufy care is done,
        A welcome refpite twilight brings;
        And in the ear of Labour's fon,
        The lulling fong of *Quiet* fings.
All, all is ftill and peaceful as the grave,
Save where the *Delaware*'s diftant billows roar,
                            When

When driven by rushing gales, the yielding
    wave
Throws its white waters on the echoing shore.
Hark the shrill *quail* with deep swoln note
Breaks the dumb silence of the scene:
The waking breezes sullen round it float,
Fold their soft wings, and sink to rest again.

Hail, lonely hour! enchanting *Silence* hail!
    When no intrusive found thy realm invades.
When fervent thought can pierce *Night*'s
    closest veil,
    And rise exulting o'er surrounding shades;
Say, will *Day*'s glories with *thy* clouds compare,
Where boisterous *Tumult* rolls his thundering
    car?
    Or, can *Apollo*'s blazing beams diffuse
      O er the sad heart, surcharg'd with grief,
      So kind a balm---so sweet relief,
    As thy soft winds and od'rous dews?
Ah! well thy power I know, while wander-
    ing here,
Far, very far from all my heart holds dear;
Where, while remembrance brings their image
    near,
Down my pale cheek tear follows tear;
               And

And the big figh, in vain fuppreft,
Urges a paffage from a fwelling breaft:
Yet do I know thy foothing power e'en here,
Though far---ah me, how far from all my heart
  holds dear!

To ETHELINDE.

1792.

NO longer let me weep a prey to love,
 Sad victim to ill-fated paffion's fway;
A thoufand *fighs* will ne'er their fource remove,
 Nor *tears* its fond remembrance wafh away.

Ah me!---when finks the heart by *griefs depreft*,
 And *Hope* denies her balmy foothings fweet,
And bufy *Memory* wrings the bleeding breaft;
 Then, furely, *then* is wretchednefs complete.

Come *Hope*, in *Ethelinde*'s enchanting form,
 Come bid my ufelefs tears forbear to flow;
Check the wild paffions in my breaft that ftorm,
 Rude as the gufts o'er *Erie*'s furfs that blow.

Why fhould I grieve?---no fwain with artful
  tongue
Has broke the vows I ventur'd to approve;
For *Alma*'s TRUTH my eafy heart has won,
 Whofe form is *beauty* and whofe voice is *love*.

        Does

Does he not feel?---why then that frequent figh
  When grief or ficknefs cloud my penfive face?
Or why that pleafure fparkling in his eye,
  When cheerfulnefs and health refume their
    place?

Why does his cheek with fudden flufhes glow,
  From a fhort abfence when we meet again?
Or why dejection hang upon his brow,
  When other fav'rites my attention claim?

Oh! if he loves---with paffion fuch as mine---
  Life's varying fcenes how eafy fhall I find?
How *light* will be the woes of CAROLINE?
  How *rich* the pleafures fhar'd with *fuch a
    mind?*

But---if I muft a *common lot* deplore---
  Oh! if my ALMA chufe fome happier fair,
Then will I fly to fome forgotten fhore,
  And wafte my forrows on the defert air.

Ha!---will the foreft's echoing glooms be
    found
  More cheering than the voice of *Ethelinde?*
What!---can *eternal abfence* heal *my* wound,
  Or blot his lov'd idea from *my* mind?---

No

No, furely, no---firm as the earth's broad bafe
　　Are my affections round his *virtues* twin'd;
And *Time*, beneath whofe touch *all* elfe decays,
　　Serves but the ligaments more clofe to bind.

Then will I ftay, a votary to his charms,
　　And, kneeling *victor* at *Submiffion*'s fhrine,
Clafp the *bleft woman* in my conquering arms,
　　And *all the heart* that once was *mine* to *her*
　　　　refign.

To the fame.

1792.

AH! ceafe the " dirge like lay," my *Ethe-
linde* ;
　　Wipe off the tear that quivers in thine eye,
Nor let the bofom of my beft lov'd friend
　　Heave with the deep but unavailing figh.

On the broad pinions of unwearied *Time*
　　Our months and days are fwiftly borne away,
And each fucceeding hour, in conftant chime,
　　Configns fome dear enjoyment to decay.

Age fteals the rofe from the dejected cheek,
　　And plants his enfigns on th' unwilling brow;
Cheerfulnefs fighs---and *Wit* forgets to fpeak,
　　Loft in eternal torpor---Oh what woe !

But

But *Grief*, (ah me, how well the truth *I* know!)
 Grief, with officious hand, propels us on,
Urges our fpeed, left *Time* fhould move too flow,
 And ere we reach *Life's noon*, our fun goes
  down.

Ceafe then to weep, my beauteous *Ethelinde*,
 Ceafe thine own rugged path with thorns to
  ftrew;
Oh check thofe griefs I know not to befriend,
 Nor give aloofe to fuch immoderate woe!

What! fhall *my* cares on ALMA reft alone?
 Shall all *thy* wifhes to MYRTILLO fly?
And fhall the heart that meets no kind return,
 Burft---coward like---and bleed its channel
  dry?

No, *Ethelinde*, with generous pride I burn,
 ALMA, the noble ALMA, I refign;
And tho' my heart *awhile* its lofs may mourn,
 It *never* to relenting fhall incline.

The gracious *Power* whofe word hath given
 us *life*,
 And mixt our cup with *pleafure* and with *pain*,
Will ftrength afford to *pafs* the mental ftrife,
 Or ftrength at leaft the conflict to *fuftain*.

F f 2   Oh!

Oh! would but man enjoy the bleffings given,
　　How many tears had never learn'd to flow!
How few deep fighs had wing'd their courfe to
　　　　heaven!
　　How few the hearts furcharg'd with help-
　　　　lefs woe!

For *us* young *Evening* fheds her foft perfumes;
　　For *us* blith *Morn* expands her golden eyes;
For *us* the *Sun* heav'n's azure arch illumes;
　　And *forefts* bloom for *us*, and *oceans* rife.

But oh! the ingrate man, with felfifh mind,
　　He fpurns the blifs which heav'n defign'd
　　　　his own;
His airy wifh outftrips the hafty wind,
　　And grafps at raptures *never to be known.*

In efforts vain he toils away his days,
　　Purfuing *Fancy* in her mad career;
Though ftill deceiv'd, he ftill her call obeys,
　　And finks at laft---the victim of *Defpair*.

Such is vain man's---and fuch hath been *our* lot,
　　Such the dim mift that dark'd our earlieft years;
Fixt on our happieft hours a lafting blot,
　　And bath'd each following day in *heart-
　　　　wrung tears.*
　　　　　　　　　　　　　　　Where

Where are the golden joys we once have known?
Where the calm comforts which for us have
    bloom'd?
Smooth, gliding scenes of peace! they all are
    gone,
All by oblivious *Sorrow---all* entomb'd.

Oh! sad regret, the feeling heart beats full,
    Vain prove th' attempts wild *nature* to subdue:
My lyre is struck with wandering hand and dull,
While lawless tears the pausing strings bedew.

---

*On seeing a Print, exhibiting the Ruins of the
Bastille.*

1792.

AT each return of the auspicious day
    Which laid this mighty fabric in the dust,
    Let joy inspire each patriotic breast
To bless and venerate its august ray;
Let *Gallia*'s sons attune the harp of joy,
And teach the trump its boldest notes t' em-
    ploy;
Let clarions shrill the deed declare,
And blow their son'rous notes afar;

F f 3   Let

Let mufic rife from ev'ry plain,
  Each vine-clad mount or daified dell,
And let *Æolus* float the ftrain
  Acrofs old Ocean's ample fwell.

Ah ! fee the *Baftille*'s iron walls thrown down,
  That bulwark ftrong of *Tyranny*;
See her proud turrets fmoke along the ground,
  Crufh'd by the giant arm of *Liberty!*
Her gloomy *tow'rs*---her *vaults* impure,
  Which once could boaft eternal night;
Her *dungeons* deep---her *dens* obfcure,
  Are urg'd unwilling to the light.

Oft in thefe dreary cells, the *captive*'s moan
  Broke the dead filence of the midnight watch
When *Memory*, pointing to the days long gone,
  To wafting forrows woke the feeling wretch.

Here everlafting Darknefs fpread
  Her veil o'er fcenes of mifery,
Where *Sicknefs* heav'd an anguifh'd head,
  And roll'd a hopelefs eye.
Here drown'd in tears, pale *Agony*
Spread her clafp'd hands toward the fky,
While all convuls'd, *extreme Defpair*
  Swallow'd the earth in fpeechlefs rage,
  Or phrenzied gnaw'd his *iron cage*,
Tore off his flefh, and rent his hair.

                                    Such

Such were thy glories, O Baftille!
Such the rich bleffings of *defpotic pow'r*,
Whofe horrid *dæmon* quaff'd his fill,
Daily of bitter tears and human gore:
But now 'tis o'er---thy long, long reign is o'er,
Thy thunders fright the trembling hofts no
    more;
Thy fhafts are fpent---thy fons no more engage
To add new triumphs to thy train,
To bind new victims to thy chain;
For thy moft valiant fons are flain
By the fierce ftrokes of kindled patriot rage.
Roll'd in the duft, behold thine honours lie,
The fport---the fcorn of each exploring eye.

Hail gallant Gauls! heroic people hail!
Who fpurn the ills that Virtue's fons affail,
Whofe hearts benevolent, with ardour bound
The hard-got bleffing to diffufe around:
Oh! be your ftruggles bleft, and may you fee
Your labours rivall'd by pofterity;
'Till the fmall *flame* (which firft was feen to rife,
'Midft threat'ning blafts, beneath *Columbian*
    fkies,
Which, as it taught its fplendours to expand,
Arofe indignant from Oppreffion's hand,
                                And

And blaz'd effulgent o'er the mighty plain)
Luring your heroes o'er the ftormy main,
'Till this fmall flame, fed by their nurturing
    hand,
Not only canopies your native land,
But far extending its prolific rays,
Envelopes neighbouring empires in the blaze.
And thou, FAYETTE ! whom diftant lands de-
    plore,
As now *felf-banifh'd* from thy native fhore;
Tho' *zeal miftaken*, may a fhadow throw
Athwart the laurels which adorn thy brow;
Yet fhall they bloom---for in thy generous
    breaft
No foul like *Coriolanus* is confefs'd:
To *Gallia* ftill thy warmeft wifhes tend,
And tho' an *injured exile*, ftill a friend!
When grateful nations tell thine acts to *Fame*,
America fhall urge her oldeft claim,
Point to the *worthies* whom her fons revere,
And place FAYETTE with thofe fhe holds moft
    dear.

To

To the Memory of *Mrs.* HENRIETTA ANNA
MARIA DUBUISSON.

October, 1792.

OH! lovely vision! art thou gone?
　Doft thou repofe in Death's dull fhade?
Are all thy boafted glories flown?
　Doft thou too reft among the dead?

Oh, faireft flower that ever bloom'd
　To deck life's variegated fcene,
How fhort liv'd have thy beauties been?
No fooner open'd than entomb'd!

With rifing joys *Hope* ftrew'd thy way,
　And *Hygea*'s rofes deck'd thy brow;
Lovely, and young, and good, and gay,
　Thou wert---but ah! what art thou now?

Cold---lifelefs---dead---a fenfelefs clod---
　To death's chill grafp an early prey;
Frail as the tenants of the fod
　Which fhrouds thee from the face of day

Let frantic *Mirth* be penfive here;
　Here let *Youth* weep its tranfient bloom;
Here let vain *Beauty* drop a tear,
　For *Harriet* moulders in the tomb.

Come,

Come, weeping Mufe, come form a wreath
　　To deck the turf where beauty lies ;
Where the foft winds of Evening breathe,
　　Where Morning's fweeteft dews arife.

But wherefore mourns my heart thine early
　　　doom,
　　Or ftrays in weeping filence round thy grave ?
　　Can the dull ear of Death my fighs receive ?
Or dwells the æthereal being in the tomb?

No, burfting from Death's dark confines,
　　And wand'ring on the gales of even,
It wings its flight to happier climes,
　　And gains at laft---its long wifh'd heaven

Tell me, fair effence, when releas'd from clay,
　　Thy pinions open'd in a land unknown,
　　Did no kind angel hafte on purple plume,
To hail thee fafe---and guide thee on thy way ?

Did not the echoing *Lyra*'s melting ftrain
　　Obliterate the *memory* of each tear,
　　To *rapture* foothe each yet remaining fear,
And urge thy wond'ring fpirit from its chain?

It did---it did---the folemn ftrains
　　Seem to vibrate on my enchanted ear ;
　　And wilder'd with the floating tones I hear,
Life's ruby current warbles in my veins.
　　　　　　　　　　　　　　' Welcome

' Welcome from the hands of *Pain*,
 ' Welcome from *Sin*'s baneful pow'r,
' Welcome from *Death*'s drear domain,
 ' Thou fhalt feel their ire no more.

' All that thou haft heard below,
' All that Angel pow'rs can know,
' Peace eternal, joy divine,
' Everlafting love are thine.

' Let the garland we affume,
 ' *Amaranth* with *myrtle* join'd,
' Flow'rets of perpetual bloom,
 ' Thy triumphant temples bind.

' Lo! the walls of Paradife!
 ' Lo! the pearly gates unfold!
' Darting fplendours down the fkies;
 ' Lucid gems and fparkling gold.

' There no *Sun*, with dazzling beam,
 ' Gilds the glowing cheek of morn;
' There no *Moon*, with fmile ferene,
 ' Waits mild Evening's calm return:

' There dwells UNCREATED LIGHT,
 ' Blazing with unfading ray;
' Ne'er we know returning night---
 ' Bleft with everlafting day.
      ' Hark!

' Hark !---I hear the warbling throng
' Hail thee to thy native home ;
' Hark ! their *Lyras* bid thee come---
' Hafte, fair Angel,---hafte along !

To the Memory of Mrs. Scriba *and her infant
Daughter.*

1792.

THE blafts of *December* are heard on the
 hills,
They have fcatter'd their high-drifting fnows
 o'er the plain;
The breath of rough *Boreas* the fountains congeals,
 And *Flora* bemoans her blight'd honours in
 vain.

The *Tulip* is faded---its tinges are fled---
 The *Violet* fhrinks from the loud-howling
 gale ;
And the foft dewy *Rofe* droops its languifhing
 head,
 And ceafes its balm-breathing fweets to exhale.

Thy wide defolations, oh *Emblem of Death !*
 Spread glooms and dejections acrofs the fad
 mind ;

          And

And we trace a loft *friend* in each bare dreary
 heath;
And we hear their laft figh in the voice of
 the wind.

Yet the gambols of *Spring* fhall thy rigours un-
 bend,
 And cherifh the fcenes *Maia*'s abfence that
  mourn ;
But the *Winter* of *Death* hath no folace---no
 friend---
 Nor' buds the green *Spring* for the duft-bear-
  ing *Urn*.

On the cheek of our LAURA how late bloom'd
 the *Rofe*,
 And *Innocence* fhot from her eyes its foft ray ;
But the blufh is extinguifh'd---no more that
 cheek glows---
 And thofe eyes drink no more the effulgence
  of day.

Wife, Sifter, Friend, Parent, ah names dear in
 vain !
 As fragile and fair as the gay clouds of dawn ;
Ye are vanifh'd, alas ! like the breeze on the
 plain,
 And all, but your mournful *remembrance*, is
  gone.

My fpirit the days that are paft oft reviews,
  And penfively treads where her joys were
    once ftrewn;
While a fond retrofpection her forrows renews,
  And fhe weeps o'er the hours that for ever
    are flown.

Like fome beautiful flow'ret, whofe delicate
    form
  Still delights, tho' o'erthrown by the tem-
    peft's rude breath;
Thus *Laura*, tho' preft by *Affliction*'s cold ftorm,
  Yet cheerfully fmil'd on the bofom of *Death*.

Tho' the arrows of *Anguifh* affaulted her frame,
  And the night like the day brought no footh-
    ing repofe;
And tho' faft finking *Life* rent each languifhing
    vein,
  Not a fingle complaint, not a murmur arofe.

' Ceafe for *me*, weeping friends, the SUPREME
    to invoke;
  ' I leave the rough pillow of *Agony*'s bed,
' To *reft* in the Regions of Glory'-----She
    fpoke,
  And th' unfetter'd fpirit exultingly fled!

                 And

And thou, too, ELIZA, the grasp of *Disease*
    Hath crush'd thy young blossom and wasted
        thy sweets;
And the *Cherub* that long'd for the mansion of
        Peace,
From the darksome abode of *Affliction* re-
    treats.

Yes, the wings of that moment which speeded
        her flight
To the bosom of LAURA, beheld her con-
    vey.'d
Where the uncloying scenes of perpetual de-
    light
Can never admit of a pause nor a shade.

There, surely the day of distress hath an end ;
    There, *parting* and *weeping* for ever are o'er ;
There, the *Winter* of *Death* finds a solace, a
    friend ;
And *there* buds the green *Spring*, to be rifled
    no more.

To ETHELINDE.

1792.

HAIL to the heart, whose gen'rous pride,
    Can burst the iron bars of *grief*,
Can *Love*'s fantastic ills deride,
    And from itself procure relief.

If

If *tears Oppreſſion*'s hand would gild,
Or ſighs a feeble reſpite yield;
Or if the woes remember'd oft,
By repetition grew more ſoft:
Then might we court the weeping muſe,
O'er our ſad boſoms to diffuſe
Her ſoothing pow'r---in *melting lay*
To teach us *ſing* our griefs away.
But ah! how well *(too* well) *I* know
Who weeps, he but *indulges* woe;
And every briny tear that flows
Binds to the heart its griefs more cloſe.

Riſe then, my ſoul, with ardour riſe,
    Expand thy wiſhes far and wide,
Go contemplate the ſtarry ſkies,
    Go emulate thy SEX'S PRIDE.

Ah! vain attempt---on pinions ſtrong
    She ſoars beyond the panting wind;
And all enamour'd of her ſong,
    She leaves thee, wondering muſe, behind.

Shame to the heart, whoſe tranquil beat
    Ne'er felt contending paſſions keen;
Ne'er knew the vict'ries of *defeat*,
    When *Reaſon* joy'd o'er *Folly* ſlain.

                                Yes

Yes---while among the ftars fhe fhines,
    And " vifits worlds conceal'd from fight,"
A humbler theme I chufe for mine,
    The Dufky Dawn and Mifty Night.

I'll drink the fparkling dews of morn,
    And watch *Apollo*'s earlieft ray;
Or greet the fhepherd's mellow horn,
    That lulls the clofing hours of day:

Or, bending o'er old Ocean's ftream,
    Mount the tall *Pico*'s loftieft brow,
And, guided by *Cylene*'s beam,
    Paufe o'er the *diftant* world below:

Or, hanging o'er fome cavern dark,
    Where troubled waters heave and fwell,
Lift to *Charibda*'s angry bark,
    Or howling *Scylla*'s fearful yell:

Or, mingling with th' enthufiaft throng,
    Who to *Melpomene*'s harp afpire,
Mimic CALISTA's *melting fong*,
    Or penfive ELLA's *weeping lyre:*

Then mourning thro' fome foreft's gloom,
    From *flumbering couch* wake *Echo pale*;
And pluck the bloffoms of the dale,
To deck fome lonely tomb.

G g 3

Such

Such be my fongs, while *Ethelinde*,
  Smiling, my artlefs labours views,
Reward---the beft that can attend
  The flights of CAROLINA's mufe.

A VERSION *of Mrs.* BARBAULD's *Tenth Hymn.*

1793.

OFFSPRING of woe, what mean thofe fighs
  That from thy burfting bofom heave?
What mean thofe gufhings from thine eyes?
  What haft thou feen to make thee grieve?
Alas! alas! I've feen the *Rofe*
To the warm *Sun* its leaves expofe;
Elate, it drank his golden ray,
And fpread its beauties to the day.

Again I look'd---that very beam
  Which op'd its dewy blooms at *Morn*,
Smote it at *Noon*, and on the ftem
  Had only left the rancling thorn!
A ftately *Tree* grew on the plain,
  Wide to the winds its boughs were fpread,
Deep in the earth its roots were lain,
  And firm its mighty trunk was made.

Again

Again I look'd---the *Eastern Blast*
Had bid its emerald glories waste;
With greedy tooth, th' insatiate *Worm*
Had rudely pierc'd its noble form,
The *Axe* had lopt its limbs away,
And all foretold a swift decay!

I've seen the lovely *Insect* throng
  Desporting on the beams of morn,
They danc'd the bubbling stream along,
  On the light plumes of *Zephyrs* borne;
Their azure wings were star'd with gold,
  Their bodies ting'd with tyrian hue
Soft down'd---their numbers were untold,
  And quick as lightning's glance they flew.

Again I look'd---the *Evening*'s cool
  Had chill'd their limbs and check'd their
      flight,
The *Breeze* had brush'd them in the pool,
  They died before the mists of night;
The *Swallow* chose them for her food,
  They fill'd the *Pike*'s voracious maw,
And of so great a multitude,
  So gay, so fair---not one I saw.

Proud of his strength, I've seen vain *Man*,
  His cheek with youthful beauty glow'd,
He walk'd, he danc'd, he leapt, he ran,
  And quick his vig'rous pulses flow'd:

                                   Eloquence

Eloquence dwelt upon his tongue;
　　Science his fwelling heart embrac'd;
The mountain *Echo* learnt his *fong*,
　　And ev'ry charm his nature grac'd.

Again I look'd---on the bare ground
　　Stiff and immoveable he lay;
Horror and fear prevail'd around,
　　And check'd the cheerful fports of day:
His hands---his feet no motion prov'd,
　　No fong employ'd his tuneful breath;
From light, and love, and fenfe remov'd,
　　A prey he fell to *rav'nous Death!*

Oh let me weep! this *rav'nous Death*
　　Lawlefs o'er earth extends his fway;
Creation feels his blighting breath,
　　Shrinks from his touch and fades away.

Since *Shrub*, and *Beaft*, and *Man* in vain
　　Againft the *mighty Spoiler* ftrive,
The *Sun*, and *Moon* and *Starry train*
　　Shall not his ruthlefs pow'r furvive:
They too his baleful grafp fhall feel;
　　Earth from her bound'ries fhall retire,
And *Sea* and *Mountain*, *Rock*, and *Hill*,
　　And *Space* and *Time* fhall all expire!

The

The following Lines were occafioned by Mr. RO-
BERTSON*'s refufing to paint for one Lady, and
immediately after taking another Lady's likenefs.*

1793.

WHEN LAURA appear'd, poor APPEL-
 LES complain'd,
That his fight was bedim'd, and his optics
 much pain'd;
So his pallet and pencil the artift refign'd,
Left the blaze of her *beauty* fhould make him
 quite blind.

But when fair ANNA enter'd the profpect was
 chang'd,
The paints and the brufhes in order were
 rang'd;
The artift refum'd his employment again,
Forgetful of labour, and blindnefs and pain;
And the ftrokes were fo lively that all were
 affur'd
What the *brunette* had injur'd the *fair one* had
 cur'd.

 Let the candid decide which the chaplet
  fhould wear,
 The *charms* which *deftroy,* or the *charms*
  which *repair.*

To

To NATURE.

1793.

YES, Nature! thou art lovely, every scene
Is form'd to yield the throbbing heart delight;
Whether thou art bedeck'd in changeful *green*,
Or shrink'st beneath a shroud of sparkling *white*;
Whether when *Morning* mounts her crimson car,
Wakes the young gales, and gilds the eastern
    main!
Or when grey *Evening* lights her fav'rite star,
And shapes fantastic glide along the plain;
For in thy *Gaiety* the *Lover* finds
    Some faint resemblance of his darling fair,
And trusts the rivulet or courteous winds
    May to her ear his tale impassion'd bear;
And when hoar *Winter* storms along the skies,
    And frights old *Ocean* with the fearful roar,
    The *Wanderer* forlorn, treads the bleak shore,
Mingling with waves and winds his tears and
    sighs:
    Yet 'tis a *solace* to his misery,
    The *howling whirlwind* and the *surging sea.*
How oft, Oh *Summer!* have thy jocund hours
Flown disregarded o'er my head?
                                    Alas!

Alas! I courted not *their* softening pow'rs,
  Since all I lov'd from me was fled.
Ah! then I hied me to the pebbly shore,
  And o'er the waves would cast a tearful eye,
  With the vain hope my CYRILLE to espy,
And press him to my aching heart once more:
  The war of *rushing storms* and *Ocean's howl*,
  Were the lov'd soothers of my anguish'd soul.
Cheer'd with his love again, thy charms,
    O *Spring!*
Rise with redoubled softness on my view;
  I love the breath of *Morn*, mild *Evening*'s dew,
And all the varying scenes thy reign can bring;
Yet, 'reft of all thou hast, ah! I should not
    repine,
While LOVE and CYRILLE I could claim as
  mine.

ARRIA's TOMB.

1793.

PRIDE of the peaceful solitary *Night*,
  While now thou cheer'st her solemn gloom;
Through these damp shades a weeping *Wan-
    derer* light,
  And guide my pensive steps, to *Arria*'s tomb:
                                    There

There will I vent the anguiſh of my ſoul,
  Bathing my locks in *Night's* unwholeſome
      dew,
While fierce around my head the ſhrill gales
      howl,
  And ſpectres pale, the ſhades of Night purſue:
But ſee, a *ſpirit* fleets before mine eye ;
Ah! well I know that anguiſh loaded ſigh ;
It is my *Arria's* form.; yes, dear forlorn!
Thy *Georgianna* weeps upon thine urn.
Thou feeble ghoſt, whoſe tears yet ſeem to fall
  Down a dejected cheek, all cold and pale ;
As ſad thou glid'ſt along the moon-gilt wall,
  And liſt'neſt to the *Night-bird's* chilling wail.
Dear weeping lilly, did not once Health's *roſe*
  Bloſſom upon thy cheek with lovelieſt grace ?
Did not once *Peace* within thy breaſt repoſe,
  And tranquil Cheerfulneſs beam through thy
      face ?

Oh, LOVE ! what haſt thou done ? thy lawleſs
      pow'r
  Subdu'd a heart too gen'rous to deceive ;
  But, ah! unpitied, it but beat to grieve ;
Scorn, cruel *Scorn!* embittering every hour.
  Shut from the world, ſhe bore her griefs alone,
  And of life careleſs, wept her hours away ;
While *Death*, exulting o'er his precious prey,
  Cropt the ſweet bloſſom ere it yet was blown.
                              Oh,

Oh, thou hard heart, where PITY *never* dwelt !
  May dire *Affliction* mark thee for her own ;
May'ſt thou endure pangs *worſe* than *Arria* felt,
  And no one pity thee, nor heed thy moan ;

May pale *Remorſe* on all thy ſteps attend,
  Shewing a form thy folly would not ſave ;
May thy ſad life be ſpent without *one friend*,
  And not *one tear* be ſhed upon thy grave !

To a CANARY BIRD.

1793.

BEAUTIFUL bird, of ſaffron plume,
  Whoſe warbling whiſpers tell the approach
    of night,
With ſoften'd cadence uſhering in the gloom,
  The ſolemn gloom devote to calm delight.

Tell me, confin'd within thy wiry cell,
  The little notes thou chanteſt ſo ſerene,
Say, are they *plaints* thy breaſt that ſwell,
  And is *Captivity* thy theme ?

Or, fever'd from thy lovely mate,
  Her loſs doſt thou bewail ?
And all thy little wrongs relate
  In melancholy tale ?

        H h   Ah,

Ah, no! fo foft, fo fweet a ftrain
Vibrates not like the moan of *pain*;
Such tones as from *thy* bofom flow
Ne'er left the burfting heart of *woe*.

Yet, peaceful, inoffenfive gueft,
Could *freedom* make thee ftill more bleft,
I would unbar thy prifon gate,
And let thee go, to feek thy fate.

But ah, I know, unfkill'd in flight,
    Through the dark defert fhould'ft thou ftray,
Thy wings would tire, and ere the mifts of night
    Some cruel bird would on thee prey.

Or elfe thy little frame expos'd
    To the raw blafts, and midnight air;
Hungry, and faint, and uninclos'd,
    Thou would'ft, my fongfter, perifh there.

Stay then fweet PAN, and when the morning's
        light
    Steals through the op'nings of thy grated dome,
    Do thou thy pleafing hymning pow'rs refume,
Praifing the Author of each new delight:

And *I*, on bended knee moft fure,
    Humbly *my* lays with thee will join;
Nor will my mattins be lefs pure
    For mounting up to *Heaven* with thine.

                                    THE

THE BIRTH DAY OF COLUMBIA.*

1793.

COME round *Freedom*'s facred fhrine,
Flow'ry garlands let us twine,
And while we our tribute bring
Grateful pæans let us fing;
Sons of Freedom join the lay,
'Tis COLUMBIA's natal day.

Banifh all the plagues of life,
Fretful *Care* and reftlefs *Strife*;
Let the memory of your woes
Sink this day in fweet repofe;
Ev'n let *Grief* itfelf be gay
On COLUMBIA's natal day.

Late a *defpot*'s cruel hand
Sent Oppreffion through your land;
Piteous plaints and tearful moan
Found not accefs to his throne;
Or if heard, the *poor forlorn*
Met but with reproach and fcorn.

PAINE, with eager virtue, then
Snatch'd from TRUTH her *diamond pen*,

H h 2   Bade

* Addreffed to the members of the CINCINNATI of the
ftate of New-York, on the FOURTH of JULY.

Bade the flaves of tyranny
Spurn their bonds, and dare be free:
Glad they burft their chains away;
'Twas COLUMBIA's natal day.

Vengeance who had flept too long,
Wak'd to vindicate our wrong,
Led her vet'rans to the field,
Sworn to perifh ere to yield;
Weeping Memory yet can tell
How they fought, and how they fell.

Lur'd by virtuous WASHINGTON,
(Liberty's much favour'd fon,)
Vict'ry gave your fword a fheath,
Binding on your brows a wreath,
Which can never feel decay
While you hail this blifsful day.

Ever be its name rever'd;
Let the fhouts of joy be heard,
From where *Hampfhire's* bleak winds blow
Down to *Georgia's* fervid glow;
Let them all in this agree,
" Hail the day which made us free!"

Bend your eyes toward that fhore
Where *Bellona's* thunders roar,

There

There your *Gallic brethren* fee
Struggling, bleeding to be free!
Oh! unite your pray'rs that they
May foon announce *their* natal day.

O thou Pow'r! to whom we owe
All the bleffings that we know,
Strengthen thou our rifing youth,
Teach them *Wifdom, Virtue, Truth*;
That when *we* are funk in clay
They may keep THIS GLORIOUS DAY!

JULY THE FOURTEENTH.

1793.

HARK! hark how the clamours of war
 Thro' *Gallia*'s wide regions refound;
Bellona has mounted her car,
 And fcatters her terrors around:
Captivity burfts off her chains,
 Her fhoutings are heard on the heath,
Her vet'rans are crouding the plains,
 Refolv'd upon *Freedom* or *Death*.

But fee! from her battlements high,
 Plum'd *Vict'ry* undaunted alight;
Her ftandard fhe waves in the fky,
 And urges her fons to the fight.

Their fwords all indignant they clafh,
 They rufh round the *Baftille*'s ftrong walls.
Ah ! heard you that horrible crafh ?
 The *tow'r* of proud *Tyranny* falls !

The minions of defpotifm fly,
 Purfu'd by deftruction and wrath,
Fear wings their fad flight, and their *cry*
 Difturbs the deep flumber of *Death*.
Hafte, hafte, *man's difgrace* difappear,
 Vile wretches, of nature the blot,
And wherever your hamlets you rear,
 May *fhame* and *diftrefs* be your lot.

But *Gallia*, all hail ! may thy chiefs
 A temple to *Liberty* raife ;
And there may their feuds and their griefs
 Be loft in its altar's bright blaze.
And when they remember *this day*,
 Bedeck'd with the *laurel* and *vine*,
May anguifh and care flee away,
 And their voices in anthems combine.

And *then* may the warblings of fongs
 Be heard from *Columbia*'s green vales,
While Echo the wild notes prolongs,
 And whifpers them foft to the gales.

        And

And oh! let the zephyrs fo fleet
 Bear the fweet fwelling tones o'er the main,
And *there*, let them fondly repeat
 In the ear of each *Frenchman* the ftrain.

To *Mifs* MASON, *at New-Rochelle*.

1793.

ENQUIRING Fancy plumes her wings,
 To feek thee on HASPEDOC's fhore;
And *Friendfhip* true, her tribute brings,
 To glad the lonely vacant hour.

And all attentive would fhe glide
 Along thy footfteps; mufing flow,
Whether thou climb'ft the mountain's fide,
 Or cheer'ft the clovery dell below.

Where art thou now? led by the evening's cool
 Stray'ft thou along fome echoing foreft's
  fhade?
Or on the graffy margin of fome pool,
 Beneath fome willow art thou flumbering
  laid?

Where the fwoln throated *threfher* throws
 His warblings on the winding gale,
And the foft fcented frail *wild rofe*
 Sprinkles its odours in the vale?

Or

Or doſt thou bend o'er ſome ſtupendous cliff,
  Whoſe awful ſhadow frowns along the deep ;
And ſee'ſt from far the rough winds ſweep,
Through the high ſurging *ſound*, the ſcudding
      ſkiff ?

  Or elſe, where courteous BARTOW's dome
    Raiſes its hoſpitable head,
  Perhaps thou wandereſt down the gloom
    Of the *long alley*'s verdant ſhade ?

Where'er thou art, the ſcene I know ;
  Through all thy fav'rite paths have trod ;
Have mark'd the gay field's varied glow,
  And, pauſing gaz'd upon the flood.

Where yon gay *locuſts* ſhade the green,
  And gently whiſper to the breeze ;
Where chirps the *wren* their boughs be-
      tween,
  And flow'rs and ſhrubs conſpire to pleaſe :

There ALFRED oft at cloſe of day,
  Attun'd his numbers ſoft and ſlow,
And ſung the ſilent hours away,
  And fed each panting gale with woe :
And *I*, when high the clear full *moon*
Had hung her lamp amid *night*'s noon,
Have roam'd along this beauteous glade ;
                              And

And all regardlefs of the blaft
That whiftled round my naked head,
   My faddeft weeping hours have paft
E'en here, till many a dewy fhow'r
Had filver'd o'er my fragrant bow'r
And damp'd my locks; then quite oppreft,
Late have I fought the couch of reft.

Beauteous ROCHELLE ! along thy rocky fhore
Full many a bard his tuneful ftrains fhall pour,
And as the numbers float along the ftream,
Thy ruftic beauties fhall compofe his theme:
   Thy wild romantic iflands green,
      Thy limpid waves that filent glide
      To meet old *Ocean's emerald tide,*
         Thy fhelving banks, thy rude cliffs fteep,
         Thy nodding forefts, dark and deep,
   And fruitful meadows fpread between.
And though perhaps the gentle poet's name
Be ne'er recorded in the *fcroll of Fame*;
Yet, when he refts beneath the valley's clod,
Thy GENIUS weeping, fhall bedeck his fod;
Thy flow'rs fhall bloffom *fweeter* round his
      grave,
And *foftlier* towards his couch fhall creep thy
      pearly wave.

                              THE

THE

HUDSON.

NILE's beauteous waves, and TIBER's fwelling
 tide
Have been recorded by the hand of Fame,
And various floods, which through Earth's chan-
 nels glide,
 From fome enraptur'd bard have gain'd a name;
E'en THAMES and WYE have been the Poet's theme,
 And to their charms hath many an harp been
  ftrung,
Whilft Oh! hoar GENIUS of old *Hudfon*'s ftream,
 Thy MIGHTY RIVER never hath been fung:
Say, fhall a *Female* ftring her trembling lyre,
 And to thy praife devote th' advent'rous fong?
Fir'd with the theme, her genius fhall afpire,
 And the notes fweeten as they float along.
Where rough *Ontario*'s reftlefs waters roar
 And hoarfely rave around the rocky fhore;
Where their abode tremendous north-winds make,
 And reign the tyrants of the furging lake;

       There,

There, as the shell-crown'd genii of its caves
Toward proud LAWRENCE urg'd their noisy waves,
A *form majestic* from the flood arose;
A coral bandage sparkled o'er his brows,
A purple mantle o'er his limbs was spread,
And sportive breezes in his dark locks play'd:
Tow'rd the east shore his anxious eyes he cast,
And from his ruby lips these accents past:
' O favour'd land! indulgent Nature yield
' Her choicest sweets to deck thy boundless fields;
' Where in thy verdant glooms the fleet deer play,
' And the hale tenants of the desert stray,
' While the tall evergreens* that edge the dale
' In silent majesty nod to each gale:
' Thy riches shall no more remain unknown,
' Thy wide campaign do I pronounce my own;
' And while the strong arm'd genii of this lake
' Their tributary streams to LAWRENCE take,
' Back from its scource *my current*† will I turn,
' And o'er thy meadows pour my copious urn.'
  He said, and waving high his dripping hand:
Bade his clear waters roll toward the land.
Glad they obey'd, and struggling to the shore,
Dash'd on its broken rocks with thund'ring roar:
                                        The

---

* Cyprus, hemlock, firr and pine.

† All the waters of Lakes George, Champlain and Ontario empty in the river St. Lawrence, except one small stream, which, running an opposite course, forms the Hudson.

The rocks in vain oppofe their furious courfe;
From each repulfe they rife with tenfold force;
And gath'ring all their angry pow'rs again,
Gufh'd o'er the banks, and fled acrofs the plain.
Soon as the waves had prefs'd the level mead,
Full many a pearly footed Naïad fair,
With hafty fteps, her limpid fountain led,
To fwell the tide, and hail it welcome there:
Their bufy hands collect a thoufand flow'rs,
And fcatter them along the graffy fhores.
There, bending low, the *water-lillies* bloom,
And the blue *crocus* fhed their moift perfume;
There the tall *velvet fcarlet lark-fpur* laves
Her pale green ftem in the pellucid waves;
There nods the fragile *columbine*, fo fair,
And the mild dewy *wild-rofe* fcents the air;
While round the trunk of fome majeftic pine
The blufhing *honeyfuckle*'s branches twine:
There too *Pomona*'s richeft gifts are found,
Her golden *melons* prefs the fruitful ground;
The gloffy crimfon *plumbs* there fwell their rinds,
And purple *grapes* dance to autumnal winds;
While all beneath the *mandrake*'s fragrant fhade
The *ftrawberry*'s delicious fweets are laid.

Now by a thoufand bubbling ftreams fupplied,
More deep and ftill the peaceful waters glide,
And flowly wandering through the wide campaign,
Pafs the big billows of the grand CHAMPLAIN:

There,

There, when *Britannia* wag'd *unrighteous war*,
  A *fortress** rear'd her ramparts o'er the tide;
Till brave Montgomery brought his hosts from far,
  And *conquering*, crush'd the scornful Briton's pride.
The openings of the forests green, disclose
  Ticonderoga (long since known to fame:)
There fiercely rushing on th' unwary foes,
  The gallant Allen† gain'd himself a name.
Hence flows our stream, meand'ring near the shore
  Of the smooth lake‡ renown'd for waters pure,
Which gently wanders o'er a *marble bed*,§
  Cool'd by projecting rocks, eternal shade.
Amid those airy clifts (stupendous height!)
  The howling natives of the desert dwell:
There, fearful *Echo* all the live long night
  Repeats the *panther's* petrefying yell.

FORT-EDWARD.

But wherefore river creep thy waves so slow?
  Or why so mournfully pursue their course,
As though thou here had'st known some scene of woe,
  Whose horrors fain would fright thee to thy source?
      I i   Alas!

  * St. John's, besieged and taken by the American army under General Montgomery.
  † Colonel Ethen Allen, who took Ticonderoga by surprise.
  ‡ Lake George.
  § Almost the whole bed of Lake George is a smooth WHITE rock.

Alas! alas! the doleful caufe is known;
  'Twas here M'CREA,* guided by favage bands,
  Fell, (oh fad fuff'rer!) by their murderous hands,
And *this flood* heard her laft expiring groan!
This flood, which fhould have borne the nuptial throng,
  Found her warm blood deep tincturing its ftreams!
Thefe woods, which fhould have heard her bridal fong,
  Wildly refponded all her hopelefs fcreams!
CRUEL in MERCY, BARBAROUS *Burgoyne!*

Ah! fee an *aged fire*, with filver hairs,
(Whofe goodnefs trufted much, *too much* to *thine*,
  Bathing his *mangled daughter* with his tears!
Hear a diftracted *lover*'s frightful voice!
  See, as he bends to kifs the clotted gore
Senfelefs he finks! but Death hath clos'd *thine* eyes,†
  And Mem'ry weeps, but will *reproach no more.*

In *Edward*'s fortrefs, here a grand retreat
The Britons plann'd, but ere it was compleat
New Albion's vet'rans, with undaunted force,
Stood like a barrier and oppos'd their courfe.
Here broader fwells the tide, and the ftrong oar
Is heard to dafh the waves: the fhady fhore
Sounds with the peafant's ftrokes, and the *tall wood*
The hand of *Commerce* bears along the flood;
                     Unnumber'd

---

* Near Fort-Edward the beautiful Mifs M'Crea was cruelly murdered by Indians, who were fent by General Burgoyne to efcort her to her lover, one of his officers, to whom fhe was to have been married in a few days.

† He died in 1792.

Unnumber'd herds of *cattle* graze the plain,
And in the valley waves the *yellow grain;*
The *green maize* ruftles on the mountain's brow,
And the thick *orchard's* bloffoms blufh below:
For the luxuriance of the cultur'd foil
Amply rewards the hardy ruftic's toil.

Now the fair *Hudfon's* widening waters tend
Where SARATOGA's ancient forefts bend,
Where GATES, the *warlike* GATES, Columbia's boaft,
Vanquifh'd the proud *Burgoyne's* aftonifh'd hoft!
Victorious chief! while here thou glad'ft our eyes,
For thee, from the full heart a pray'r muft rife;
Of the poor *orphan* all his friends remov'd,
And the fad *widow* reft of all fhe lov'd:
Thefe, *while thou liv'ft,* fhall blefs the hero who
Refcued *Columbia* from a cruel foe,
A *parent* to the *orphan'd child* reftor'd,
And bleft the *widow* with her *much lov'd lord,*
Reveng'd the caufe of many a foldier flain,
And fixt on Britifh arms a lafting ftain!
And when the hand of Death thine eyes fhall clofe,
And chanting angels guard thy foft repofe,
Then will they, grateful, o'er thy cold tomb mourn,
And, weeping, hang a garland on thine urn.

Through many a ' blooming wild,' and woodland
    green,
  The *Hudfon's* fleeping waters winding ftray;

Now 'mongft the hills its filvery waves are feen,
　And now through arching willows fteal away :
Then burfting on th' enamour'd fight once more,
　Gladden fome happy peafant's rude retreat ;
And paffing *youthful* TROY's *commercial* fhore,
　With the hoarfe MOHAWK's roaring furges meet.
Oh, beauteous MOHAWK ! 'wilder'd with thy charms,
　The chillieft heart finks into rapt'rous glows ;
While the ftern warrior, *us'd to loud alarms*,
　Starts at the thunderings of thy dread COHOES.*
Now more majeftic rolls the ample tide,
　Tall waving elms its clovery borders fhade,
And many a ftately dome, in ancient pride,
　And hoary grandeur, there exalts its head.
There trace the marks of *Culture*'s funburnt hand,
　The honied *buck-wheat*'s† cluftering bloffoms view,
Dripping rich odours, mark the *beard grain* bland,
　The loaded *orchard*, and the *flax field blue*.
ALBANIA's gothic fpires now greet the eye ;
　Time's hand hath wip'd their burnifh'd tints away,
And the rich fanes which fparkled to the fky,
　'Reft of their fplendours, mourn in cheerlefs grey.
There many an ancient ftructure tottering ftands ;
　　　　　　　　　　　　　　　　　　Round

* Next to the Niagara the grandeft falls on the continent,
70 feet high.
† This grain, when in bloom, can be fmelt at fuch a dif-
tance, and fo rich is the fcent, that it may be faid, that,
" Many a league,
" Cheer'd with the grateful fmell old HUDSON fmiles,"

Round the damp chambers mouldy vapours creep,
And feathery-footed *Silence* folds her hands,
　While the pale genii of the manfion fleep.
Yet thither *Trade*'s full freighted veffels come;
　Thither the fhepherds mercantile refort:
There *Architecture late* hath rais'd her dome,
And *Agriculture*'s products fill her port.
The graffy hill, the quivering poplar grove,
　The copfe of hazle, and the tufted bank,
The long green valley, where the white flocks rove,
　The jutting rock, o'erhung with ivy dank;
The tall pines waving on the mountain's brow,
　Whofe lofty fpires catch day's laft lingering beam;
　The bending willow weeping o'er the ftream,
The brook's foft gurglings, and the garden's glow:
Thefe meet the wandering trav'ller's ardent gaze;
From fhore to fhore enraptur'd Fancy ftrays;
Each parting fcene his anxious eyes purfue,
Till HUDSON's city rifes to his view:
There, on the borders of the river rife
The *azure mountains* tow'ring to the fkies,
Whofe cloudy bluffs, and fpiral fteeps fublime,
Brave the rude gufts, and mock the ftrokes of Time.
High on the healing *firr tree*'s topmoft bough
　The folitary *heron* builds her neft;
　There in fecurity her offspring reft,
Regardlefs of the ftorms that rave below.

Wakeful remembrance, on thine ember'd plain
  Will paufe Esopus,* and indulge a tear;
  Will bid again the fcenes of woe appear;
Will bid the mouldering manfion blaze again.
She calls to mind when Britain's lawlefs bands
  Wag'd impious war with confecrated fanes;
Streach'd againft Heav'n their fanguinary hands,
  While *fear*, nor *awe*, their barbarous will reftrains.
O Hudson! Hudson! from thy frighted fhore
  Thou faw'ft the burfting flame mount to the fky;
Thou heard'ft the burning buildings fearful roar;
  Thou heard'ft the mournful fhrieks of Agony.
See, from his couch defencelefs *Sicknefs* driv'n!
  See bending *Age*, exhaufted, creep along!
Weeping, they turn their hopelefs eyes to heav'n,
  And pitious wailings murmur from their tongue.
Here a diftracted *widow* wrings her hands,
  While griefs too keen forbid her tears to flow:
There all aghaft a wretched *parent* ftands,
  Viewing his beggared babes in *fpeechlefs woe!*
Why did thy hand, O *defolating War!*
  Thy bloody banners o'er our land unfurl?
Why did thy cruel *hirelings* come from far,
  Murder and fire o'er every plain to hurl?
So as they glutted their dark fouls with death,
  Be their attendants fhame, remorfe and pain:
                                        While

* Efopus was burnt by the Britifh in 1777. Befides this place and Hudfon there are feveral towns and villages upon the river, viz. Red-Hook, Poughkeepfie, New-Windfor, New-burgh, New-Malborough, Fifh-Kill, &c.

While each fack'd village on th' enfanguin'd heath
Shall from its fmoking afhes rife again.

Low funk between the Alleganian hills,
   For many a league the fullen waters glide,
   And the deep murmur of the crouded tide,
With pleafing awe the wond'ring *voy'ger* fills.
On the green fummit of yon lofty clift
   A peaceful runnel gurgles clear and flow,
Then down the craggy fteep fide dafhing fwift,
   Tremendous falls in the white furge below.
Here fpreads a clovery lawn its verdure far,
   Around it mountains vaft their forefts rear,
And long ere Day hath left his burnifh'd car
   The dews of Night have fhed their odours there.
There hangs a louring rock acrofs the deep;
   Hoarfe roar the waves its broken bafe around;
Through its dark caverns noify whirlwinds fweep,
   While *Horror* ftartles at the fearful found.
The fhivering *fails* that cut the fluttering breeze,
   Glide through thefe winding rocks with airy fweep:
Beneath the cooling glooms of waving trees,
   And floping paftures fpeck'd with fleecy fheep.

WEST-POINT.

Dafh ye broad waves, and proudly heave and fwell;
   Roufe aged *Neptune* from his amber cave,
   And bid the nymphs the pebbly ftrand who lave,
Round this grand bulwark found their coral fhell:
                                             For,

For, nightly bending o'er thefe ftreams,
Bafe TREASON plotted murderous fchemes;
Then ftealing foft to ARNOLD's bed,
Her vifions vague around him fhed;
And while dark vapours dim'd his eyes
She bade thefe forms illufive rife:
Firft ANDRE came; his youthful air
    Allur'd the falling chieftain's eyes;
But when the glittering bribes appear,
    A thoufand ftrange ideas rife:
He faw Britannia's marfhall'd hofts,
Countlefs, advance toward his pofts;
Honour he faw, and *Wealth*, and *Fame*,
With every good that wifh can frame,
Attend their train; he long'd to ftretch
Beyond his *virtuous brethren*'s reach;
His heart *polluted*, vainly figh'd
To *bound* and *fwell* in TITLED pride.
Now fair COLUMBIA's armies come—
His hand hath feal'd their mournful doom;
And in an unrelenting hour
He yields them up to Albion's power:
Then *Murder* bloats with horrid pride!
A thoufand fall on every fide!
And coward *Cruelty*'s bafe bands
Dip in warm gore their barb'rous hands:
Then the broad-fword difplays its force,
    Drench'd to the *very hilt* in blood!

                                    While

While the *brave warrior*, and the *frantic horfe*
Wallow together in the purple flood!.
Then rofe a NAME; and lo! from far
He hears the hum of chariot wheels;
' *Divinity*' within him feels,
And thunders forth, THE SOVEREIGN LORD OF WAR.
His anxious eyes he ftrain'd for more;
But fickle *Fancy* dropt the fcene;
TRUTH's radiant rays around him pour,
And fhew'd the wretch 'twas all a *dream!*

——————

Fierce burfting from between the fturdy hills,
More high the wealthy river's bofom fwells;
Their circles broader now the waves expand,
Howl to the winds, and lafh the anfwering ftrand;
Then rolling flow, they kifs the flinty mound,
For valiant WAYNE's victorious acts renown'd:
'Twas there *Bellona* rear'd her ftandard high,
And bellowing engines pour'd forth ftorms of fire;
While fmoky columns flow to heav'n afpire,
Obfcure the fun, and hide the glowing fky:
Ranks rufh'd on ranks, and the bright blade
Its path through many a bofom made,
While furious men regardlefs tread
Upon the dying, and the dead!
O what a piteous fcene of woes!
The blood in bubbling currents flows;
The fiends of battle fhriek aloud,
Deftruction hurls his fhafts abroad,

And

And all the rocky caverns round
With sullen groans of *Death* resound!
But valor swell'd in FLEURY's breast;
He sigh'd to give his vet'rans rest;
And listless of the deadly aim
With which Britannia's volleys came,
He rush'd among the awe-struck croud,
And bore away their banner proud.*

For *this brave deed*, hath raptur'd Fame
Twin'd many a chaplet round his brow;
And long as lasts COLUMBIA's name
The fragrant blossoms fair shall blow;
And when the hand of *Death*, so cold,
Shall wrap him in the valley's mold,
A modest stone shall mark the place;
And there Affection's hand shall 'grave,
" Here FLEURY lies, the warrior brave!"
And all the simple line who trace,
Shall heave a sigh or drop a tear,
And bless the soldier mouldering there!
Soon as the ridgy mountains leave the eye,
Tall mural rocks† shoot proud into the air;
In shapes fantastic lift their turrets high,
Fit for the *shadowy forms* who revel there:

The

* At the storming of Stony-Point Lieutenant Fleury struck the British standard with his own hand.

† These rocks rise for many miles nearly perpendicular, some of them 600 feet.

The hardy PINES that on their fteep fides grow,
(Whofe *naked roots* from chink to chink extend;
Whofe boughs afpiring, tow'rd the denfe clouds tend,)
Appear like *fhrubs* to the ftrain'd eyes below.
The wandering *goat* adventures to the brink,
And peeps acrofs the fretted edge with care;
Then from the awful precipice fhe fhrinks,
As though relentlefs *Ruin* hover'd there.
Yet there, when Night hath bid the world be mute,
The fleeplefs *failor* often clambers high,
And from fome fhadowy nook his fonorous flute
Sends mournful accents to the neighbouring fky:
And while the flood refleots the broad moon bright,
Conceal'd the budding *laurel*'s fweets among,
There the fad *lover* pours his penfive fong,
Filling with mellow founds the ear of Night.

But now the advancing fight admires
The rifing fanes and glittering fpires
Of EBORACIA's ftately tow'rs,
Which catch the Morning's fplendid beam,
And fhining o'er the frothy ftream,
Gild with refraoted light the long extended fhores.
Alas! how late the rude foe revel'd there,
(Their engines bellow mournful o'er the main,
And every ftreet gleams with the difmal glare,)
Murder, and *Want*, and *Sicknefs* in their train:
Beneath the burning torch of *War* confum'd,
Her walls in fmoking ruins lay fcatter'd round;

While

While horrid fires her HOLY DOMES illum'd,
Whofe blazing fpires fell thundering to the ground,
Gilding the gloomy bofom of old Night.
　　Then from the deadly prifon's walls arife,
　　Of *Hunger* fierce, the agonizing cries,
Filling the liftening foul with wild affright!
But now the " crimfon toils" of War are o'er,
Her dreadful clamourings meet the ear no more;
The graffy paftures, lately dy'd with blood,
Now on their bofoms hold fome dimpling flood;
And the raz'd buildings, whofe high polifh'd ftones
Sunk difregarded 'mongft half mouldering bones,
From their own afhes, *phœnix like,* arife,
And grandly lift their turrets tow'rd the fkies:
The bufy bands of *Commerce* croud her ports;
　　Full in her harbours fwells the fnowy fail,
The fpringing breeze, the dancing ftreamer courts,
　　And the deep veffel bows before the gale;
While from fair *Naffau*'s ifle,* or *Jerfey*'s fhore,
The lab'ring *peafant* turns his heavy oar;
His broad boat laden with inviting fruits,
Delicious wild fowl, with falubrious roots,
And tafteful pulfe; or elfe he draws the car,
　　Fill'd with the tenants of the briny *fea*,
Or fedgy *creek*, or wood-edg'd *river* fair,
　　And hies him to this bufy mart with glee:
　　　　　　　　　　　　　　　　Where

* Commonly called Long-Ifland.

Where from the early dawn, a hardy throng
Spread various works the loaded shores along;
Sound the harsh grating saw, or hammer loud,
Or blow the roaring furnace, sable brow'd,
Or ply the heavy hulks, propt up in air,
From smoking cauldrons, with ebullient tar,
Or guide the groaning wheels, and straining steed,
To where the sons of *Trade* their wealth unlade.
PRIDE of COLUMBIA! EBORACIA fair!
What happy region will with *thee* compare
For Nature's bounties fam'd? where swells the shore
With *soil* so *fertile*, and with AIR SO PURE?
Two mighty rivers* round thee roll their streams,
    From the green bosom of the vasty sea,
Wooing the winds so cool, when *Sol's* fierce beams
    Would singe the verdure of the thirsty *lea*.
O may the braying *trumpet's* shrill tongu'd roar
Be heard among thine echoing wilds no more,
Nor purple blood thy lilied vallies stain,
Nor sounds of death afright the restless main,
Nor panting *steeds* neigh to the *clarion's* blast,
    Mocking the vengeful sword, and glittering spear;
    Nor wounded *warriors* 'midst the hurtle drear,
Trampled beneath their coursers, sigh their last;
But may thy virtuous sons unrivall'd stand,
The boast of *Science* and their native land,

K k   Led

* The HUDSON and the EAST-RIVER or SOUND, which meet at the south-west end of the city.

Led by the hand of Truth, may they attain
The height for which have thoufands figh'd in vain;
Nor may a wifh *ambitious* ever rife,
Save this, to be more *virtuous* and more *wife;*
And by no defpot's iron laws confin'd,
Enjoying the vaft freedom of the mind;
But while they throng the domes of *Liberty,*
    May they her facred precepts ne'er profane;
Nor while they boaft themfelves ' the virtuous *free*'
    One *flave* beneath the cruel yoke retain.
May thy fair daughters Wifdom's laws obey,
    Each *thought ungentle* from their breafts repel;
And fkill'd in pious lore, to all difplay
    'Tis not in *beauty* they *alone* excel.
And may the GREAT SUPREME, when fhowering
        down,
    In rich profufion, all the joys of Peace,
Thine offspring for his favourite people own,
    And hearts beftow the donor's hand to blefs:
Then fhall thy 'habitants indeed be bleft;
    Regions far diftant fhall revere thy name,
And nations long of every good poffeft,
    Stile *thee* UNEQUALL'D in the Scroll of Fame.
And thou, O RIVER! whofe majeftic ftream
    Hath rous'd a *feeble hand* to fweep the lyre,
    Thy charms fome loftier poet fhall infpire,
And *Clio's* felf fhall patronize the theme:

                                    To